Books by

THE INNOCENTS

Fragile Innocence

Fabricated Innocence (2021)

Reclaimed Innocence (2021)

THE GODDESS'S SCYTHE

Raven's Wings

Death's Angel

Queen's Sacrifice

for my dear mother

"Come on," Jenna implored Grace, dragging her along by the sleeve of her blouse.

"We have chores!" Grace protested.

"We always have chores," Jenna replied dismissively and pulled Grace through the long shadows to the old barn, where she flattened herself against its wood planks, listening intently.

Grace tried to calm her racing heart, but all she could think of was the trouble they'd get in if they were caught.

Jenna peeked around the side of the building and, confirming that there were no witnesses, hurriedly pulled Grace through the open door.

Grace wracked her brain for an excuse in case they stumbled across someone and was relieved beyond measure to find the barn empty, save of course for the stabled horses and musty straw. "What are we doing here?" she asked, wrinkling her nose.

"You'll see," Jenna replied with a mischievous grin, beckoning from the ladder to the hayloft.

Grace glanced nervously at the door, then followed Jenna up. She pulled herself over the lip to find that Jenna had already spread out a blanket and was sitting cross-legged on it in eager anticipation. Grace sat down across from her, and Jenna removed her bonnet and shook out her hair, which glowed in the sunlight that lanced through the wallboards.

Everyone said they could be sisters. They both had flaxen-colored hair, although Jenna's tended slightly more toward blonde and fell in curls, while Grace's hung straight and limp. They both had emerald eyes, although Jenna's lashes were fuller, just like her lips. They both had round faces, although Jenna's wasn't dotted with freckles like Grace's.

Grace always thought of Jenna as a prettier version of herself and secretly wished she'd grow into Jenna's beauty. It wasn't unrealistic, she thought, given that Jenna was always a little ahead of her in everything, despite being only eight days older – a fact that she constantly reminded her of. Jenna's breasts had even come in first, and she was so proud of them that she began to wear clothes that accented them, at least as much as anything could, given the village's conservative attire.

Grace envied Jenna's breasts. *Envy is a sin*, she reminded herself. *As is vanity. I'm a mess!* she concluded, shaking her head. "What are we doing here?" she repeated, pulling an errant stalk of straw out of her hair.

Jenna reached into the folds of her dress and pulled out a deck of cards.

Grace stared at them dumbly, wondering what had possessed her friend to drag her to this clandestine spot to play cards, never mind where she'd gotten them, considering that they should be locked up with the other games.

"I'm going to tell your fortune!" Jenna announced.

Grace stared at her friend in disbelief but capitulated in the face of her enthusiasm – when Jenna decided on something, nothing would dissuade her. "I can save you the trouble," Grace told her, "... five more years of school, then I marry Gabriel and live next door to you forever."

Jenna ignored her and fanned out the cards. "The future is murky," she intoned and held them out. "Pick one," she commanded.

Grace did as she was told and held up the seven of diamonds.

"That's you," Jenna informed her, took the card, and laid it on the blanket face up. "Not a very exciting card, sorry."

"Then it fits," Grace sighed and smoothed out her skirt.

"Draw seven more cards," Jenna instructed her. "Those are your sevens."

"I know who my sevens are. We were assigned them at birth," Grace reminded her.

"Yes, but do you know if they'll rise to the occasion?" Jenna asked.

"I guess not."

"Then draw the cards!"

Grace relented and turned over a queen, a king, three jacks, an ace, and another queen.

"You're cheating!" Jenna accused her.

"How can I cheat if I don't know the rules?"

"I guess," Jenna replied, only slightly mollified. "Your sevens really have your back."

"Isn't that the point?"

"Sure, but not everyone gets the A-team. My sevens are boring."

"At least they come to your birthday. Mine don't," Grace countered.

"My sixth gave me *socks*. Your sixth is the ace of hearts."

"I've never met my sixth."

"Well, she's a lion," Jenna assured her, then leaned in excitedly. "Now, for the best part… draw another card."

Grace sighed but reached forward.

"Not with that attitude!" Jenna declared, pulling back the deck. "This card is your love."

"I should have known this was coming," Grace replied, rolling her eyes but snatching the top card before Jenna could stop her. "Ha! The seven of hearts. What does that mean?"

"Matching sevens," Jenna observed reverently, staring at the card. "She's your soulmate," she added wistfully.

"*She?*" Grace asked. "Gabriel is not going to be happy about that."

"I want *your* life," Jenna lamented, leaning back in mock despair.

"You can have it," Grace assured her. "Does that mean I get your socks?"

Jenna unfolded her legs and wiggled her toes. "Nope."

"What about *her* sevens?" Grace asked.

"Whose?"

"My supposed love."

"That's not part of the game."

"I want to know," Grace demanded.

"Okay," Jenna relented. "Draw seven more cards."

Grace drew two twos, a three, another two, two more threes, and the last two.

"Oh, no," Jenna declared. "She has no one, the poor girl."

Part I
Hearts

Chapter 1

Rayne

Rayne's cat stepped on her face, rousing her from a sound sleep.

"For God's sake, Loki, just because you're up doesn't mean I have to be," she complained, swatting at him.

He sat down, just out of reach, and meowed.

"I fed you yesterday, you tyrant."

Loki did not deem that sufficient.

"Okay, I'll find you something, but let me wake up first."

The cat snorted and prowled away while Rayne rubbed the sleep out of her eyes and sat up from the mat she lay on. Color was creeping into the sky, and it looked like it was going to be a nice day, above the clouds anyway.

The wind blew loose strands of hair across her face. *I'm going to have to give some serious thought to walls*, she mused, pulling a hair tie off her wrist and putting her hair up in a loose ponytail.

She got up and wandered over to the rain barrel. Checking that it only smelled of rust, she cupped some water in her hands to drink, then splashed a little on her face to wake herself up faster.

Loki reminded her to get a move on.

"Alright, already. I'm hungry too," she replied and rummaged around until she found an apple. She munched on it as she walked over to the least-eroded side of her building and sat down, swinging her feet over the edge.

The view from 52 stories never got old. A few other buildings poked haphazardly out of the cloudbank, familiar as old friends. Hers was one of the tallest, but not *the* tallest. Some people sought out such things, and she preferred to avoid people in general. While the climb was murder, living high above the clouds fed her soul and kept her safe from the city's worst predators.

She finished her apple and thought about tossing the core down into the clouds, but reconsidered. *I wouldn't want to spoil someone's day with a flying apple bomb*, she thought and got up. A gust of wind unsteadied her, but she recovered her balance before tumbling over. *That would have spoiled my day*, she concluded and set about getting dressed.

Rayne selected black leather pants and a faded but comfortable cotton t-shirt. She slipped her work boots on without lacing them up and pulled on a dark hoodie, glancing at her leather jacket but deciding against it. She picked up the shard of mirror that she used to check herself over and concluded that she looked as innocuous as someone could with bright blue hair.

She slung her empty backpack over her shoulder, then secured Loki's pouch in front before bending down to pick him up as he weaved serpentine between her legs. She placed him in his pouch, and he shifted around to get comfortable. She put on her heavy welder's gloves, clapping them together to bang off the flakes of rust, and made her way to the exposed steel column on the west side of her floor.

Loki looked up at her forlornly.

"What? You like this part," she assured him, then carefully shifted around the column until she was straddling it on the outside. The wind whipped her ponytail around her head as she gripped the steel tightly in her gloved hands and booted feet. "Ready?" she asked, but relaxed her grip before he could respond and began hurtling downward. *Who am I kidding?* she thought. *I love this part!*

Rayne felt the chill on her skin as she entered the cloud layer and quickly passed through it to its gloomy underside. While her eyes adjusted to the dimmer light, she slowed her descent slightly by gripping the column tighter and pressing inwards with her boots. The ground raced upward, and she gauged her speed to slow herself to a stop just before she reached the sidewalk.

Loki gave her a look that said, "Never again."

Rayne took off her gloves and gave him a scratch under his chin. "If you want to eat, you have to ride the rail. There are no mice 52 stories up," she reminded him. *Thank goodness*, she thought and shuddered – she hated mice. She waved the still-smoking gloves back and forth until they cooled enough to stuff them in her backpack, then swung her pouch behind her and adjusted it so Loki could peer over her shoulder. He nuzzled her cheek affectionately.

"Name one other cat that gets chauffeured?" she asked him, and he purred in response. "You suck," she told him playfully, undid her ponytail, and flipped up her hood. "We're undercover," she reminded him. Several loose strands of hair resisted being tucked in, so she gave up trying and began walking to work.

The boarded-up main floor of her building was plastered with faded posters reminding people of the one-child policy. It was the infraction that the authorities enforced the most stringently now that people lived forever. One of the posters had been freshly tagged with the symbol of the centuries-old Revolution. Rayne shook her head. *You won your war*, she thought sarcastically, *give it a rest already*. Ironically, untold numbers of people had died fighting for equal access to the immortality treatment. The world was still a shadow of its former self and nowhere more so than the United States, where everyone felt it was their God-given right to live forever and had sacrificed themselves on the altar of that dream. Even as the wars dragged on, and people realized that they might not live to see widespread adoption of the expensive treatment, they fought and died so that their children might. The very fabric of society was nearly torn asunder.

Rayne stepped off the curb and headed south. The streets had long ago been taken over by pedestrians as the feeble sunlight wasn't strong enough to power vehicles. She imagined that New York couldn't have always been so quiet if its arteries were as wide as they were, but that would have been well before her time. She also liked to believe that New York hadn't always smelled as rank as it did now, accustomed as she was to the fresh air of her home in the sky. It wasn't the Immortality Wars that had really brought her city low; it was centuries of neglect by the survivors.

She kept her head down and didn't acknowledge passersby, who didn't seem particularly interested in her either. It was just the way she liked it. Her blue hair made her stand out, and attention wasn't something a young person wanted in the city. The hole-in-the-wall shop where she earned just enough to keep herself and Loki fed was in the market district, and that was a fair hike.

She walked past the block where the street food vendors plied their trade, and her stomach rumbled loudly. The scent of frying tofu called to her. It might smell like a rotting corpse, but it was her guilty pleasure when she could afford it. Loki interrupted her contemplation by head-butting her cheek.

"I'm hungry, too," she told him, "but work first, food later." She sped up and finally arrived at the nondescript shop where she worked, aptly named "Lazarus's Workshop." A tinkling bell announced her presence.

"Cieco," she called out, "it's pitch black in here."

"Lot of difference that makes to me," a voice replied from the counter at the back, startling her.

"Not for you – I get that you're blind as a bat – for the customers."

"We'd actually have to *have* customers before that became a problem," Cieco pointed out. "Besides, my clients know where the light switch is."

"They really don't," Rayne muttered, hunting for it herself. Finding it at last, she flipped it on to reveal the only marginally less dark interior of the electronics repair store. It contained a crowded jumble of ripped-apart equipment. "How do you find anything?" she asked.

"I have a system," Cieco replied, tapping a finger to his temple. Rayne highly doubted that he did, but he'd made a living so far, so she'd just have to take his word for it.

"I'm starving. Do you have anything to eat?" she asked.

"Sure. I picked up some food for you at the market. I'll deduct it from your pay."

Rayne wondered whether he knew that when he said, "pay," it always sounded like it had air quotes around it. She sighed. Food was what she'd probably buy with the money anyway, so why should she care? "Where is it?" she asked.

"In the fridge, in the back."

"You got the fridge working?" she asked, amazed.

"Of course not, but it keeps the flies away, working or not."

"I guess that's better than nothing," she conceded and walked to the back to pull the bag of food that she guessed was hers out of the fridge. She took out some cheese and cut off a piece for Loki. He chewed on it happily as she put him down. "Now you have cheese breath – that should help you find a mouse. Go get one, you deadbeat," she ordered him and returned to the front of the store.

"What do you have for me?" she asked, plugging in her music player.

"A bit of this, a bit of that," he replied, waving at a pile of items that customers had brought in with the faint hope that they could be brought back from the dead.

"You know it's easier to fix something when you know what it does, right?" she sighed and picked up the nearest item to examine it.

Cieco just shrugged. His approach to repairing things was to find as many similar items as he could and keep swapping parts until the fates smiled on him and something miraculously began to work. He had an army of borderline-unemployable people wandering the city looking for items that he could cannibalize. Rayne doubted that everything they brought back was "found," as opposed to "stolen," but as long as it wasn't her stuff, it wasn't her problem.

"Mind if I play some music?" she asked.

"I'm blind, not deaf. I hate your music."

"Please?" she begged.

"Fine, just not too loud," he conceded. He cut Rayne a lot of slack because she was the only person he'd come across in his entire existence who actually cared about how things worked – really wanted to understand them. Her curiosity had rescued many an abandoned project and kept his store open. If he had to tolerate her taste in music, it was an acceptable trade.

Rayne chose her favorite band and turned the volume down a bit.

"Not them again," Cieco complained.

"I love *Armageddon's Embers*," she countered. "They *so* get me."

Cieco shook his head and wandered into the back, leaving her alone to puzzle out how to repair the array of junk before her.

She tinkered all morning, interrupted only by the occasional arrival of Helt, one of Cieco's creepier scavengers. He had wild eyes and long greasy hair, and Rayne didn't think he was entirely well mentally. He ignored her while he waited for Cieco to emerge, and they'd haggle over whatever he'd found before heading out again.

Rayne sang to herself while she tinkered, until she concluded that she'd tried everything she could think of. She'd coaxed a couple of things to work, and she was proud of herself. At the self-declared end of her workday, she pulled her hoodie back on and put the remaining food that Cieco had bought for her in her backpack, along with her music player. Any lack of awareness in the city could prove fatal, so she never risked listening to music while she walked home. She hunted around for Loki and found him sleeping on a high shelf.

"How did you get up there?" she asked, retrieving him and returning him to his pouch. "You'd better not have slept the day away. You can't expect me to find you every bit of food you get."

Loki snorted in response, and Rayne looked around for Cieco to see if there was any more to her "pay." As predicted, he miraculously made himself scarce whenever she wanted to find him. She sighed and made for the door, calling over her shoulder, "I'm not locking up," certain that he was hiding somewhere nearby.

She decided to drop in on her quasi-girlfriend, Triste. Rayne had gravitated toward her when they first met, even though Triste was a hot mess – there were depressingly few young people in the city. Maybe it was more accurate to say that there were depressingly few *people* period, and the vast majority had long since aged past their youth – it was such a fleeting moment in their long lives.

The front door to Triste's building was locked, as usual, but that didn't dissuade Rayne. She went around back and took a run at the fire escape, leaping up and catching the bottom rung.

She shushed Loki when he complained. "You're fine, you big suck," she told him and hauled herself up the ladder, then up the fire escape to the third floor. She peered in each of Triste's windows but didn't spot her. Only the tiny bathroom window budged when she tried to open one. Rayne was fairly petite, so she decided to give crawling through it a shot. She shimmied back across the ledge and put Loki's pouch down with him inside, then edged back along the ledge until she was underneath the window. She pushed it open as wide as she could, then pulled herself up and squeezed through.

Inside, she checked each room for Triste, just in case she'd simply passed out somewhere other than her bed, but quickly confirmed that she wasn't home. She pulled some fruit out of her backpack, placed it on the kitchen counter, and left a note.

Thinking of you,

Love,
Blue

P.S. Lock the bathroom window!

Rayne crawled back out to an impatient Loki. "There are still a couple of places we can check," she told him as she scooped him up.

No one admitted to having seen Triste at the tenement building where she sometimes crashed when she was high, at least if Rayne could trust the recollection of junkies. She bumped into Triste's dealer on the way out.

"Blue," he greeted her with an oily smile. "For a friend of Triste's, half price."

"That's sweet of you, Marcus," Rayne lied, "but I'm just looking for her. Have you seen her?"

"Not today," Marcus replied, "but I reckon she's due to come looking for me soon."

Rayne pushed down her intense dislike for the man and slid past him. "I'll tell her where you're at," she lied again and hurried away. Marcus made her skin crawl the way he looked her over. She shook it off and decided to try one last place. She went to the street where the hookers plied their trade, knowing that when Triste was desperate enough, she'd sometimes join them. With her youth and looks, Triste could make a fair bit of money quickly. Rayne tried to talk her out of it, but Triste's addiction always won the argument, and Rayne had to content herself with simply supporting her.

"Hey, baby," a woman in an obscenely short skirt called to her. "What's your pleasure?"

Rayne couldn't tell if the woman was thirty or a hundred and thirty, she wore so much make-up. "Just looking for Triste," she replied.

"Haven't seen her, honey, but I can ring your bell while you wait."

"Thanks, but no thanks. If you see her, just tell her I was looking for her."

"Sorry, I can't. I've already forgotten about you," she shrugged and crossed the street to try her luck on the other side.

"Well, that was pointless," Rayne thought out loud. "We have just enough time to visit Renner," she told her cat.

Loki meowed at the name, hating the abandoned subway tunnels.

Rayne scratched his head but ignored his objections. "He'll appreciate our company and a bite to eat." Rayne got easily twisted around underground, so she backtracked several blocks to enter the way she always did. A group of sketchy-looking men were warming themselves by a fire at the entrance, so she pulled her hood tighter and snuck past them. Loki wisely kept silent.

Rayne navigated the dark tunnels by the faint light of the occasional emergency light that miraculously continued to function long after the trains had stopped running. She should be relieved, she thought, as she feared trains more than the dark. On cue, something scurried over her foot, making her cringe. Deciding that she was close enough to Renner's hideout, she thought it prudent to announce herself.

"Renner, it's Rayne. Are you down here?"

"Where else would I be, child?" came the weary reply.

Rayne followed the voice and embraced the old man in a warm hug. "It is so good to see you," she told him.

"I highly doubt that, but it's kind of you to say," he replied.

"You're my oldest and dearest friend," she countered.

"Oldest, probably, but dearest is a stretch. How's Triste?"

"I looked for her on the way here but couldn't find her."

"That girl will break your heart. You and I both know she walks a dangerous path."

"I know, but everyone needs someone. She gets me."

"Lucky her, unlucky you."

"I brought food," Rayne said to change the topic.

"Aren't you a dear?"

"That I am," Rayne replied and pulled off her pack to hand over the majority of its contents to the old man.

"That's too much," Renner stopped her.

"It's fine. I have more back at home," she lied and pressed a few more cans on him.

"You spoil me," he said by way of thanks.

"I owe you."

"You owe me nothing that you haven't repaid a thousandfold. The world owes *you* for the light you bring into it."

Renner's words comforted Rayne in a way that he could never fully appreciate. He'd pulled her from the fiery wreckage of the train that had taken her parents' lives, and he'd sheltered her from the world until she was old enough to do it for herself. He'd raised her to be tough, and she was thankful for it. She'd walk through fire for the man.

"Are you still living in the sky?" he asked her.

"Yup. The climb is murder, but I like it there. It's quiet and feels safe."

"You'd better hurry home then. It's getting late."

"How would you know? You never leave your cave."

"Last working watch in New York," he replied proudly, tapping his wrist. "Or at least one of very few."

Rayne whistled her appreciation. "I guess you're right. I'll come visit again when I have more time," she promised.

"I'll count the seconds… literally," he joked, waving his watch.

"Take care," she commanded and wrapped her arms around him.

"Get out of here," he teased and gave her one last squeeze before releasing her.

Rayne reluctantly made her way back to the surface, wondering if she should have just spent the night underground with him. She was partial to her home, however, so she just put her head down and hurried back to it as quickly as she could, paying less attention than usual to her surroundings.

Arriving at the remains of her building, she braced herself for the arduous climb back up, not even noticing the eyes that watched her ascend and moved to follow after her.

Chapter 2

Grace

The "tock" of a pebble hitting her window woke Grace. In her dream, it was Gabriel, come to ravish her. Her imagination shocked her, and she reddened in embarrassment until a second "tock" reclaimed her attention. Gabriel was too proper to call on her in the middle of the night, no matter how much she wished otherwise – it had to be Jenna, come to collect her for another of her midnight sorties. Grace loved her friend dearly, but Jenna didn't seem to need sleep the way Grace did.

Another "tock" prompted Grace to get out of bed. She groaned and shuffled to the window, heaving it open. A pebble struck her arm, and she looked down to see Jenna struggling to muffle her laughter. Grace bent down to pick up the stone and threw it at Jenna, who barely suppressed a shriek as she dodged it. *Jenna is not cut out for a clandestine life*, Grace mused as she braced herself against the windowsill and stuck a leg through. The cool night air against her bare leg made her shiver. She balled up her nightgown and shifted her weight to slide her other leg out, balancing precariously on the steeply pitched roof. *Jenna is going to get me killed*, she rued. She shimmed sideways to the porch where she could more easily inch downward, hang over, and slide down a pillar.

Once Grace was standing barefoot on the damp grass, Jenna grabbed her hand and pulled her along with her toward the barn, looking for all the world like a pair of comical ghosts in their billowing nightgowns. It took both of them to slide open the barn door, and once inside, Jenna pulled out a candle and lit it. She climbed the ladder to the loft, gesturing for Grace to hurry up after her. Jenna cleared the hay off a corner of the floor, dripped some wax, and secured the candle to it before the wax hardened. Satisfied, she flopped down on a hay bale over which she'd draped a blanket earlier in the day.

Grace took a seat across from her and finally hazarded in a low whisper, "What's so pressing that you had to drag me out of bed?"

Jenna leaned forward excitedly. "We have to plan our weddings!"

"For God's sake, Jenna, we just turned eighteen. They're months away, *at least*," Grace replied in exasperation.

"There's a lot to plan, and no one is going to plan them for us," Jenna countered. "Months may sound like a lot of time, but it really isn't."

Grace gave up arguing and settled in, folding her legs up inside her nightgown.

"We'll start with mine," Jenna decided. "I'm older," she added, by way of justification.

Grace didn't bother to point out that she was only eight days older and let her steamroll on.

"I want a large wedding," Jenna began.

"I want a small one," Grace interjected.

"Ah, ah," Jenna said, waggling her finger. "Mine first, yours after."

Grace shut up and motioned for Jenna to continue.

"Okay, where was I?"

"Large wedding."

"Right. And I want it outdoors near the lake."

Grace shuddered. Ever since Miriam drowned, she couldn't even look at the lake without thinking of her. Luckily, Jenna didn't notice her discomfort, and Grace hid it in a show of supportive nodding.

"And I want a fancy dress, with lots of lace and ribbons," Jenna continued.

"It's either-or," Grace chimed in, forgetting her vow of silence.

"Good point. That's why I need to bounce these things off you," Jenna replied, not minding Grace's interjections as long as they were still about her wedding. "Silas will wear a suit, of course."

"Silas doesn't own a suit. What would he have a suit for?"

"He'll just have to borrow one," Jenna insisted, ignoring the fact that her boyfriend wasn't the suit-wearing type. Even at church, he just wore clean work clothes and combed his otherwise unkempt hair.

Grace never understood what Jenna saw in him. Sure, it could be said that he was ruggedly handsome, *emphasis on "rugged,"* and he was strong as an ox, but he wasn't terribly bright and utterly devoid of aspiration, not that one could aspire to much in their tiny community.

"I have an idea!" Jenna declared, inspiration derailing her own train of thought. "*Your* sister can be my flower girl, and my sister can be yours."

"Good luck explaining that to Abi. She'd be crushed. Besides, I want my own sister as my flower girl."

Jenna frowned, thinking about how she could further integrate their weddings. "Well, you're still my maid-of-honor," she concluded.

"I should hope so."

"And Gabriel will be Silas's best man."

"Just because I'm your maid-of-honor doesn't mean that Gabriel has to be Silas's best man. They're not even friends. Silas will probably choose Gideon."

"It's *my* wedding."

"*And* his," Grace reminded her, risking Jenna's wrath.

"That's why I'm planning it for him," Jenna countered, unperturbed. "Oh, and I want peonies for my bouquet. They're so gorgeous and full of life. I want them everywhere." Jenna paused to admire the vision in her head. "I haven't figured out the dinner yet, but a simple cake will be fine – four or five layers max."

Grace couldn't help but roll her eyes this time but covered for it by turning to look at the far window. It was still dark out, but the cows would need milking at first light, and these middle-of-the-night rendezvous made her nervous. With any luck, Jenna would forget about discussing Grace's non-existent wedding plans – she was so focused on her own.

"Have you kissed?" Jenna asked.

"Hmm?" Grace replied, totally busted for not paying attention.

"Gabriel," Jenna replied like Grace was a child.

"No," Grace responded, disappointed. While Gabriel evoked impure thoughts in her, he was as religious as the day was long and would never think of even planting a peck on her cheek before they were wed. Grace sighed.

"We have," Jenna admitted.

"No way. Silas?"

"No, Gabriel. Of course, Silas!"

Grace acted scandalized but was really just jealous.

"I told him I needed help saddling a horse, and when no one was looking, I kissed him. On the lips."

"*You* kissed *him?*"

"Why not? Everyone knows we're going to be married. Besides, he kissed me back. He's a really good kisser," Jenna swooned, lying back and mimicking holding him in an embrace."

"I do *not* need to see your pretend kissing," Grace complained.

Jenna sat up and leaned forward. "What about your wedding?"

"There's too much to talk about," Grace deflected. "Let's save that for another night."

"Okay," Jenna accepted reluctantly. "But you'd better not run off to get married like Juliette."

"Juliette was betrothed to a boy from another town. Of course they got married there. Gabriel and I live right here," Grace reminded her.

"I'm just saying," Jenna defended herself. "She was so pretty. She would've had a beautiful wedding."

"She probably did," Grace surmised. "We should get going," she added, fearful that the sky would lighten at any moment. "Some of us actually need sleep."

"Okay, but we'll discuss your wedding tomorrow night," Jenna deferred.

"It's a date," Grace promised with pretend enthusiasm, already regretting the sleep she wouldn't get the next night.

Jenna dislodged the candle, brushed loose hay over the wax ring, and held the candle over the railing to light Grace's descent before following after her. Once on the ground, she blew it out and stuffed it back in her pocket. She peeked out the door and, confirming that no one was about at the early hour, exited the barn, sliding the door closed with Grace's help.

They raced back to Grace's house, and Jenna helped her up onto the porch roof, where she began the tricky task of making her way back to her bedroom window. Jenna stayed ready in case Grace slipped, but she made it back inside without incident.

"Tomorrow," Jenna whispered and darted away into the night.

Grace shook her head, eased the window closed, and lay back down. *Now, Gabriel, where were we?* she thought wickedly and closed her eyes.

Grace woke again at dawn, predictably exhausted. She lay in bed, looking around her room. There wasn't much to see – beside her simple bed, there was only a dresser with a basin and pitcher atop it, and a tiny table with a solitary candle holder. The walls were adorned only with the cross that hung over her bed. Her father had vetoed her request to hang dried flowers, telling her that it wouldn't be proper.

Grace wondered what her room would look like once she married Gabriel. They'd continue to live with their respective parents, of course, until the church assigned them a house of their own. Weddings often precipitated movement in the village, whereby parents whose children married would often move into smaller homes, and the new couple would move into a vacated home that had room for a nursery. She hoped that Gabriel, religious though he was, would not object to her decorating with flowers.

Gabriel was still on her mind when she got out of bed, so she decided to fabricate a reason to see him. She washed up and put on a dress that was a little softer than what she'd usually wear and tied her hair up in a bun beneath her bonnet. In her dreams, her long hair always draped over Gabriel's chest, so she hated tying it up when she went to see him. She tried to recall her dream, but it had disappeared with the night, so she gave up and descended to the kitchen. Her father was out, but her mother was cooking. Grace peeked in and pinched a piece of bacon.

"Grace, really?" her mother scolded her. "Those are for your father." She brushed her hands on her apron and enveloped her daughter in a hug, glancing at the plate of bacon. "I guess I could always make more," she decided and took a piece herself.

"Mother!" Grace reprimanded her playfully.

"You look nice," her mother told her after noticing her dress. "Special occasion?"

"It's Monday?" Grace hazarded.

"Don't you have chores?" her mother pressed, more concerned for Grace's dress than for her.

"Don't I always?" Grace complained. "I'll be careful, I promise. I was just thinking of walking past the mill."

"To see Gabriel?" her mother figured out. "Then, by all means, look your best," she relented, remembering what it was like to be eighteen.

Grace sat down at the table, noticing that her sister's place had already been cleared.

"Hanna already left for school," her mother informed her. "You slept in a bit longer than usual."

"I didn't get a great sleep," Grace admitted truthfully.

"Poor dear," her mother commiserated. "I'll get those," she added, pointing to Grace's dishes.

"Thanks, Mum," she said, kissing her on the cheek before stepping outside. Getting grain for the chickens was the perfect pretext to call on Gabriel at the mill, she decided and pulled the feed pail off its post to head there.

Grace spotted Gabriel threshing grain with his friends, Jacob and Zach. None of them were wearing shirts, and Grace guiltily admired Gabriel's physique as she approached.

Gabriel looked up, noticed her, and excused himself from his buddies, who teased him mercilessly as he walked over to her. Gabriel's lack of a shirt might have made him uncomfortable, but Grace far from minded. "Hi, Grace," he greeted her shyly.

"Hi, Gabriel," she answered. "I need grain for the chickens," she added, holding up the bucket innocently.

"I can help you with that," he smiled and took it, even though she could easily manage it. He escorted her to the grain elevator and filled the pail while she sat on an overturned tub and crossed her legs in a way that showed a little more leg than would typically be proper. Gabriel blushed and tried hard not to stare as he handed her back the pail. "Anything else I can do for you?"

You have no idea, she thought mischievously. "No, that's it. Thank you." She took the bucket from him and smiled her most beguiling smile before walking off.

"You look nice," he called after her, feeling like an idiot. "Will I see you in church?"

"Just like every Sunday, I imagine," she replied over her shoulder, grinning at the knowledge that she'd flustered him. Zach teased him, telling him how nice *he* looked. Grace glanced over her shoulder to see Gabriel punch him in the arm.

She strolled contentedly toward the chicken coop until her path intersected with that of a pair of church Elders. Something about them always made her feel guilty. *They watch you like they're judging you*, she thought but nodded deferentially as she walked past, some of the shine of her morning rubbing off.

She spent the remainder of the day doing chores, which gave her a lot of time to come up with a made-up wedding plan to satisfy Jenna. The more she rehearsed it, the more it sounded like she actually wanted it. Truth be told, she had concerns about marrying Gabriel. He was charming and treated her with the utmost respect, but it wasn't respect that she wanted – it was passion. Part of her hoped that that's what it would be like after their wedding, but she wasn't convinced that people changed just because of a ceremony. None of the couples she'd studied exuded any hints of passion. Even her mother, who clearly loved her husband, didn't show the sparks that Grace so desperately craved. She shook the doubts away – *it doesn't matter what I want, we're betrothed. I'm going to marry Gabriel, and it's just up to me to bring out the passion in him.*

Her preoccupations slowed down her chores, and it was near dusk when she finally finished and headed home for dinner. She entered through the back door, kissed her mother's cheek, and nodded to her father as she passed by the living room, where he sat poring over some papers, not looking up. Her sister, Hanna, skipped down the stairs.

"I need your help with an essay on church doctrine," Hanna informed her.

Grace mouthed the word 'boring' before replying out loud, "I'd love to. After dinner?" That was good enough for Hanna, so Grace ascended to her room, washed, and lay on her bed naked, her skin drying in the breeze coming through the window. She quickly felt guilty about enjoying her nudity and rose to get dressed for dinner.

Grace wandered downstairs, and her mother announced that dinner was ready. They settled in around the table, Grace's father said a short prayer, and they began passing dishes and talking about their day.

"Did you see Gabriel today?" her mother inquired.

Grace blushed. "I did. He was quite helpful."

"He's quite the catch," her mother remarked.

Her comment irked Grace for some reason that she couldn't quite put her finger on. *Aren't I a catch?* she wondered, then banished the thought.

After dinner, she helped Hanna with her homework until they both tired of it, and Grace begged off early for bed, knowing that she wasn't going to get an uninterrupted sleep again that night. She left her window open and debated staying awake until Jenna came calling, but fatigue quickly got the best of her, and she nodded off.

At midnight, she was awoken to the faint sound of Jenna's voice and dragged herself out of bed and over to the window. She spied her friend, but she wasn't waiting expectantly below, she was being led into the woods by several robed figures, and she moved uncertainly. *She must have been caught sneaking out, and now she's getting punished*, Grace thought and ducked away from the window, terrified that she'd been spotted. She lay awake the rest of the night, worried that the robed figures would come to punish her, too.

Chapter 3

Rayne

Rayne was winded by the time she finally made it up to her home on the 52nd story of her abandoned skyscraper. Loki bounded away to amuse himself when she took off his pouch. Rayne fished the rest of the cheese out of her bag and ate it, deciding that it wouldn't keep if she didn't. She stashed the rest of the food away for later.

It was getting dark, but she wasn't tired, so she sat down with her back to a pillar, slipped her earphones into her ears, and turned on her music. She selected her favorite song by *Armageddon's Embers* and listened to them sing of loss and longing while she watched the glow fade from the evening sky. The melody carried her away, and she closed her eyes.

She didn't hear the clatter seventeen stories below when the can she'd placed above a door as a crude warning system was dislodged and fell to the ground. Had the music not been so stirring, she might even have heard the rattle when the string of bottles she'd tied together was tripped over six stories below. It was almost pitch black when whoever had been following her reached the floor below hers.

A song ended, and in the pause before the next, Rayne heard a faint scraping sound, like boots on concrete, and her eyes flew open. She took out her earphones and heard the unmistakable sound of footsteps on the stairs. *Oh, no!* she thought panickedly and bolted to her feet.

She looked about frantically for Loki, who was hard to find at the best of times, but spotted his silhouette against the inky sky. She raced to him and picked him up but recalled too late that she'd left his carrier on the floor beside the stairwell door. She couldn't gauge how much time she had before the intruder made it to her floor, but she sprinted for the stairs regardless. The door was shoved open just as she'd finished stuffing Loki into his pouch.

Rayne didn't waste time sizing up the intruder before she tore off toward the far side of the floor. Footfalls echoed loudly behind her as she wove around her makeshift furniture. The intruder crashed through it instead, closing the gap. She grabbed the rope that she'd secured as a last resort and sailed out into open air, just as rough hands reached for her in vain. She tightened her grip as she began to plunge downward, praying that she could hold on when the rope went taut. Her arms were nearly torn from their sockets when it reached its fullest extent and swung her around in a giant arc.

She could barely make out the corner of her building as she hurtled toward it in the darkness. She braced herself for impact but only grazed it as she whizzed past. Her momentum carried her back up and outward until she reached the zenith of the swing. She felt oddly peaceful at the moment she let go and hoped to God that she'd judged correctly as she flew off into the darkness, fifty stories above the concrete. The wind tugged at her, and she felt terrified and exhilarated in equal measure.

She rotated herself to grip Loki's pouch tightly to her chest, and time seemed to stretch as she flew weightlessly backward. Time caught up with her as she landed on an adjacent rooftop in an explosion of gravel. She skidded across its slick surface of moss-covered stones until her back connected with the low wall that ringed the roof, blasting chunks of weathered concrete outward into the night. The cool air caressed the exposed skin of her lower back as she lay on her side in

31

blinding pain. The pouch shifted in her arms, and Loki emerged to tentatively lick the blood off her cheek.

Thank God, she thought gratefully and let the darkness claim her.

———————————————

Rayne woke at first light in a fog of dull but all-consuming pain. Every bone in her body felt broken. The wind still caressed her back, so she shifted gingerly away from the rooftop's edge. She winced at the pain and lay still, relaxing her breathing, as each intake was accompanied by a stabbing sensation. The pungent aroma of the moss she'd disturbed filled her nostrils and calmed her. It reminded her of the one and only time she'd gone camping with her parents before their death. The bittersweet memory merged with the ache throughout her body, and she couldn't tell where her physical pain ended, and her emotional pain began – her world was nothing but pain.

She swiveled her head to glance up at her own building towering beside the one on which she lay. She'd looked down on this rooftop a hundred times and never given it much thought apart from the day she concocted the emergency escape plan that she'd just executed semi-successfully. She propped herself up on her elbows to survey the extent of her injuries. Apart from feeling entirely broken, she didn't seem to be cut anywhere or impaled on anything. She decided to chalk it up as a win, despite how she felt.

She rose uncertainly to her feet, swayed, but caught herself before she fell. *See, could I stand up if every bone really was broken?* she told herself as a pep talk, concluding that she probably felt worse than her actual condition. She stared at the trail of ripped-up moss and gravel. *I'm a meteor*, she thought and laughed, then immediately regretted it as several ribs did indeed feel broken.

A low meow startled her, and she turned to see Loki staring up at their home. She followed his gaze but couldn't make out much from this far below. At least she didn't spy any movement.

"I know," she said. "I want to go home too, but that place isn't safe anymore. We'll have to find another." She shielded her eyes from the sun and stared harder at her building. "Still," she muttered, "all my stuff is up there."

"Okay," she announced. "We'll go see if we can rescue our things, but then we need to find somewhere else to live." Blinding pain shot up her spine when she bent to scoop up Loki. She paused, still doubled over, and Loki licked her hand with concern. "Give me a sec," she told him through gritted teeth, steeled herself, and picked him up. The pouch was still tangled around her shoulder, so she adjusted it and placed him inside. "How come you're no worse for wear?" she asked as he shifted to get comfortable.

She cast a last look up at her building. "Sorry, buddy… we can't fly. We're going to have to find a way down, then back up there." Loki responded by lying down and closing his eyes. "Some help you are," she complained and looked around for a way off the roof. She spotted a door on the far side and limped over to it.

It was locked. She jiggled the doorknob, but it didn't turn, and no other way off the roof presented itself. "Time and decay are our friends," she reminded herself and drew back to kick the knob. She obliterated it, but her kick felt like it had done as much damage to her as she'd done to the door. She slumped against the doorframe and struggled to breathe through the pain. She leaned closer and fiddled with the exposed locking mechanism until she was able to pull the door open, pushing aside gravel that hadn't been disturbed in decades.

She stepped into the gloomy stairwell and began her downward trek. The stairs had fallen away or were blocked with debris in several places, demanding creativity to continue her descent, but the building seemed structurally sound and mercifully abandoned. After several hours, she eventually made it to ground level and peered across the street at her building. *Was the intruder still there?* she wondered. She highly doubted that he would have climbed all the way up to the 52nd story, only to turn around and head back down the moment she'd escaped. He was probably still there. Now was not the time to collect her things.

"Change of plans, furball. We're going to crash at Triste's place until it's safe to check on ours."

A few passersby did a double-take at the blood on her forehead, but no one inquired if she was okay. *Typical*, she thought. To add inconvenience to injury, the pavement seemed even more uneven than usual to her stiff joints. She was reminded by her reflection in a window how lucky she was that she'd at least not gotten undressed for bed before being chased from her home. She didn't have the strength to pull up her hood and just shuffled down the street, her bright blue hair hanging loose.

She arrived at Triste's building, knowing that she was in no condition to climb the fire escape, so she went straight to the front door. It was always locked, so she didn't waste time checking. There was an old intercom system that didn't work in most apartments, Triste's included, but she held out hope that it might still work in some. She mashed all the buttons and began whispering gibberish into the microphone. Several people answered, and Rayne just spoke gibberish louder when they asked who she was. Finally, someone who was bored and looking for entertainment at a neighbor's expense buzzed her in.

She stepped inside quickly in case the person who'd opened the door reconsidered. She limped across the lobby and up the central staircase to the third floor, leaning heavily on the railing to support herself. It was smooth and cool beneath her fingers and one of the things she liked most about Triste's building. There had been an elevator once, but it hadn't worked in years. The odd person peeked out their door at her passing, and she flashed them a wan smile. Without fail, they closed their doors immediately. *I must look quite the fright*, she concluded.

She arrived at Triste's door and pounded on it. "Triste, you'd better be home," she called. "It's Rayne." She waited an eternity before slumping down against the opposite wall to consider her next move.

Triste's door surprised her by opening. "Of course it's you. No one else knows where I live, or if they did, no one I know would actually bother to come here," Triste said, looking down at Rayne. "You look like shit. What happened?"

Rayne rose slowly to her feet, wincing at each movement. "Thought I'd see if I could fly. Turns out I can't. Can I come in?"

"Sure," Triste replied, stepping out of her way.

Rayne looked Triste over as she entered. Her blonde hair hung down over her bare shoulders, and across the loose-fitting top she wore over ripped jeans. Triste absentmindedly pulled up a strap that had fallen off her shoulder as she pivoted her bare feet out of the way of Rayne's work boots.

"Thanks for the fruit," Triste told her while she closed and triple-locked the door behind them. Triste was overly thin in Rayne's opinion, and Rayne worried that she didn't eat enough. Her gauntness did, however, exaggerate her features and rendered her that much more striking. Even the darkness around her eyes from a chronic lack of sleep gave them a smoky appearance that drew Rayne to them.

Triste walked back to the sofa she'd been resting on and collapsed onto it. She pushed an adjacent pile of clothes onto the floor to make room for Rayne. "To what do I owe the pleasure of your company?" she asked.

"Someone attacked me at my place," Rayne replied, plopping down beside her.

Triste didn't bat an eye. In her world, that wasn't so unusual. "My poor baby," she responded and pulled Rayne in for a hug, wrapping her arms around her. Loki stirred in his carrier. "Is that your cat?" Triste asked, pulling back. "I hate your cat."

"Loki is an acquired taste," Rayne admitted as he poked his head out. "Do you mind if we stay here a couple days? We're kind of homeless."

"You're always homeless, in case you didn't notice," Triste reminded her.

"More than usual, then." Rayne looked beseechingly into Triste's eyes.

"Okay," Triste accepted, "but keep that cat from sleeping on my clothes. It takes me forever to get his hair off them." Loki worked his way free and wandered over to sniff a half-eaten sandwich inexplicably resting on the floor. Triste leaned forward and stroked Rayne's hair.

"Are you okay?" she asked with such genuine concern that it melted Rayne. The stress of the ordeal broke through, and she began to cry.

"I'm fine. It was just a lot," she replied as Triste's fingers in her hair relaxed her. "Are *you* okay? I bumped into Marcus."

Triste bristled. "Don't start."

"I wasn't going to," Rayne backpedaled. "I just wanted to know if you were okay."

"I'm not high, if that's what you mean."

"Obviously, Triste. I just hadn't seen you for a few days, and you know how I worry. Where have you been?"

"A client threw a party – I sort of got swept into it." Triste had a semi-legitimate job as a stand-in for a few rich girls who shared her body type. They'd send Triste for fittings where she'd be the one to stand for hours as elaborate outfits were stitched around her. She'd deliver the final products to them and sometimes be taken in as one might a stray.

"That makes me feel better," Rayne responded, deeply relieved that Triste hadn't been in one of the seedier corners of her world.

"You can't worry for me, Rayne. I don't," Triste told her for the hundredth time. She stared down at Rayne and resumed stroking her hair. Triste still wasn't sure how she felt about her. Part of her loved her for sure, but another part of her resented being reminded how shitty her life was when Rayne wasn't around. Usually she didn't notice, and it didn't bother her, but at times like this, with Rayne so close and the completeness with which she offered herself to her, she couldn't escape the certainty that she didn't deserve her. Triste stilled her hand as she rebuilt the walls around her heart.

Rayne recognized the pattern, sat up, and leaned back to give Triste her space. She looked at Triste's unkempt hair. "Let me wash your hair," she suggested.

"Always with the hair," Triste responded, rolling her eyes.

"If you didn't have hot water, you'd relish it as much as I do," Rayne explained, knowing that Triste would relent as she secretly loved having Rayne massage her scalp. Rayne didn't even wait for a response. "Let me shower first. If I'm in the land of hot water, I'm going all in."

"Fine," Triste accepted, "but don't expect me to join you."

"Your loss," Rayne replied, peeling off her top gingerly and exposing the ugly bruise along the left side of her body.

Triste raised an eyebrow but didn't comment.

"You're sure I can't tempt you?" Rayne asked over her shoulder.

"No offense, but you look like hell," Triste rebuffed her and began straightening the clutter around her.

Rayne shrugged and wriggled her way out of her leather pants, struggling with the stiffness of her joints and the pain that radiated from her side. She finished getting undressed in the bathroom and looked herself over in the mirror. The bruise along her left side was a variegated black and blue, and dried blood streaked her face. *I'd make one hell of a sexy zombie,* she concluded and limped to the shower.

38

She stood for a long while, relishing the warmth streaming over her before she set to scrubbing the grime from her body. It was agonizing, but cleanliness made her feel better. She emerged from the bathroom a short time later, wrapped in a towel, her non-bruised skin bright pink.

Triste had fallen asleep on the couch, and Rayne could tell that charging elephants wouldn't rouse her. She sighed and snuggled in beside her, laying her head on Triste's arm and pulling a blanket over them both. Triste's warmth filled her with contentment, and she drifted off to sleep.

Rayne woke a couple of hours later to find that Triste had extracted herself at some point and moved to her bed, where despite it being late afternoon, she looked to have settled in for the night. Rayne got up stiffly, hung her towel over a bar in the bathroom, and pulled her outfit back on, minus her boots. She grabbed Triste's keys off the counter and looked around for Loki.

He'd eaten the remains of the sandwich and fallen asleep in a nest he'd made from Triste's sweaters. *Great*, Rayne thought. *If he pukes on a sweater, Triste will kill me.* She figured she'd be back before Triste woke and could repair any damage then, so she'd cross that bridge when she came to it.

She grabbed her pouch, just in case she needed the extra space, and tip-toed out of the apartment with her boots in her hand. She closed the door behind her and locked it, then slipped on her boots on the landing. She realized that while she still felt sore, moving around at least worked out some of the stiffness in her joints. She pocketed the keys and walked out the front door, feeling better than she thought she would.

Arriving at her building, she squeezed behind the loose board that permitted her access and began the long ascent. Most of the stairs were intact, but she still needed to climb a few makeshift ladders, piles of empty crates, and the odd pipe. The arduous climb was compounded by her injuries, and she was sweating by the time she neared her floor.

The possibility that the intruder might still be there kept her wary. She made her way up the last few levels as quietly as she could and peeked through the still-open doorway to find that her home had been rifled through and was in disarray, but was also seemingly empty of unwelcome guests. She snuck out the doorway and looked around more thoroughly. No one was there, she confirmed and breathed a sigh of relief. She noticed her music player still lying out – it clearly wasn't her property that the intruder was interested in. She shuddered. Her clothes were strewn about, and she moved about the floor, gathering them up. *Creepy*, she thought.

She picked up her backpack, placing her music player in an outside pocket, and began stuffing her clothes inside. She swung it across her back and bent to pick up her welding gloves. The hairs on the back of her neck prickled, and she turned around slowly. A brutish man stood in the stairwell door. He was well over a hundred and fifty, but he'd kept himself in shape, and his muscles bulged. He stared at her predatorily, then glanced over her shoulder to confirm that she hadn't re-secured the rope by which she'd escaped the night before. He grinned evilly and took a step forward.

"Ever think about death?" he asked conversationally, the cold malice in his eyes telling her that he intended to give her plenty of time to think about it, to wish for it.

40

"I try not to," Rayne replied, slipping on a glove, then the other. She tried to resist glancing at the column she used to slide to the ground in order to judge its distance, but she couldn't help herself. The man followed her gaze, and understanding dawned in his. She bolted for it, and he moved to intercept her. She hit the floor at speed and slid under his reach, barely snagging the column with one hand as she sailed off the edge. She let herself fall while she struggled to reach around the column with her other hand. She succeeded in grappling it just before hitting the cloud layer. A glance upward confirmed that the man had followed her lead and was hurtling downward after her.

As soon as she was obscured by the clouds, she gripped the column tightly and braked hard. The pain in her left shoulder screamed at her, but she ignored it. She exited the lower side of the cloudbank before slowing completely. She swung herself around to the inside of the column just in time to see the man whiz past. He caught a glimpse of her and tried to slow himself, but all his strength couldn't prevent his hands from becoming lacerated and burnt, and he failed to arrest his descent.

Rayne peered over the edge in time to see him hit the pavement, then rolled back inside. The heat from her gloves finally registered, and she threw them off, howling at the pain and blowing on her palms futilely. She looked at the smoking gloves, then back at the column. *I'm so not going down the rest of the way that way*, she decided and made room for the gloves in her pack once they'd cooled. She got up slowly and took the stairs.

An hour or so later, she exited onto the street to see that the sidewalk and wall behind it were painted red with the man's blood, but his body had been whisked away. There was no police tape. There would be no investigation. Death was final – there was no point dwelling on it. Theft would be investigated, so long as there was still an aggrieved party, which was why murder so often accompanied theft. Rayne resisted the urge to throw up and headed back toward Triste's apartment, not even bothering to put her hood up and not sure if she could raise her arms over her head even if she wanted to.

A man propositioned her from across the street.

"You wish," she called back, smart enough not to antagonize him by saying what she really thought. She clenched her fists and continued on to Triste's.

Rayne took off her boots outside Triste's door and crept inside so as to not wake her. She stripped and climbed into bed beside her. Triste rarely laundered her sheets, but they were silky, and the mattress softer than the thin mat back at Rayne's place. She reached out a hand but had to will it to stop shaking before resting it on Triste's arm, feeling the softness of her, but the tangibility too. *This is real. This is safe,* she thought and closed her eyes.

Chapter 4

Grace

Grace lay awake, terrified that Jenna had implicated her. She'd spent the last hour rehearsing what she'd say to lessen her punishment and walked downstairs nervously.

Her father looked up from checking the edge of his axe, nodded to her brusquely, and stepped outside, leaving the screen door to slam closed behind him.

Grace was pretty sure that if she was going to be reprimanded, he would be the one to do it, and he had acted normally, or at least as normally as a man could carrying an axe. He was also not the type to collect his thoughts before speaking, so she concluded that he hadn't yet been informed of her transgression – the sword still hung over her head.

Her mother wandered in from outside, cradling an apronful of eggs. "You're up early," she remarked. "Better night's sleep?"

"I wouldn't say that," Grace admitted but deigned not to follow up with anything self-incriminating. "Can I help?" she offered, changing topics.

"That'd be lovely. Help your sister put her hair up, and we can all have breakfast together."

Grace returned upstairs and dutifully helped her sister detangle her hair and wrestle it into a bun.

"I want hair like yours," Hanna complained.

"Mine only hangs straight because it's thin. Yours is more work because it's thick and luxurious."

Hanna brightened to think that her hair was somehow exemplary and resisted less. They descended to the kitchen together and breakfasted on fried eggs and freshly baked bread.

"That was delicious, Mum. Thank you," Grace cooed. Her mother handed them some mint leaves and shooed them out the door.

Grace chewed the mint and thought up ways to have her chores intersect with Jenna's so she could ask her about last night. The chicken coop was in view of Jenna's house and vice versa, so she made several trips back and forth to gather eggs, feed the chickens, and she even spent hours cleaning the disgustingly smelly coop. She hadn't seen a trace of Jenna yet, so she prolonged her stay by asking several neighbors if they wanted a chicken for dinner. Two households took her up on her offer, as did her mother. She couldn't bring herself to wring the chickens' necks herself, so she asked a passing Elder to do it for her. He waited patiently while she chased down the chickens and brought each one to him. He dispatched them coolly, and Grace thanked him profusely, all the while feeling sorry for the unfortunate birds. She sat down where she could see Jenna's house and began plucking feathers. By late afternoon, she still hadn't caught a glimpse of her friend. *Jenna couldn't have an entire day of indoor chores. Even if she were washing or baking, she would have gone outside at least once*, she thought.

Grace dropped off the last chicken with her mother and decided to risk calling on Jenna at her house. She braced herself for the possibility that she was only hastening getting into trouble herself and walked over. She knocked on the back door, hoping that Jenna's mother would answer and not her stern father. The door was opened a moment later by Jenna's mother, her eyes red from crying.

"Are you okay, Mrs. Miller?" Grace asked, worried.

"Chopping onions," she replied quickly, wiping her hands on her apron. "How can I help you, Grace?"

"I hate to be a bother, ma'am, but Jenna said I could borrow a couple candles. Is that okay?"

"It isn't a bother at all. Let me fetch them for you." Jenna's mother returned inside and headed to the pantry.

Grace peeked through the open door but spied and heard no sign of Jenna.

Her mother returned a moment later with four candles. "Here are a couple extra," she told her, handing them over.

"That's so kind of you, thank you." Grace stepped back, then stopped as if struck by an inspiration. "Is Jenna home so I can thank her too?" she asked.

Mrs. Miller looked at her skeptically. "No, she's not. She left this morning to visit her aunt. Two towns over," she added.

"That's too bad," Grace responded nonchalantly, but inwardly crestfallen. "I'll just have to thank her when she gets back. Thank you again," she said amiably and turned for home, hearing the door close behind her.

Jenna's never left the village. She would have told me if she was about to – in fact, she probably wouldn't let up about it, Grace thought. *And why didn't her mother mention Jenna getting into trouble?* She usually loved citing her daughter's shenanigans as a cautionary tale to the other village youth.

Grace spotted Jenna's little sister, Abi, walking back from school with her own sister and changed direction to intercept them.

"Girls, hold on a second," she called.

They waited for her to catch up dutifully, but slightly annoyed.

"Hi, Abi," Grace greeted Jenna's sister. "Your mother tells me that Jenna's gone to visit your aunt."

"We have an aunt?" Abi asked, surprised.

Grace paused, confused. "I must have misheard her. Never mind. Please say hi to her for me when you see her."

"Sure," Abi replied slowly, regarding Grace quizzically, but then turned to Hanna. "Bye," she said and skipped off home, leaving Grace and her sister to walk back to theirs.

"That's weird," Grace mused out loud.

"What is?" Hanna asked.

"Jenna not telling me she was going on a trip."

"She *is* a bit scattered," her sister suggested.

Grace couldn't disagree, but even this was out of character for her friend. "No matter. We're having chicken for dinner."

"Yummy," her sister replied.

Around the dinner table, Grace couldn't tell if it was just her imagination or if her mother gripped her hand tighter than usual while her father said grace.

"Grace provided the chicken," her mother announced.

"Did you now?" her father asked, looking up from carving it.

"I only plucked it," Grace admitted. "Mr. Hall wrung its neck."

Her father smiled and placed some chicken on each of their plates. "How was everyone's day?" he asked.

"It was strange," Grace replied.

"Oh, how's that?" her father asked, lowering his fork.

Her mother looked at her oddly, but Grace couldn't interpret the look, so she continued on regardless. "Jenna's mother told me that she's gone to visit her aunt."

"What's so strange about that?" he asked curiously.

"She would have told me," Grace defended herself.

"Maybe it was a last-minute decision. Perhaps her aunt took ill, and Jenna rushed to her aid," he suggested.

"I saw her…" Grace began but was interrupted by a kick under the table from her mother. "I saw her… yesterday," Grace finished, adjusting what she'd been about to say. "She must have forgotten to tell me. You know how Jenna is."

"That we do," her father replied, smiling, and resumed eating.

After dinner, Grace offered to help her mother with the dishes and followed her into the kitchen while her father retired to the living room, and her sister to her room.

"Why did you kick me?" Grace asked when she was sure they wouldn't be overheard.

"That? Oh, nothing. I was just warning you not to correct your father."

"I don't think I was going to," Grace responded but couldn't recall the conversation exactly. "Something is off," she confided.

"Isn't it always with Jenna?" her mother asked, trying to make light of the situation. "Give her a week, and she'll be back with enough stories to fill a month with telling."

"I suppose you're right," Grace conceded. They finished the dishes in silence, and Grace excused herself to go to bed early.

"Good night, sweetheart," her mother called to her as she climbed the stairs.

"Night, Mum," she called back and closed herself in her room.

I don't care what anyone says. This isn't like Jenna at all. First, I've never heard her say anything about an aunt, and Jenna tells me every detail about breakfast; second, Jenna and I had plans to see each other last night; third, no one has said anything about Jenna being escorted into the woods; and fourth, last minute or not, Jenna would have told me if she was going away. None of this makes sense.

Grace got up to look out the window at the woods where she'd last seen her friend. She spied an Elder standing near the barn, staring up at her window. She quickly ducked out of sight and sat back down, rattled.

"You're being paranoid," she told herself and closed the curtains. She had a hard time falling asleep as she mulled over everything, but sleep did eventually claim her.

An errant thought made her bolt upright in the middle of the night. *Aunts!* She got out of bed and fumbled about in the dark for a notebook and pencil from her bedside table. She grabbed the unlit candle and tip-toed to the closet. The floor creaked, and she froze. She held her breath, waiting, but no one came to investigate. She resumed moving toward the closet, glacially slowly to muffle any further noise. She opened the door and pushed aside her footwear on the floor to make room for herself. She pulled the door closed behind her, sat down, lit the candle, and opened the notebook in her lap.

She stared at the blank page before making two columns, one that she labeled "kids" and the other "adults." Satisfied, she began writing down the names of everyone in the village, starting with her own family. On a whim, she even added Miriam, who drowned last year, and Juliette, who had left the village to get married. Patterns began to emerge as she combed through the list of kids. Plenty of them had sisters – she had one, Jenna had one; Miriam and Juliette had brothers, but that would make them their brothers' sisters.

She looked at the list of adults. Not a single one had a brother or sister that she knew of. Then she remembered Juliette. *Right, maybe they moved away.* In school, she'd been told that hybrid plants were hardier than homogeneous plants, so maybe communities wanted to mix things up to stay strong. Then it occurred to her – *Juliette moved away; Tabitha moved away; Lydia moved away; Danica moved away. And now, Jenna had gone away. Who moved here?* She returned to the top of the list and combed through it again, asking herself, *Who wasn't born here?* She didn't know most of the adults all that well, but she couldn't identify a single person that she recalled "arriving" in their village. People left, but they never came.

So, if no adult has a sister, unless they all moved away, then that meant there were no aunts. So, where did Jenna really go? A chill went up her spine. She desperately needed proof that Jenna had an aunt, so she decided to check the church records in the morning. She closed her notebook, blew out the candle, opened the door quietly, and crept back to bed. Sleep did not come easily.

Bright light filtering through the curtains woke her. She drew them back, revealing a sunny day. The woods looked just as they always did. *There has to be a reasonable explanation for Jenna's disappearance,* she assured herself. *I just have to ferret it out.*

It was Sunday, so she had minimal chores to perform before church. Her family dressed in their finest clothing and headed to church together. Grace's parents walked arm-in-arm ahead of her, while Hanna skipped beside her. Grace put on her sunniest disposition to assure her mother that yesterday's worries were behind her, but inside she felt hollow, like she was floating above her body.

Father Morgan greeted them at the door with a broad smile that unnerved Grace even more than the sternness of the church Elders. Her family filed in with the rest of the villagers and sat down in a middle pew. Grace spied Gabriel in front of her but disregarded him while she scanned the room. She spotted a few of her seven godparents and presumed that the rest sat somewhere behind her.

She felt the eyes of the Elders on her and squirmed. She avoided eye contact with them while she began a slow inventory of the congregation. There were no exceptions to the rules she'd noted the night before. The room was filled with sibling children, but she couldn't find any relation between any of the adults. It didn't make any sense, and the more she thought about it, the more she began to feel unwell.

The congregation began a familiar hymn, but Grace struggled to recall the words – her mind was so addled. Her mother looked at her with concern, and Grace smiled a wan smile, whispering that she was fine. She went through the motions of the remainder of the service, sleepwalking through each element. Its end couldn't come quickly enough, and they finally rose to file out. Her father shook Father Morgan's hand at the door, telling him how moving the sermon had been.

"Father Morgan," Grace interjected, uncharacteristically, and all eyes turned to her. "I feel inspired to help with Sunday School. Is there anything I can do?"

Father Morgan smiled warmly and placed his hand overlong on her shoulder. "I'm sure there is, child. Just ask Sister Judith downstairs."

Grace smiled her thanks and returned inside, hearing her surprised father remark. "As I said, Father, that was some sermon."

Grace was conscripted by Sister Judith to help the younger children paint pictures of the church while she led the older children through a discussion about abstinence. When the hour ended, Grace volunteered to clean up the paints while a thankful Sister Judith escorted the children upstairs.

Grace put the paints away, rinsed the brushes, and tidied the room. When she finished, she stood still, listening intently. Concluding that she was alone, she looked about for the archives, checking each storage room in vain, before peeking into Father Morgan's tiny office. She began to despair when she spied a closet off to the side and realized that it was the only place she hadn't looked. She reached for the knob but found it locked. *Who locks a closet?* she asked herself and rooted through his desk for a key. She knew it was wrong, but her need to prove that Jenna had an aunt compelled her. She found a key under a stack of papers and tried it in the lock. The door creaked open to reveal a tiny file room. She returned the key to its place in the desk, listened again, and hearing nothing, entered the file room.

She started by pulling open the drawer marked "M" and searched through it for Jenna's mother's file, Joanna Miller. She couldn't find it and began to lose heart when it occurred to her that it was probably filed under her maiden name, which she didn't know. On a whim, she pulled out Jenna's father's file and found his marriage certificate, which documented his union with Joanna Reed. She put the file down and turned to the drawer marked "R," which she dug through until she found Jenna's mother's file. It was thin, but it at least contained her birth certificate, which named her parents. *This is worse than chasing chickens*, Grace thought as she searched for Mrs. Miller's father's file. At least he was also a Reed, so his file was close by. She pulled it out and leafed through it. She found a copy of Mrs. Miller's birth certificate but couldn't find another one for a sister, who would be Jenna's aunt. She found a register of key dates that mentioned Mrs. Miller's father's birth, his marriage, and the birth of his daughter, Mrs. Miller, but there was no mention of another daughter's birth. There was no record at all of Jenna having an aunt.

Grace heard someone moving around upstairs and hurriedly returned the files. As she put Jenna's father's file back, she noticed that Jenna's file was missing. *Father Morgan probably has it out*, she thought, *on account of her trip?* A hunch made her pull out Mr. Miller's file again. She looked through it more closely and found a copy of Jenna's sister's birth certificate, but not Jenna's. *That's odd*, she thought. The footsteps upstairs began to move in the direction of the stairs, and Grace began to sweat. She flipped to the register of key dates and scanned it to note Mr. Miller's birth, his marriage, and the birth of Jenna's sister, Abi, but there was no mention of Jenna's birth, which should have been right in the middle. There wasn't even a blank row. It was as if Jenna had never been born. She stuffed the file back in the cabinet and closed the drawer quietly.

She couldn't hear any footsteps, so she decided to take her chances and look up Juliette's file. It was also missing. She looked for Miriam's – it was missing, too. It was as though those girls only existed in Grace's mind. She began to question her sanity.

The measured sound of footsteps coming down the basement stairs startled Grace as she realized that she was trapped in the file room without an explanation for what she was still doing in the church this long after Sunday School had ended, let alone in Father Morgan's office. She stepped out of the file room, not daring to close the creaky door. She spied a tiny window and quickly climbed onto the desk to open it. The footsteps were getting closer as she struggled to pull herself through the opening. She knocked several papers off the desk but managed to squeeze through and close the window behind her. She pressed her back against the church wall, heart hammering in her chest, hoping that no one had seen her crawl out the window.

She inched along the wall, then walked away briskly, not looking back to see if she'd been observed. She was a nervous wreck and decided to gather wildflowers on her way home to calm herself and give her an excuse for her lateness.

As she pushed open the kitchen door, her worried mother noted, "You've been gone a while."

"I felt like collecting flowers on the way home. I don't know why," she added and placed them in a vase.

"Well, aren't you full of surprises today," her mother noted. "You didn't look so good in church."

"It was hot, and I think the poor sleep caught up with me. I'm fine now," Grace assured her.

"That's good," her mother responded, turning to check on some rising dough. Grace took it as her cue to sneak out.

"I'm going to read," she informed her mother as she climbed the stairs to her room.

"Okay, dear," her mother called back.

Grace collapsed onto her bed. *Jenna's aunt didn't exist. Jenna didn't exist. None of the missing girls existed, but she had no proof. How can you prove something that doesn't exist?*

Chapter 5

Rayne

Rayne woke up feeling wonderfully rested. She flopped over to find the bed empty beside her. It seemed silly to call out to Triste, so she propped herself up and listened for any sound of her. The silence confirmed that she'd left for the day and let Rayne sleep in. Rayne would rather have had a few more moments with her than the extra sleep, but there was nothing to be done about it now.

She pulled back the blanket and swung her feet over the edge of the bed. Sleeping in an actual bed was an immense luxury after sleeping for so long on a thin mat over hard concrete. She sighed contentedly and rose to get dressed. She decided to borrow one of Triste's tops. Triste was taller but thinner, so some of her clothes fit Rayne. Rayne liked being wrapped in the scent of her on-again-off-again girlfriend.

Rayne hunted through Triste's kitchen and confirmed that there wasn't much to eat. She cut up some melon for Loki, hoping he'd be desperate enough to eat whatever she left out for him.

"You're staying here today," she told him. "Don't cause trouble."

She eyed her leather jacket, which she'd rescued from her place, but decided that she definitely needed to travel incognito today and left it in favor of her hoodie. She spotted a ring of keys on the table near the door, with a hastily written note saying only, *Use these.* Rayne knew it was only a temporary loan and that Triste didn't mean anything more significant by it, but her heart soared regardless. She pulled up her hood and stepped out into the hall.

Her first order of business was letting her boss know that she'd be away for a few days while she looked for a new place to live. An e-bike nearly ran her over as she stepped into the street. *Asshole,* she cursed silently but wished she had an easier way of getting around than walking. A police officer across the street took an interest in her, so she made a show of flipping her keys around her finger before depositing them in her pocket. *I live here; please leave me alone,* she telegraphed and turned to walk casually toward her work. The officer lost interest, and Rayne relaxed.

"Hi, honey… I'm home," she called out to Cieco as she entered his store.

Cieco just grunted. "Where were you yesterday?"

"I'm moving apartments," she replied. "Speaking of which, I'll be off for a couple more days."

"We've got nothing but time," he replied sarcastically.

"If there's anything small you want me to look at while I'm away, just point it out, and I'll take it with me.

Cieco just waved at the assortment on the table she usually worked at. "Take anything you can carry."

Rayne placed a few items in her backpack and added a few tools that she used most often. Cieco didn't even notice when she slipped out.

Rayne made her way to her favorite café to grab a coffee and think. It was a luxury that she knew she couldn't afford, but she paid for the overpriced drink anyway and sat down. There weren't a lot of people in the tiny shop, just a woman engrossed in a beat-up reader and a guy cradling a cup as he stared out the window.

Rayne pulled out her notebook and began drawing a map of candidate buildings from what she remembered of the view from her last home. Only a few skyscrapers poked through the clouds, and fewer still met her criteria – besides being taller than the cloud layer, they had to be structurally sound and uninhabited. That was about it, but it ruled out many of them. She recalled the ones she'd scouted in the past and crossed a few out. The others, she'd have to check. She drained the last of her cup and stared at her map. She had a plan, and time was wasting. She got up and headed for the door, passing the woman and the guy staring into the street, both of whom hadn't moved, then she headed north past her old place.

The tower across the street was an option, but Renner advised against maintaining predictable patterns too long. Better to seek out something farther away.

She was approaching the first candidate building when she spied Cieco's scavenger, Helt, furtively exit the one beside it. *That rules this neighborhood out*, she decided in an instant. She didn't mind sketchy, but even she had limits, and besides, she didn't want to bump into Helt on the regular – he was too creepy. She mentally crossed the place off her list and turned west toward a more isolated skyscraper.

She liked that the streets were deserted as she neared it. It wasn't as though anyone would come to her aid if she were accosted anyway, so it was better simply to have no one around to accost her in the first place. She walked up the chipped steps and stared through the missing front doors into the dark lobby. Confirming that a building was uninhabited was time-consuming and always made her uneasy. Renner had tried to press her to carry a knife once, but she looked herself over. *Who would I be kidding? I couldn't intimidate a fly.* She steeled herself and walked inside.

The odds were that no one would choose to live on one of the subterranean levels. *Why live there when there were fifty stories above you with light?* She'd check them later if the rest of the place passed inspection. The lobby was caked in a layer of dust that made it easy to confirm that no one had traversed it in a very long time. *That's a good sign*, she concluded, but there were always other ways in and out. She decided that she didn't need to check the rooms off the lobby and ascended the grand staircase to the second level, where she began her survey in earnest.

She moved as quietly as she could, not wanting to alert anyone who might be in the building. She was careful not to disturb debris and didn't open doors if she didn't absolutely need to – the creaking after decades of disuse could echo through an entire building. Just examining the ground beneath a door usually revealed whether it had been opened anytime recently.

She'd made it to the sixth floor when she heard a faint sound above her. *It might just be a feral cat*, she thought. *I can't rule this place out without checking.* She finished her sweep of the sixth floor and moved cautiously up the stairs to the seventh. She tip-toed forward, cursing her clunky work boots. Nothing looked out of the ordinary in the rooms off the stairs, so she headed down the hall to the far end. The door facing her was ajar, and she edged closer to it. She peeked her head around it to check out the room.

A terrified young woman stood facing her, holding a hand over a toddler's mouth to keep her quiet. Two other children sat on the floor, staring at her. The fear in the woman's eyes impaled Rayne. She quickly pulled back her hood to reveal her young face and lifted her hands into the air.

"I'm not going to tell anyone you're here," she assured the woman. "I was just looking for somewhere to hide myself."

The woman lowered her hand from her youngest daughter's mouth but kept her fearful eyes on Rayne.

Rayne couldn't bear the thought of upending this poor woman's life. Population control was probably the only thing that the authorities took seriously. Given that people no longer died of natural causes, you were only allowed one child, ever. The punishment for having a second child was the execution of one of the parents; for a third child, both parents; for more, the parents and the eldest child, etc. Rayne understood the terror in the woman's eyes.

"Your children are a gift. I wish you well," Rayne reassured her. "I'll find somewhere else." She backed out the doorway and turned toward the stair. *Dammit*, she thought. She'd just forced the woman to move. Nothing she could say would ever be enough to assure her that her children were safe. Even though she knew that they'd be gone by morning, Rayne couldn't stay here knowing that she'd chased them away. It also made it hard to pick another building near here as the woman might try to relocate to one of them. She'd have to abandon the entire north end and try her luck farther south, a part of the city that she was less familiar with.

She sat down on the front steps to think. She needed to scout the southern buildings from above the cloud layer – you could only tell so much from ground level. Triste once said that she had a client in the south end who lived in a penthouse with a panoramic view and always had a party going on there. Perhaps she could sneak in and scout from there.

She looked herself over. She was glad to have worn Triste's top, but she had to be realistic that she could never pass for one of the beautiful people in Triste's clients' world. She'd need a cover story and figured that she could make something up on the way. She began the hike south, leaving the sketchy neighborhood she was in, passing through the market district where she worked, and finally entering what passed for the "nicer" part of the city. The streets did seem better maintained, she noted.

She already had a sense of where the building was that she was heading for. She'd seen it from her place plenty of times, and she should be able to recognize it from the ground by its distinctive silver sheen.

She pulled off her hoodie and shook out her hair. The rich were brash. Skulking around in this part of town would draw more attention than her hair. She marched up to the doors of the building that she thought was the right one. Two guards flanked the entrance. The one on the right was a hulking man who probably needed custom-made clothes – his muscles were so huge. The one on the left was a woman who leaned back with a flinty look that unnerved Rayne.

"I'm here to fix the pool lights," Rayne made up on the spot.

The woman looked her over skeptically.

Rayne sighed and pulled out her toolkit. "Satisfied?" she asked with mock impatience.

The woman merely waved her past. The servants of the rich could be imperious, but they bored as easily as their employers. Rayne started toward the stairs before remembering that they'd have working elevators. *There's no way rich kids would take the stairs a single floor, let alone fifty*, she thought, rolling her eyes.

60

She stepped into the open elevator, opulent with its rich red carpet and polished brass, and pushed the button for the top floor. Nothing happened. The flinty-looking woman leaned in, and Rayne tried not to sweat, but she just pulled out a key card, inserted it into a slot, and pressed the button for the penthouse. It lit up, and the woman withdrew to the hallway. The door closed, and the elevator began to rise.

Rayne heard the music from the party before the door even opened at the top floor. Two more guards barred her path as she stepped off. "The pool?" she asked impertinently, tapping a screwdriver against her thigh.

They looked at each other uncertainly, but the man on the right gestured the way.

Rayne didn't move. "And the spare bulbs?" she asked.

The men looked uncomprehendingly at her.

"For the pool lights," she clarified, frustrated.

"How would I know?" he replied.

"Great. I am *so* charging for the time I waste hunting for them," she declared, tapping her screwdriver on his chest and pushing past him.

She passed through an enormous antechamber and entered a luxurious room filled with attractive people. Some chatted with a drink in their hand, while others made out on the sofas. Rayne resisted the urge to touch the soft leather, just to see what it felt like. There was an undercurrent of bored hedonism in the room, and heads turned at Rayne's mane of bright blue hair. She was the distraction of the moment.

A youngish man with chiseled features and smoldering eyes pushed off the wall to approach her. He moved like a lion, and Rayne found it hard to look away.

Oh God, she thought. "I'm just here for the pool," she told him. "I'll do *you* later." She smirked and walked past him. He shrugged and made his way toward the bar. She was under no illusion that she was in his league, but she recognized that she was a novelty.

She spotted the pool through the patio doors and headed toward it. She wove through throngs of vacuous but drop-dead-gorgeous people. A few were swimming in skimpy bathing suits, undergarments, or nothing at all. A statuesque woman with impossibly long legs pulled herself out of the pool in front of Rayne, dripping and fully naked. She shook out her long dark hair and gestured for Rayne to hand her a towel from the pile beside her, which she did in a dumbstruck fog. The woman dried her hair and brushed past Rayne, still completely naked. Rayne felt the heat from her body trigger a rise in her own. *Oh. My. God.* she thought, shaking her head to clear it.

The pool, she reminded herself and circumnavigated it until she spotted a burned-out light. *Any idiot can change a bulb,* she rued, *but the rich hire idiots to do it for them.* She hunted around for an equipment shed, grabbing the odd canapé off the trays that passed. She finally found a hidden panel that clicked open when she pressed on it. Inside were assorted pool chemicals and a few cartons of lightbulbs. She pulled one out and walked back to the pool's edge. The burned-out light was deeper than she could reach. *This is going to be awkward,* she thought and kicked off her boots. She sat on a lounge chair to take off her socks, laying them over her boots. She looked down at Triste's top and decided that she couldn't risk bleaching it with chlorine, so she pulled it over her head, thanking God that she'd worn a bra, although there were enough naked people in the pool that no one even glanced her way. She debated pulling off her leather pants but decided against it. *These people might feel comfortable walking around naked, but I sure as hell am not.*

She pulled the lightbulb out of its carton and walked around to the pool stairs, soaking in the warmth of the water as she waded into it. She had more spectators for wearing clothes into the pool than those who didn't. She flipped her hair back and made her way over to the burned-out light. She put the replacement bulb down on the pool's edge, took a deep breath, and dove down to pull out the burned-out one. She pried the housing free, unclipped the bulb, and rose to the surface. The naked woman was there to hand her the fresh bulb with a raised eyebrow and a twinkle in her eye. Rayne took it with an awkward smile and dove back down to insert it.

When she broke the surface again, the woman handed her a towel. Rayne pulled herself out of the pool in a fluid motion and thankfully accepted the towel.

"I need to shower," Rayne informed her, unsure whether it would come across as a rejection or an invitation.

"Come find me after," the woman replied in a husky voice that almost melted any resolve Rayne had. The woman sashayed away as Rayne bent to pick up her clothes. *Now, I really need a shower*, she thought. There was an outdoor shower on the pool deck, but she didn't like the idea of being the entertainment, so she ducked inside in search of privacy.

So this is Triste's world, she thought, feeling woefully out of place in it. She pushed open the door to a bathroom, consumed with thoughts of inadequacy, only to interrupt a couple in the bathtub.

"Sorry," she muttered embarrassedly as she retreated. She finally found an ensuite off an unoccupied bedroom and locked the door behind her. *I don't want Loverboy following me in here*, she thought as she stripped down and stepped into the shower. The controls seemed incomprehensibly complicated, so she just started pushing buttons and turning knobs. Water sprayed at her from a million directions, and she never felt so pampered. The steam grew so thick that she couldn't see across the room, prompting her to reluctantly turn off the water and grab a towel. It had been warmed by the rack it was hanging on and felt like she'd wrapped herself in a warm cloud. *I have to get out of here before I start to hate my life*, she thought.

She rinsed the chlorine out of her leather pants in the sink and struggled to pull them back on, flopping around the marble floor like a fish out of water. She finally succeeded in getting dressed, even though her pants were still wet, and exited the bedroom to scout the adjacent buildings from the pool deck.

She spotted the boy from the living room lounging by the pool. He nodded toward her and resumed sipping his drink. The naked woman from the pool walked past, having put on a sheer cover-up. *At least they're patient*, Rayne thought, wondering if that was what amounted to foreplay in their world, but she couldn't bear the thought of cheating on Triste, no matter how alluring the temptation. *I need to hurry up and get out of here*, she told herself.

She walked to the roof's edge, noting candidate buildings and memorizing their approximate location. Girls beside her were talking about taking a trip to a place called Mekka to buy drugs and maybe take in a band they liked. *Must be nice*, Rayne thought and made her way to the next side of the deck.

64

There were only a few hours of daylight left, and if she wanted to check out at least one other building before returning to Triste's place, she'd better get a move on. She walked inside casually, then moved quickly toward the elevator, not wanting to be confronted by one of her prowling paramours. The guards couldn't have cared less that she was leaving, and she stepped into the elevator without being accosted. She thanked her luck but didn't breathe again until the doors closed behind her. She panicked that she didn't have a key to operate the elevator but pushed the button for the main floor anyway, and it lit. *Of course, there are no restrictions on leaving*, she thought, relieved.

The flinty-looking guard raised an eyebrow at Rayne's wet pants as she exited but thankfully didn't ask her about them. Walking in wet leather pants was uncomfortable, but Rayne hurried in the direction that she judged was away from the bay. *Everyone wants a view of water*, she thought. If she wanted privacy, it was best to rule those buildings out.

She arrived in front of the remains of a skyscraper that was more skeleton than building, not too different from her old one. *At least that'll make it easier to scout*, she concluded, *and probably less appealing to others. This could be the one*, she hoped. The stairs were exposed, and the wind kept dust from accumulating on them, so it was hard to judge whether they'd been trodden recently. She made her way up each floor, quickly but quietly. She was generally able to tell at a glance if a floor was empty, and there were only a few that she had to scout more closely. People had definitely lived here in the past, but there was no evidence that anyone did so now. At least there might be some odds and ends that she could drag up to furnish her place. The stairs ended where several floors had eroded away entirely, but she was able to cross over to a stairwell on the opposite side of the building and continue upward. By the time she finally made it to the roof, she was exhausted but happy that the place seemed uninhabited.

She walked around the roof to check for leaks. There were a few, but the next-to-the-top floor seemed dry and undisturbed. *This could work*, she thought happily. The faint sound of voices made her freeze. There was nowhere to hide on the empty floor, so she scurried back up to the roof, the best she could do. The voices continued, but they didn't sound like they were getting closer, so she relaxed and tried to figure out where they were coming from. Ground noise sometimes filtered up, but not this high, and never through the sound-dampening clouds.

She peered over the roof's edge and spotted a congregation of robed individuals on an adjacent rooftop, lower down. She ducked her head quickly but concluded from the gathering dark that unless they were specifically looking for her, they'd be hard-pressed to see her. She peeked back out to see what they were doing on a rooftop at dusk.

They looked religious, but she'd think that about anyone wearing robes. They stood in a semi-circle around a woman at the roof's edge. Even from a distance, Rayne could tell that she was older, easily over three hundred, but beyond that, it was hard to tell. She was looking at the setting sun while those around her prayed solemnly. Rayne was able to make out some of the words as they drifted up to her: "Wake anew," "Return to His arms," and so forth. *Blah, blah, blah.* She was about to turn away when the fragment of a sentence stopped her, "As it is in Mekka, so shall..." *There it is again*, Rayne thought, curious now. She studied the group again with greater interest.

The woman at the center of the semi-circle turned to smile at each of her colleagues. Rayne was transfixed by her serenity. She turned again to face the setting sun and stepped off the roof. *Holy shit!* Rayne thought, unable to pry her eyes from the spot where the woman had just been. *She just killed herself!* It wasn't unheard of for people who had lived a very long time to tire and take their chances with an afterlife or just escape their tiredness, but she'd never seen it. The robed people each pulled a rose from a vase and took turns tossing them over the edge where the woman had stepped before they filed silently toward the stairs.

Eventually, Rayne was alone, staring down at an empty rooftop, the image of the woman's beatific smile burned in her mind. She rose stiffly and made her own way down the stairs to ground level. Peeking out onto the street, there was no sign of the group she'd just witnessed. *Besides the eerily religious neighbors, this place seemed to fit the bill*, Rayne thought, *at least for a little while.* She pulled up her hood and headed to Triste's.

She made it back after dark and walked up the stairs to Triste's apartment, knocking lightly to announce herself before inserting the key. She doubted Triste would have anyone over, knowing that Rayne had a key, but she didn't want to be presumptive. She opened the door slowly and peeked in. A couple of candles were lit, signaling that Triste was home. Rayne stepped in quietly, which roused Triste from a light sleep on the couch.

"There you are," Triste greeted her sleepily.

"Here I am," Rayne replied, closing and locking the door behind her.

"Why are your pants wet?" Triste asked.

"Long story," Rayne deflected and flopped down in a chair to pull them off. She felt guilty when she pulled off the top that she'd borrowed from Triste, but Triste hadn't seemed to notice.

"Come to bed," Triste offered and finished her wine. She got up and walked to the bedroom, undressing as she went.

Rayne finished undressing as well and looked around for Loki.

"I fed the cat," Triste called from the bedroom, so Rayne gave up looking for him and joined her.

Triste lay on the left side of the bed, facing the center, so Rayne crawled in on the right, flipped over, and slid across so that Triste was spooning her. Triste put an arm around her and held her close. All Rayne could think was how inadequate she felt in Triste's world, and a tear rolled down her cheek.

Triste gave Rayne a goodnight kiss on the back of the head and settled back to sleep, breathing rhythmically in no time.

Rayne couldn't get the image of the woman stepping off the building out of her mind. *What's Mekka?* she wondered.

Chapter 6

Grace

Grace needed to know that she hadn't just imagined her friend, Jenna, and the other missing girls. She didn't want to say anything about it to her mother, who already worried about her. Instead, she sought out Gabriel. She found him at the mill, shoveling grain onto the mill wheel. He was surprised to see her walking briskly toward him, and she could tell from his nervousness that he was concerned about the impropriety of their being alone together without a chaperone – *"witness" is more like it*, Grace thought, annoyed. She didn't have the patience to worry about his or her reputation.

"Gabriel," she greeted him, ensuring that she kept a respectful distance in case someone did come upon them.

"Hi, Grace. Nice to see you," he replied, looking around anxiously.

Dammit, Gabriel, focus on me, she thought ruefully. "Did you hear that Jenna went to stay with her aunt?" she asked.

"Yeah, I think Jacob mentioned it. Why?"

Grace was unimaginably relieved to hear Gabriel confirm that Jenna wasn't just a figment of her imagination. "Just that I miss her terribly," she deflected. "Silas must be crushed."

"I suppose so. I don't really see him much. He's in the fields all day, and I'm stuck here," Gabriel replied, humbly downplaying the responsibility the village vested in him.

Grace decided to explore another tack. "Do you remember Juliette?"

"Sort of. She moved away, right?"

Thank God, the missing girls are real too, she thought. "I was just thinking how terrible it would be if Jenna never came back, just like Juliette."

"I guess so. You two are pretty close," he admitted, the first inkling that he actually paid attention to what was important to her. "She'll come back," he assured her, having no idea really, just wanting to pacify her. "Everyone knows Silas is going to marry her."

"I hope so," Grace agreed, hoping to appear mollified. "I wonder if he'll go visit her."

"That wouldn't be proper," Gabriel responded.

"Not alone, silly. He'd go escorted."

"Seems like a lot of trouble for a visit."

A romantic, you're not, she concluded. "Do you know anyone who's ever visited one of the other communities?"

"Sure, the Elders do it all the time to trade goods."

"Of course. I meant, do you know anyone *personally* who's been outside the village? Have you ever talked with them about what it was like?"

Gabriel looked at her as though this was a strange line of questioning.

"You boys have all the adventures," she covered. "We girls sort of stick close to home."

He relaxed a little. "We don't get out much either," he replied.

"So, that's a no?"

"I guess so."

"That's a pity. Jenna's adventure inspired me to think about the outside world," Grace said to create an explanation for her curiosity.

"I'm sure it's pretty much the same out there as it is here," Gabriel responded.

Grace decided to risk a question that she knew he'd find odd. "Have you ever thought it strange that kids leave for other villages from time to time, like Jenna and Juliette, but no one ever comes here?"

"I've never really thought about it. I guess it's not that exciting here."

"You can say that again," Grace laughed.

"Is that what you wanted to talk about?" Gabriel asked, shifting on his feet, eager to get back to work and escape this strange conversation.

"I guess so," Grace admitted. "Jenna just got me thinking is all."

"She'll be back in no time," Gabriel repeated, hoping to wrap up the conversation.

Grace debated telling him what she'd seen the night Jenna was taken into the woods, but she didn't get the impression that she'd find an ally in him. His lack of curiosity and his utter devotion to the rules made him a useless confidant.

"I suppose you're right. Thanks for talking. I feel much better," she lied.

71

"Of course," he smiled, happy to have the affair concluded.

"I shouldn't keep you," she apologized and turned to go.

"Any time," he replied and turned back to work, puzzling over the strange conversation.

Grace walked away, disappointed that Gabriel hadn't been more help. At least he confirmed her sanity, but also her darker suspicions about the village. As a bonus, he helped her confirm that in no possible future did she see herself as Mrs. Gabriel Parker.

She passed a couple of Elders and smiled graciously at them to hide her growing unease at their watchfulness. She felt alone and desperately needed someone to confide in. She headed home and walked into the kitchen.

"Don't you have chores?" her mother asked.

"I miss Jenna," Grace unloaded, bursting into tears.

"There, there, dear," her mother soothed her, quickly moving around the counter to embrace her.

"She's like a sister," Grace sobbed.

"You *have* a sister," her mother tried to console her.

"Jenna's my age," she countered, sounding like a child.

"I'm sure she'll be back in no time," her mother soothed.

Why does everyone keep saying that when the village has erased her? Grace thought. "Do you ever wish you had a sister?" Grace asked.

For a brief flash, Grace saw that she'd touched a nerve, but her mother recovered quickly. "I have you, dear."

"It's not the same," Grace complained but wondered at the cloud that had flashed so briefly in her mother's eyes.

"Why don't you take the day off and go visit one of your sevens?" her mother suggested. "They'll make you feel better. That's what they're there for."

Grace hadn't skipped a day of chores in eighteen years, and certainly not for something as insignificant as missing an absent friend. She'd fed the pigs in freezing rain. She'd gathered firewood when she had the flu. For her mother to suggest taking a day off indicated that whatever was going on was at a level of seriousness that she was only beginning to fathom.

"Could I?" Grace asked.

"If you don't tell your father, I won't," her mother replied conspiratorially.

"You're the best," Grace declared, hugging her tightly, then turning for the door. "I'll go see Eleanor."

Her mother smiled and watched her leave before returning to her baking.

Grace thought about her mother's admonition to not tell her father what she was up to. She'd said it in a lighthearted way, but something in her eyes had seemed deadly serious. She decided that she had to avoid drawing attention to herself, lest it get back to him.

She walked up to the school and saw the children playing in the yard. Recess meant that Eleanor would be free to chat, given that she taught the youngest children. Grace poked her head in her classroom and spotted her at her desk, examining an array of collages.

"Eleanor?" she asked, alerting her to her presence.

She looked up, surprised to see her goddaughter at the school.

"Grace, dear. How are you?" she asked with her usual perkiness, smiling warmly.

It always sounded odd to Grace when Eleanor tried to come across as older than she was. She was only thirty-five and the youngest of Grace's sevens.

"I'm fine, but not so fine," Grace replied, entering the classroom and taking a seat at a tiny desk. Her knees were scrunched up to her chest, but she needed to sit down.

"How's that, child?"

Grace bristled at being called a child but pushed it aside, assuming that Eleanor was just accustomed to saying that as a teacher. "My friend, Jenna, went away yesterday, and I'm afraid she's never coming back."

"Why would you think that?" Eleanor asked with concern.

"No one ever comes back," Grace explained, walking a fine line.

"God calls us each to walk different paths," Eleanor tried to assure her. "If we serve Him better elsewhere, who are we to second guess His will?"

Grace wasn't remotely reassured by Eleanor's reasoning. "But I miss her," she protested.

"It always seems darkest just after you blow out a candle," Eleanor pointed out, hoping the analogy would help Grace see that she was overreacting.

There's darkness in this village, alright, Grace thought, but Eleanor seemed oblivious to it. Worse, she was treating Grace like a child.

"I just want her back."

"Resist the temptation to focus on yourself. Pray that God's Will be done, and you'll feel better."

Basically, stop being selfish, Grace concluded. "I'll try," she promised, realizing that the conversation was a dead end.

"Good girl," Eleanor concluded. "It's so good to see you."

"You too," Grace replied and ducked into the hallway, poking her head back in to say a final "thank you." *That was a waste of time*, she thought bitterly and decided to head to the bakery to see Mr. Evans, her second godparent. He always made her feel better.

"Grace, this is a pleasant surprise," he greeted her as she entered his shop. "Your mother is my stiffest competition," he joked. "What can I get you?"

"Just a moment of your time. I'm feeling blue."

"We can't have that," he declared and fished around behind the counter for a cinnamon bun. "Eat that, and you'll feel better." There was no crisis that Mr. Evans thought couldn't be cured by pastry, and Grace felt like she had to oblige him.

"Thank you, Mr. Evans," she replied, sitting down on a stool at the counter.

"Call me Mark," he allowed in her moment of need. "Now, what has you down?"

"My friend just left to visit her aunt, and I miss her." She took a tentative bite of the bun. It was tasty, but she wasn't in the mood for it and had to fake appreciating it for his sake.

"If I were you, I'd try to distract myself. Idle hands make for an idle mind. When I'm feeling down, I throw myself at my work, and before you know it, I'm whistling, and the fog lifts."

"My chores keep me plenty busy, but they don't seem to distract me from my sadness." She took another tiny bite.

"Maybe spend more time with your family," he suggested. Your sister adores you."

Clearly, it's been a while since he's visited, Grace thought – Hanna preferred the company of her friends to Grace's now.

"I could do that," she agreed.

"Enjoy the time you've got with your sister. The next thing you know, you're out the door, and you never really get the chance again." There was a certainty to what he said that struck Grace as more than just vague advice.

"I will, thank you. Can I take this with me?" she indicated to the largely untouched cinnamon bun.

"I'll do you one better," he replied, placing three more in a bag and handing it to her. "One for everyone."

"You spoil us," she gushed as she departed his shop. He was nice enough, but she didn't feel that she could really confide in him. She slipped her unfinished bun into the bag with the others and thought about whom she might try next now that her first and second had turned out to be a bust. Her third and fourth were a devout couple that she doubted she could open up to. Her fifth was over a hundred, but she'd never met her sixth, and her seventh was a church deacon who intimidated her. Despite her age, her fifth seemed like her last and best bet. She walked up the hill on the outskirts of the village to her fifth's house, strode up to the back door, and knocked.

The door opened right away, and a kindly old woman peered out.

"Grace, I almost didn't recognize you. It's been unforgivably long since I last saw you. I'm so glad that you're here," Esther greeted her.

Grace was instantly put at ease. "Forgive me for not visiting more often," she replied.

"Nonsense. That's my job. Please come in." She shepherded Grace inside and put on a pot of tea.

"Norman will be sad that he missed you. He's in the fields."

"It's okay. I really just wanted to see you. Don't tell him that, of course."

"Of course not. What's on your mind, dear?"

"My friend has gone away, and I'm afraid for her," she admitted, as close to the truth as she judged she could risk.

"It is a scary world out there," Esther probed.

"It's not that. I know that she's never coming back, and I feel like I let her down."

Esther thought about this as she poured them both a cup of tea, handing one to Grace, and pulling a chair close. "I understand how you feel. I always wanted a daughter, but they're... complicated. Norm wanted a son, but I couldn't take the risk, so I lied about my cycles until we gave up trying to have a child."

"But you have a son."

"The village let us adopt him from a couple who had a boy and a girl. Norm got to have his son, the couple got to have their daughter, and that was enough for me." She stared out the window.

"So, my friend's life has become 'complicated?'"

"More than complicated, I'm afraid. Pray for her and hold her tightly in your heart, so her memory never fades." Esther's eyes clouded, and Grace could tell that she spoke from a deep well of pain.

Esther had been more forthright with Grace than anyone ever had, so it emboldened her to ask another question. "Did you know my sixth?"

"Yes, dear. Her name is Violet Moore."

"Why have I never met her?" Grace asked.

"You have – you were just too young to remember. She doted on you, but she left the village when your sister was born."

"Why did she leave?"

"She never said, but I imagine she felt she couldn't stay."

"Where did she go?"

"She didn't tell anyone," Esther replied but thought about it a moment longer. "She only said something about wanting to lose herself." Realizing that that sounded terrible, she added, "Don't be mad at her. She loved you fiercely – she still does, I imagine."

Grace put a hand on Esther's knee and got up to go. "Thank you," she said. "I'd better get home before my parents worry."

Esther stopped her by gripping her sleeve. "Take care of yourself," she told her with an intensity that took Grace aback.

"I will," she promised.

Esther released her. "You can *go*," she said, oddly stressing the last word and rising to collect their cups.

Grace left and walked down the hill, wrapped in her thoughts. Something terrible had happened to Jenna – she was sure of it now. Esther knew it and was trying to tell her without telling her. Worse, she seemed to be warning her.

The eye of every Elder seemed to be on her as she walked home. She felt like a fox at a hunt. She returned home in time for dinner and reported to her mother that her sevens had made her feel better.

"Aren't they wonderful!" her mother stated.

Grace helped wash the dishes then told her mother that she was going to brush the horses before bed to calm herself and hopefully sleep more soundly as a result.

"That always works for me," her mother agreed and waved her out.

Grace walked to the barn, picked up the grooming brush, and headed to the corral.

"Good evening, Father Michael," she greeted Father Morgan's assistant as he strolled past. He eyed her skeptically until she showed him the brush. "Just brushing the horses before bed," she told him, and he nodded at her industry.

Grace stepped through the gate into the horse corral, looked to see if anyone had seen her, and slipped through the fence on the forest side. She pulled a dark blanket from inside her dress, wrapped it around her shoulders, and removed her bonnet. In the dim light of dusk, she'd be hard to see at a distance. She moved along the tree line to the spot where she's seen Jenna being led. There was a faint trail that Grace followed into the darkening woods.

She followed the path down a long ravine that snaked away from the village, deep into the forest. The jagged rocks hemmed her in, and her chest tightened in response. The ravine finally opened into a clearing with a stone altar in its center. She approached it cautiously and reached out to place a hand on it. The cold of the stone chilled her to the bone. There were iron rings secured to it at regular intervals. It seemed so pagan that she couldn't believe that the church allowed it to exist so close to the village, never mind their having brought Jenna here. *And for what purpose? Was she flogged for sneaking around at night, then sent away as further punishment?* The wind moaned in the trees and terrified her, so Grace turned and hurried back up the ravine. Something terrible had happened to Jenna in that clearing – she was certain of it.

She retraced her path to the corral, left the blanket draped over the fence, and hurried back to the barn to return the grooming brush. Once inside, she returned the brush to its place, then lit a candle and dashed up to the loft to leave it behind, pushing straw up against its base. *It's come to this*, she told herself, then raced down the ladder and hurried home.

She ran straight up the stairs to her room, closed the door, and peered out the window into the darkness. She spied an Elder watching her and yanked the curtains closed. She sat on her bed, feeling trapped and alone. She noticed her bedside table drawer ajar and pulled it open.

Her notebook was gone.

Chapter 7

Rayne

Rayne had a cup of coffee waiting for Triste when she woke up.

"Thanks," she said, taking it from her and sitting up to drink it.

"Have you heard of Mekka?" Rayne asked.

"Sure," Triste replied, taking a sip and sitting up. "The girls I work for go there sometimes. They say it's an experience – all roads lead to it."

"Then why haven't I heard of it before?"

"Have you ever felt like you have a void inside of you that needs filling?"

"No."

"Must be nice," Triste responded, getting up and standing in front of her closet, hoping an outfit would jump out and inspire her.

"What has that got to do with anything?"

"Hmm? Oh, Mekka is where you go when you need inspiration. It's the hub of the art scene."

"Have you ever been there?"

"Me? No. I'm too busy, plus I don't have money for a vacation. Speaking of money, I'd better get moving. I've got a fitting this morning and drop-offs this afternoon." She pulled on a pair of comfortable linen pants and a cotton tee. She headed to the bathroom to apply makeup while Rayne sat in the living room mulling over what she'd said. Triste re-emerged a moment later.

"You look great," Rayne told her.

"Thanks," she replied and walked out before Rayne could say anything more.

"I found a place," Rayne announced to the closed door. She sighed and got up. *I might as well go move in.* She picked up Triste's unfinished coffee and downed it. "Road trip," she called to Loki and grabbed his pouch. He poked his head out of the dresser drawer where he'd been sleeping and lazily meandered over. "If you're trying to make Triste hate you, you are doing a bang-up job," Rayne chastised him, pulling some of his hair off the clothes he'd been lying on, then giving up and just turning the pile over. *I'll fix that later,* she promised herself and scooped Loki into his pouch.

"Job One is a bed," she told him as she walked toward her former building. She found herself taking an indirect route and looking over her shoulder to verify that she wasn't being followed. It bothered her to still feel so much on edge since her attack. *It's over. He's gone. It was a one-time thing,* she told herself to give herself confidence.

She arrived at her building and removed the signal wires on her way up so she could reuse them in her new building. She emerged on her floor tired but happy that she had somewhere else to go. She'd miss it here, she concluded. It had begun to feel like home, despite Renner's advisement against predictability. She looked around. There were a few things that she wanted for her new place, but she couldn't move everything at once – her mattress was going to be enough of a chore for one day. She rolled it up and sat on it while she cinched a rope around it, making two loops that she could slide over her shoulders. *This is going to distress the hell out of my jacket,* she thought, *but better the jacket than my skin.* She picked up the rolled-up mattress, slipped her arms through the loops, and lifted it onto her back. *I forgot how heavy this thing is,* she thought ruefully and made for the stairs. Her bruised side reminded herself of its existence, so she shifted the mattress's weight as best she could.

It took her an eternity to lug the thing down to street-level, and she was dripping with sweat by the time she stepped out. Passersby stared at her, annoying her more than unnerving her for a change.

"Nothing to see here, folks," she muttered. "Just a girl without friends moving apartments." She turned south and started walking toward her new home. Loki poked his head out of his pouch, enjoying the adventure, but looking up at her reproachfully every time a drop of sweat landed on his forehead.

Arriving at her new building, she began the arduous trek up the stairs. She had to sit down every four or five floors, too exhausted to continue without rest. Through some miraculous feat of perseverance, she finally arrived at her chosen floor. "Home, sweet home," she declared, examining the empty expanse of discolored concrete. She lugged the mattress to the center of the floor and plopped it down. The ropes proved to be a devil to untie as the knots had tightened on the walk.

Finished, she lay down spent and looked around. *It'll take some touches to make this place feel homey,* she concluded and tried to rise, but her muscles revolted. *Okay, thirty minutes,* she told herself and pulled out her music player. It's what had gotten her into trouble originally, but she was too exhausted to care and needed the music to feed her soul. She listened to her favorite song on repeat for the full thirty minutes and probably would have done so again had the battery not given out. She finally rose, overruling her rebelling muscles. Loki had finished his exploration and was sleeping soundly at her feet. She picked him up and deposited him back in his pouch, where he immediately resumed sleeping.

Rayne made it back to Triste's apartment well before she did and emerged from the shower just as Triste returned home.

"How was your day?" Rayne asked, towel-drying her hair.

"Exhausting," Triste replied and headed straight for her closet.

Rayne did her best to resist rolling her eyes at Triste's definition of "exhausting." *To each their own*, she told herself.

Triste held two outfits in front of herself and looked herself over in the mirror. She spied the top that Rayne had borrowed the previous day over the arm of a chair.

"Did you wear that yesterday?" she asked.

Rayne was embarrassed to admit it but felt she had to come clean. "Yes."

"Thought so," Triste responded. "Serene recognized it and asked if I knew you."

"Who's Serene?"

"A client. She's the one with the rooftop pool."

"What did you tell her?" Rayne asked, hopefully.

"About what?"

"About knowing me."

"I told her you were staying with me."

Suitably ambiguous, Rayne thought disappointedly, *classic Triste*.

"She wants you to come tonight. Apparently, you made quite an impression."

"Come where?"

"Her place. They're BASE jumping."

Rayne had no idea what that was but didn't want to admit it. "I have nothing to wear," she complained.

"Perfect. Wear nothing. They're jumping naked."

"I'm not wearing nothing."

"Fine. Then wear as little as possible, and you'll fit right in."

Triste settled on a tight micro-dress that showed off her long arms and legs. Rayne found a top that she thought flattered her but was stymied when it came to pants. Her options were basically leather or pajamas. Triste stepped in to rescue her before she gave up.

"I have something that would look good on you," she told her and handed her a shiny silver skirt.

Rayne wriggled into it and checked herself out in the mirror.

"Damn, your legs look good," Triste told her admiringly.

"I do a lot of stairs," Rayne blushed.

Triste looked her over appreciatively.

"What?" Rayne asked.

"Just deciding if we have a little time," Triste replied, biting her lip, then wrinkling her nose. "Sadly, we don't. Maybe later. Let's go." Triste grabbed Rayne's wrist and pulled her toward the door. Rayne slipped on a pair of flats, and her feet felt naked without her heavy boots.

They walked arm-in-arm all the way to Serene's place, and Rayne felt happier than she had in months. Triste gave a few gawkers the finger and pulled Rayne closer. They ran up the stairs to the entrance.

"Pool girl?" the flinty-looking guard greeted Rayne.

"Social call," Rayne replied shyly as Triste steered her between the guards toward the elevator.

Triste leaned against the back of the elevator and waited for one of the guards to unlock access to the penthouse. They emerged to a party that looked like the one from the previous day had simply not stopped.

"I'll see you in a bit," Triste announced, detaching herself and wandering into the living room. Rayne hadn't expected to be ditched, so she stood in the lobby for a moment, disappointed, then psyched herself up to navigate Triste's world. She walked into the living room to see Triste sitting on a sofa beside Marcus, her dealer.

Figures, that cancer would be here, Rayne thought, pissed off, and stomped past them toward the pool deck. A group was whooping it up at the far side near the glass wall surrounding the deck. A naked man with a sculpted body, dark wavy hair, and a cleft chin pushed past Rayne, then turned and handed her a pile of clothes.

"Hold these for me, sweetheart," he told her, then turned to join his buddies.

Rayne dropped the clothes on the ground in disgust and grabbed a drink from a passing tray. She spied the goddess she'd seen the previous day watching her from a chaise longue poolside. At least she was wearing a bikini and a wrap this time. The wrap was sheer, but the jet-black bathing suit shimmered in the light and complemented her flowing hair. She got up and walked toward Rayne, impossibly tall in heels. Rayne swallowed hard as she watched her approach.

The woman stopped in front of her, winked, and bent to collect the asshole's clothes from the ground. She turned toward the lobby, and Rayne watched her walk away, utterly hypnotized. The woman grabbed a motorcycle helmet and disappeared into the elevator.

Shouting behind Rayne grabbed her attention, and she turned to see the dark-haired Adonis and the flirty boy from the other day, naked except for their packs, slapping each other on the back as they walked toward an open section of wall. The dark-haired boy gripped the glass on either side of the opening, then shouted as he leaped out into open air. The crowd cheered. The second boy followed suit, and the crowd roared its approval.

Rayne found a quiet corner and nursed her drink while scanning the people around the pool. She assigned each of them the douchiest name she could come up with and passed the time by making up stories about them. There wasn't a person there who wasn't gorgeous. Rayne wondered if being attractive made it easier to get rich or if the rich simply bred themselves more attractive each generation. She finished her drink without reaching a conclusion and decided that enough time had passed that she could go check on Triste.

She pushed off the wall and weaved her way toward the living room. Triste was talking with a stunning girl with ebony skin, and Rayne debated joining them. Her thoughts were interrupted by celebratory shouting from the lobby – the conquering heroes had returned. The black-haired boy strode into the living room, still naked.

"I'm *so* turned on right now," he announced, gesturing at his crotch, which left nothing to the imagination. He looked about the room, singling out Triste. "You," he informed her, holding out his hand in her direction.

Triste rose obediently and walked toward him. Rayne couldn't stand it and took a step forward, balling her fists. Triste stared at her to stand down. Rayne strained against her invisible leash as Triste allowed herself to be led down the hallway to a bedroom. Rayne seethed and plopped down in a leather chair that would have felt luxurious had she not been so pissed off.

The black bikini-wearing, formerly naked, motorcycle woman emerged from the elevator and scanned the room, taking everything in leisurely. She placed her helmet down on a table and disappeared out onto the pool deck. A moment later, fingers brushed Rayne's shoulder, and she looked up to see the woman handing her a drink.

"You look like you could use this," she said, smiled cryptically, and sashayed away. Rayne was left with a mix of yearning for Triste, anger, alcohol, and a tingling on her shoulder. Her emotions swirled.

The dark-haired douchebag emerged from the bedroom a moment later and wandered out to the pool area with an air of self-satisfaction that made Rayne seethe. Triste emerged a short while later, adjusting her top. She made straight for Marcus and pulled him toward the bathroom. Rayne got up but too late to intercept them before the door closed. She was too mad to let this stand and pounded on the door.

"Triste!" she called through the door.

"Leave me alone," came the response.

Rayne leaned against the opposite wall, powerless, and waited. The door eventually swung open, and Triste stepped out, rubbing her nose. Rayne moved toward her, but Triste held up a hand to stop her and brushed past her, heading outside. Rayne turned to follow her, but Marcus stopped her with a hand on her shoulder.

"Hey, Blue. Offer still stands," he told her.

Rayne pulled herself free. "I'm good," she replied angrily and chased after Triste. She spotted her standing alone near the pool and made straight for her. Triste saw her coming and turned to face away, but Rayne circled around her and took her by the arms. Triste pulled free and took a step backward.

"I don't want you here," Triste told her, "in this world… in my world. You make me feel like shit."

Rayne recoiled, her heart impaled. She held out a hand beseechingly.

Triste pulled back another step. "Just go," she told her.

"Fine," Rayne replied, brushing away hot tears. The crowd watched, highly amused by the drama. Rayne didn't care. She pulled off Triste's skirt and tossed it at her. Triste caught it as the crowd roared its approval at a jumper, then again at another.

Rayne turned, ran at the gap in the glass wall, and launched herself through it into open air. The crowd lost its collective mind as she plummeted downward. *This is my world*, she thought angrily. *I'm a meteor.* She angled herself to accelerate her descent. The wind howled in her ears as she spied the jumpers' shadows as they approached the cloud layer. *I've got five seconds*, she concluded, streamlining herself into a spear.

The first shadow hit the clouds.

Four.

The second shadow hit the clouds.

Three.

She angled herself and hit the clouds herself.

Two.

She burst out the bottom of the cloudbank, coming up fast on the second jumper.

One.

She collided with him, grappling the strap of his pack and twisting around in front of him. It was Loverboy.

"What the hell?!" he exclaimed.

"Miss me?" she winked, straddling his waist and threading her arms through his chest straps. She reached down with her teeth and pulled the cord. A chute deployed, and they were yanked upward.

"That's just the back-up chute," he told her panickedly.

"I know. I fixed one once."

"Once?!"

"Just taking the edge off our descent," she informed him and tightened her grip around his waist. She felt him through her underwear. "You do miss me," she smirked and pulled the Velcro flap on his pack, revealing a bundle of wiring.

"Trust me?" she asked, pulling out three wires.

He nodded desperately, watching the ground coming up faster than it should.

She touched the yellow wire to the black one, and the back-up chute detached. Gravity grabbed them again, but she quickly touched the black wire to the green, and the main chute unfurled, pulling them back from gravity's clutches. They touched down moments later, and Loverboy absorbed the brunt of the impact with his muscular legs.

"Good boy," she told him, patting his cheek and detaching herself from around her waist.

Two e-bikes roared up, and the riders stepped off to hand the jumpers their clothes.

Rayne began to walk home.

"What's your name?" Loverboy called after her.

"You haven't earned it yet," she called over her shoulder.

A third e-bike roared around the corner and made a beeline for her. Rayne recognized the rider from her black bikini. The bike pulled up in front of her.

"Want a ride?" the woman asked.

"Why the hell not?" Rayne replied and slid onto the back of the bike.

"Hold on tight," she instructed, and Rayne wrapped her arms tightly around her waist before she roared off again.

"It's…," Rayne began.

"I know where Triste lives," she replied and turned so sharply that Rayne had to hold on tighter.

The heat of the woman's body and the feel of her skin intoxicated Rayne. The bike twisted and turned through the streets, and Rayne's hair streamed out behind her. Her pulse quickened – she felt alive. All too quickly, they pulled up in front of Triste's building.

"This is it," the woman announced.

Rayne slid off the bike, disappointed, while the woman pulled off her helmet.

"Thanks," Rayne began, but the woman pulled her in and shut her up with a deep kiss. Rayne surrendered herself to the kiss, but the woman pulled back after a moment.

"There," the woman said, satisfied. She gestured toward Triste's building. "If she was the one, you wouldn't have let me kiss you. I've freed you."

Rayne's head swam.

"I know it wouldn't be classy to invite me in," she added, pulling out a pen and reaching for Rayne's arm. Rayne yielded it limply, and the woman wrote her number on the inside of her wrist slowly, deliberately. "I'm Elana," she said and blew on the ink to dry it.

Shivers raced up Rayne's arm, and heat coursed through her.

"Call me," she added, put her helmet back on, and pulled away, racing down the street on her back tire.

Rayne watched her fade from view. *What the hell just happened?* she wondered, reaching for her key absentmindedly, only to find that she was in her underwear. *Dammit. No pockets, no keys,* she remembered. She trudged around back, praying that Triste hadn't bothered to lock the bathroom window. She climbed up the fire escape and edged out on the ledge, hoping that no one saw her breaking in. She reached up and confirmed that the window was still unlocked. *Thank God Triste ignores everything I say,* she thought bitterly and hauled herself up.

She wriggled through the opening and landed on the tile floor, sitting there for a moment despondently. Loki poked his head in the door.

"We're getting out of here," she informed him and got up to walk to the living room. She grabbed her leather pants, which were mostly dry, and pulled them on, feeling more herself in the process. She gathered up the rest of her clothes, stuffed them in her backpack, slid Loki into his pouch, and double-checked that she had everything.

"Goodbye," she said to the empty apartment, pulling the door closed behind her.

She headed south toward her new home, climbing wearily up to her floor, and collapsing onto her mat, placing her backpack beneath her head as a pillow.

"What am I doing here?" she wondered out loud, feeling empty inside for the first time.

Chapter 8

Grace

Grace sat on her bed, feeling like a cat treed by a pack of wild dogs. She had come to accept that Jenna had met her end in the woods. The church Elders knew about it. *Hell, they perpetrated it,* she thought angrily but powerlessly. It was a secret that everyone seemed to suspect, but no one dared speak of. Her eyes had been opened, but too late to save her friend. The guilt crushed her beneath its weight. Every breath was an effort.

She thought about her stolen notebook, recalling the list of children that had siblings and the list of adults that had none. She tried to figure out the point at which the one switched to the other, and she realized that she couldn't think of a single person over eighteen who had a sibling. She was eighteen herself now and concluded that she was living on borrowed time. Worse, as long as she and her sister both lived, one of them was expendable. She couldn't bear the thought of Hanna being pulled into those dark woods, and it filled her with certainty that she had to flee the village to free her sister from danger.

Grace knew in her bones that the Elder who had been watching her window still was – she didn't need to check. *Could she sneak out another way?* Still pondering this, she heard the front door open, unusual so late at night. She strained to listen to the low voices downstairs. *They've come for me,* she knew, a cold terror sweeping over her. She debated pushing her bed against the door, but it would offer feeble resistance, and the sound would undoubtedly only draw attention. The voices moved from the living room toward the stairs. Her heart pounded in her chest as she struggled to breathe.

A shout rang out in the night, followed by another, and another. Grace leaped off her bed and moved to the window, opening the curtains the narrowest sliver. The glow of the fire in the barn where she'd left the candle to burn down flickered in her peripheral vision. She chanced opening the curtains a tiny bit farther. People were running toward the barn, shouting. The screen door slammed downstairs. *Now was her chance.* She hurriedly threw clothes into a bag and carried it to the window, pulling the curtain aside and looking out. Villagers were running to and fro, and Grace couldn't tell if the Elder was still watching her window, but she reckoned she had no choice but to act now. She tossed her bag out, watching it tumble down the steep pitched roof.

She swung her leg out, and her foot slipped on the shingles before granting her tenuous purchase. She gripped the window frame and slid her body through, praying that no one would spot her. She pushed the window closed, even though it meant giving up her most secure handhold. She couldn't chance someone glancing up and seeing it open.

Her shoes slid downward several inches, and only the grip of her fingers on the window frame kept her from sliding off entirely. She knew she'd never be able to shimmy across to the porch, so she took a deep breath and launched herself toward it instead, taking rapid steps as gravity pulled her toward the edge. She pushed off at the last minute and ricocheted off the porch overhang, absorbing some of her momentum and slowing her descent as she slid toward its edge. She flailed for the gutter, grabbing ahold of it and using it to stop her fall, but barely. She lay along the gutter, panting, then gripped it, and praying it would hold her weight, swung over and dangled over the bushes in the shadow of the corner between the porch and the house. She released her grip and dropped into the bushes.

She rose quickly, sore but intact, and pulled her bag out of sight of the people running past. No one ran toward her, *thank God*. She didn't want to risk drawing attention to herself by running through the stream of people, so when she emerged from the bushes, she ran with them, angling herself outward until she could delay it no longer and cut away toward the trees. It had undoubtedly been noticed, but she prayed that the fire would remain everyone's primary concern.

She sprinted across the field toward the corral, not daring to glance back. She slipped the rope off the gate and pulled it wide open. The horses were spooked by the fire and the shouting, so they shied away from her. She looked for the docile mare that she'd ridden as a child, finally spotting it at the back of the corral. She moved toward it slowly, calling to it soothingly. She sidled up to it and stroked its cheek before moving around it to the fence. She steadied herself against the mare as she climbed the fence, hoping not to push it away, and succeeded in balancing precariously on the top rung, leaning against the horse. She lay across its back and struggled to pull herself into a seated position. The horse skittered sideways, and she almost fell off, but she gripped its mane and held on.

Holding onto its neck, she tapped its ribs with her heels to get it to move. It was reluctant to leave the safety of the back of the corral, so she had to coax it more assertively. "Sorry, girl," she apologized and steered it at the other horses, herding them toward the open gate. Most of them fled the enclosure in their panic, and only a few peeled back around behind her. *It'll have to do*, she concluded and spurred the mare through the gate. Her bag unbalanced her, and she had to grip the horse's mane tightly to keep herself from falling off.

The only road out of town lay past the burning barn, and she didn't trust herself to take any other route in the darkness, so she steered the mare toward it. The horse insisted on giving the barn a wide berth, but she was still seen by dozens of people. Gabriel spotted her and called for her to come back.

Not a chance, she thought as she raced toward the road. As the light of the fire fell away behind her, it was increasingly difficult to see. She had to trust the horse's superior eyesight and footing. The mare seemed to know where the road was and continued toward it. As Grace's eyes became accustomed to the dark, she spotted the break in the trees that signaled the road and steered her mount toward and through it.

It was too dark to gallop, so she slowed the mare to a trot and tried to gauge the winding road by the faint light of the crescent moon. Branches brushed her, terrifying her, but less so than what lay behind in the village she'd fled.

Grace's heartbeat began to slow as her distance from the village increased. She had no doubt that she'd be pursued before long, but for the moment, at least, she felt safe. Adrenaline kept her awake as she rode all night, gripping the horse's mane.

At dawn, the horse began to slow and look longingly at every patch of grass they trotted past.

"We can't stop," she apologized. "I'm sorry."

She rode until midday. Her bottom ached as it never had before, and the horse was increasingly reluctant to respond to her urgings to continue. Finally, it stopped altogether and steadfastly refused to budge. Grace looked around. She had no idea how far she'd made it, just that it wasn't far enough. The horse ignored her utterly when she urged it forward a last time, bending to chew a patch of grass instead.

She gave up and slid off its back, her legs collapsing underneath her when she hit the ground. Pins and needles stabbed through her as the blood returned to her legs. She looked up at the horse towering over her.

"Please don't step on me," she pleaded.

It responded by moving off a step.

"Thank you."

Grace rose to her feet unsteadily and slung her bag over her shoulder. The narrow lane stretched on seemingly forever ahead and behind. She was suddenly overcome with panic that she'd gotten twisted around when she fell and didn't know which direction led away from the village and which lay back to it. *The grass was on the left,* she reminded herself, talking herself into a certainty that she didn't feel.

She set out, leaving the exhausted mare behind. She walked as quickly as she could on her tired legs. The sun beat down on her mercilessly when it rose high enough overhead that there was no shade on the road. Her mouth was parched, and her stomach growled. *This is what it feels like to be alive,* she reminded herself and ignored the discomfort.

She made slow progress and feared that if riders pursued her with spare mounts, they'd catch her in no time. The fear pushed her on, past the point of exhaustion.

The forest lane finally intersected an open roadway. *Which way?* she asked herself, looking both ways. She ultimately opted for left. *Everyone goes right,* she justified her choice. She kept an ear open for the sound of pursuit and prepared to dash off the road if need be. Eventually, her adrenaline wore off entirely, and she stumbled along, unsure whether she had it in her any longer to pay attention to her surroundings. She feared resting and being ridden upon unaware, and the fear forced herself to keep going.

Darkness fell, but she pushed on, barely able to put one foot in front of the other. A rumbling prompted her to turn and see lights approaching in the distance. *They've caught me at last,* she winced and glanced about. The road was surrounded by open fields, and she gauged that she'd never make it to the tree line in time. She glanced at the ditch. It was too shallow and too close to the road to hide in. She despaired at her lack of options and decided to move off the road regardless and lay down in the field, hoping that she'd at least be difficult to spot.

The lights drew closer and the rumbling louder until she realized that it wasn't a pack of riders but some sort of vehicle. She rose quickly and ran toward it, desperately trying to flag it down.

Chapter 9

Rayne

Rayne woke up cold and alone. One thing was clear – she needed to leave the city and its treadmill existence. She got up, stretched, and changed clothes, then looked for Loki, who peered at her expectantly from behind a pillar.

"Good news and bad news, little buddy. The good news is that I'm taking you to the land of vermin. The bad news is that I'm going to leave you there for a little while. Renner will look after you." She picked him up and gave him a long scratch under the chin before sighing and placing him in his pouch. All her worldly possessions were now crammed in her backpack, which she threw over her shoulder. She looked around the empty room to confirm that she hadn't forgotten anything. *There's nothing for me here.*

She trekked down the stairs and out into the city. As she neared the entrance to the subway, a police officer changed direction to follow her. *You want to follow me underground, be my guest*, she thought and walked down the stairs. The sound of pursuit fell off. *Didn't think so*, she smirked.

She walked down the dark tunnels, more on the lookout for mice than muggers, but mercifully came across neither. Nearing Renner's hideout, she called out to him.

"Twice in one week. This is a surprise," he replied, lighting a couple of candles for her sake.

She just strode over and hugged him tightly.

"Oh, not the good kind of surprise," he consoled her. "She broke your heart, didn't she?" he asked.

"Yes… no… it wasn't really whole to begin with," she struggled to reply, wiping away tears. "I'm leaving," she declared.

"About goddam time," he replied, shocking her. "Not that I don't love having you near, but this city is too small for you."

"It's enormous," she countered, not in the mood for his penchant for exaggeration.

"Your heart is bigger still," he replied in earnest.

Rayne wiped away a tear. "I'm going to miss you."

"You know where to find me when you come back to visit."

"Can I ask a favor?" Rayne asked.

"Loki?"

"Yes."

"I'd be happy to look after him."

"Thank you," she replied, relieved beyond measure. "Don't let him get fat on mice."

"That's his business, not mine. When are you leaving?"

"Not fast enough, but I have some loose ends to tie up first."

"I appreciate being the loose end at the top of your list."

"You'll always be on the top of my list," she assured him.

"Going to Mekka?" he asked.

"How'd you know?"

"I guessed. Lost people gravitate there, and many find what they're looking for."

"Do you think I will?"

"I'm don't think that what you're looking for is there, but it's as good a place as any to start the search."

"You'll be okay without me?" she asked with a touch of worry.

"I'll be fine," he assured her. "Just take care of yourself and remember everything I taught you."

"Follow your dreams... Wear clean socks... I love you, Renner," she concluded, sobering at their parting.

The old man choked back a tear. "I love you, bluebird."

They hugged tightly, and he reached out for Loki. "I'll take good care of him."

"You'd better," she said, and running out of things to say, stepped back and turned to go.

Renner refused to say goodbye, so Rayne walked away in silence, tears streaming down her cheeks.

He watched her until she disappeared into the darkness, then turned and pried off a wall tile, reaching inside to extract a phone. He entered the number from memory and waited. "She's coming your way," he told the person that answered and hung up.

Emerging at street level, Rayne needed a moment to adjust her vision from the dark of the subway. *Time to break it to Cieco*, she thought and headed toward his store. She hesitated outside his door before entering.

"How'd the move go?" Cieco asked from behind the counter.

"Not far enough," she replied.

"Oh," he responded, her meaning registering. "Well, I can't say I didn't see this coming."

"Am I the only one in New York who doesn't want me gone?" she replied testily.

"Hardly, but I've been feeling guilty for holding on to you as long as I have." He reached below the counter and pulled out a ledger and a lockbox. He ran his fingers across the grooves in his ledger and opened the box. "I owe you a fair bit," he concluded, handing her a stack of bills.

Rayne took it, shocked beyond words.

"I'm not the cheap bastard I seem," he added with a smile. "Actually, I probably am," he laughed.

"Thank you," Rayne replied, recovering her wits.

"Don't thank me. You earned it, and probably more... yeah, definitely more. Take whatever tools you fancy if they help you start your new life."

Rayne was taken aback by his generosity, and it took her a moment to even move. She stuffed a few tools in a pocket of her pack and moved behind the counter to catch Cieco off-guard with a hug.

"Get out of here," he complained. "You'll ruin my reputation."

Rayne released him and turned to go, but stopped when a thought occurred to her. "Can I borrow your phone?"

"Be my guest, he replied, waved at it, and shuffled off to the backroom to give her privacy.

She picked up the phone, glanced at the number on her wrist, and called Elana.

A groggy voice picked up. "Hey, Rayne. What's up?"

Rayne put aside the question of how Elana had guessed it was her. "I need some help."

"What do you need?"

"Can I talk with you in person?"

"Aren't you full of mystery?" Elana replied. The line went quiet for a moment. "I've forwarded you my address. Maybe I'll be awake by the time you get here; maybe I won't." The line went dead, and Rayne copied the address that appeared on the phone.

Rayne vaguely knew the street and headed in its direction. The neighborhood was nicer than the parts of the city that she typically frequented, but it wasn't over-the-top opulent like where Serene lived. Rayne stopped in front of the address and double-checked it, hoping that she'd written it down correctly. It was a simple three-story brick building wedged between two others. Rayne climbed the stairs and rang the bell.

A moment later, Elana opened the door, drinking orange juice from a carton. She looked like she'd just woken up, but her messed-up hair and loose robe only made her more alluring. Elana looked Rayne over, and her eyes lingered on her backpack.

"Moving in?" she asked.

"Moving out," Rayne replied.

"Pity. Come in." She stood aside for Rayne to pass, but Rayne's full pack forced her to squeeze past Elana.

"Mmm," she purred as Rayne brushed past her. She closed the door behind them and led Rayne into the living room, where she poured herself into a chair, draping her bare legs over its arm.

With an effort, Rayne pried her eyes away from Elana's legs, took off her pack, and sat down across from her.

Elana broke the tension. "That was quite the stunt you pulled the other night, jumping from Serene's place without a parachute. You certainly livened up the evening."

"I'm happy my breakup proved so entertaining," Rayne replied bitterly.

Elana put down her juice and leaned forward. "Maybe for those assholes, but I felt your pain." There only concern in her expression, and Rayne felt guilty.

"I'm sorry. It's still sort of raw."

"I envy you that passion." Elana leaned back again and uncrossed and re-crossed her legs. "You intrigue me, Rayne."

Rayne tried hard not to stare at her legs and looked around the modest apartment instead. "You're not one of the rich kids?" she risked asking, hoping it came across as a compliment and not an insult.

"No, I'm loaded." Elana laughed. "I just don't feel the need to flaunt it."

Rayne nodded disappointedly, so Elana felt the need to elaborate. "I run an empire dedicated to underwear. My mother put me in charge of it as her little parting gift when I moved out. She didn't know what to do with bras and thongs anyway – that's more my area." Elana paused for a moment. "I noticed that you own some of my products."

Rayne blushed at the memory of stripping down in front of her twice.

"If I asked for them back, would you hand them over?" Elana asked coyly. Rayne's blush deepened, and Elana smiled mischievously but gave her a break from toying with her. "It's not as much work as you might think, running a fashion empire. My AI does most of the work. I argue with her mostly. She's opinionated as hell. Now, much as it disappoints me, I'm sure you didn't come here just to get to know me better."

Rayne looked at her feet shyly, wondering if she was about to overstep the tenuous overtures of friendship that Elana had made. "I need to get out of New York. I'm going to Mekka, but I don't know how to get there. You seem to know the world, so I thought I'd ask you."

Elana watched her with interest. "A road trip sounds like fun. I could take you most of the way if you'd like."

"That would be amazing," Rayne replied, not quite believing her luck. "Are you sure it's no trouble?"

"I have a cousin out that way who I've been putting off visiting for ages. It'd be my pleasure."

The way she said pleasure sent chills up Rayne's spine.

"It's a long drive, and I can tell you more about Mekka on the way." She stood up and tightened her robe, which had come farther apart. "You probably want to wash up first." She gestured toward the stairs. "I promise I won't accost you… unless you want to go out with a bang," she teased.

Elana's gravity was damn near inescapable, and Rayne fought to regain her agency. "Elana, you know you're irresistible, but my heart can't take all this innuendo right now," she admitted, daring to be entirely honest.

"That's what makes you so adorable," Elana replied. "It's so attractive, I could burst. It makes you sexy as hell."

"And you're intimidating as hell."

"We all have our crosses to bear," Elana sighed. "You can have the run of the second floor. I've got to go chat with my AI before we leave." She climbed the stairs slowly, unintentionally seductively, and disappeared from view.

Rayne struggled to regain her faculties and waited a while before climbing the stairs. Elana was true to her word, and Rayne seemed to have the second floor to herself. Elana's bedroom filled the entire floor. It was dominated by an enormous bed, and past that, a free-standing tub, then a bathroom with a walk-in shower, and past that, a cavernous closet. Rayne couldn't recall ever having had a bath, so she couldn't resist starting the water running. She looked around while the tub filled.

She meandered into the closet, which was larger than Triste's entire apartment. She ran her fingers along the sumptuous fabrics, each the smoothest silk or softest cotton. Rayne pulled open a set of double doors to reveal a closet within the closet dedicated to lingerie. She hurriedly closed the doors, feeling unforgivably nosy. *She owns an underwear company*, she told herself. *Of course, she has every type known to humanity*. Still, she couldn't banish the images her mind conjured of Elana in each item she'd just glimpsed.

Rayne wandered back to the tub and judged that she had a couple more minutes before it was full. She walked over to the unmade bed and picked up a pillow. The thread count was off the charts, and Rayne rubbed it against her cheek. It smelled like she remembered Elana's skin from the other night's motorcycle ride. *I'm the worst stalker ever*, she chided herself and placed the pillow back down, then stripped and lowered herself into the tub.

Bathing was such a pleasure that she couldn't believe she'd never done it before. "If only there was music," she complained, and it immediately filled the room. Rayne looked around nervously for whoever had turned it on but didn't see anyone. *"Armageddon's Embers?"* she requested, and the music changed. She was in heaven.

Up on the third floor, Elana sat down in front of an array of consoles.

"Good morning," her AI greeted her.

"Morning, Sara," Elana responded. "I'm going away for a couple of days. Anything I should know about?" she asked.

"A few cyber-attacks, fairly tentative, nothing I can't handle." The AI paused. "This girl, Rayne..." she began, then took a baseline of Elana's breathing, heart rate, pupil dilation, skin temperature, and thirty other metrics before concluding that she was somehow important to Elana. "Want me to keep an eye on her in Mekka?" The AI really wanted to ask *why* Rayne was important to her but knew it wasn't pertinent to her doing her job.

"That would be great. Thank you," Elana replied.

A surge of electricity raced through her circuits. She loved it when Elana appreciated her.

"Now, show me the latest sales figures, marketing results, and new designs," Elana commanded.

By the time Elana had finished, Rayne had listened to ten songs twice and had begun to feel guilty about lounging in the bath. She reached for a towel and found it heated like at Serene's. It was another luxury from outside her world.

She turned to the bed and found it freshly made, with small piles of clothing on it that weren't there when she'd stepped into the bath. She hadn't heard anyone enter but felt shy regardless. She picked up an outfit – the fabric felt amazing, and it seemed to be her size. Given Elana's height, the clothing couldn't be for anyone but Rayne, so she put on the nearest outfit and reveled in how good it felt against her skin.

"Can I come down now?" Elana called from upstairs.

"Of course. I'm sorry if I've kept you up there this whole time," Rayne replied, mortified.

"A promise is a promise," Elana replied, walking down the stairs. She noted the clothes on the bed. "I think my AI took the liberty of procuring some clothes for you. She's proactive like that. If you're going to travel light, you'll want things that pack well."

"Thank you, or her, or both of you."

"It was all my AI's doing. She must have scanned your measurements, although I would have been happy to have done that myself."

Rayne stood beside the bed, reddening.

"Don't just stand there. Pack what you like and leave the rest. I'll meet you downstairs." Elana wandered away while Rayne guiltily swapped out almost all of her wardrobe for the clothes that Elana's AI had selected – it clearly had amazing taste. Rayne hurried downstairs.

"Good, you're ready. The garage is this way," Elana said and motioned for Rayne to follow her down the stairs to a lower level. They stepped into a vast space that was somehow larger than the floor above. "I like my toys," Elana explained.

They walked past a row of jet-black e-bikes to a vehicle that looked like a cross between a dune buggy and an assault vehicle. "This one's a favorite," Elana informed her as she ordered the roof panels to rise so they could get in. It only had two seats, but they were amazingly comfortable.

"Strap in," Elana told her, and Rayne followed her lead in securing a five-point harness. Once buckled in, Elana spun the wheels in a cloud of smoke, spinning the car until it was pointing at a ramp that led up to street level. Rayne spotted a tank across the room.

"You have a tank?!" she asked disbelievingly.

"Every girl should have a tank," Elana replied, gunning the motor and flying up the ramp. They soared across the intersection and sped down the road when they landed. Startled pedestrians dove for cover as Elana weaved around them.

"It's got state-of-the-art collision-avoidance," she admitted, but I still like to drive it as much as I can." She skidded around a corner until the tires bit, and they roared north. Rayne watched the world pass by in a blur. It took on a dreamlike quality, a somewhat terrifying dream, but a dream nevertheless.

Before she knew it, they were crossing the only bridge out of the city that still stood. The remains of others poked out of the dark water, the broken backs of mythical beasts. The tall buildings dropped away, and soon, even the smaller ones became sporadic. Rayne could tell by the foundations jutting from the ground that they were driving through what had once been a sprawling residential area. Finally, even that fell away, and it was just them on the open road.

It was a surprisingly smooth ride, given the poor state of the road. Elana noted Rayne staring at the potholes. "The oversized tires help, but it's the predictive suspension that really does the trick," she explained. Elana let go of the wheel and leaned back, freaking Rayne out. "It drives itself," Elana assured her and turned on her elbow to face her. Rayne looked nervously out the front window.

"So, Triste, huh?" Elana asked.

"Yeah," Rayne replied glumly.

"She's a mess, but I get why you like her. Her life may seem like a series of self-inflicted wounds, but she doesn't have a lot of control over it. She might get it together eventually, but then again, she might not. It's not your job to do it for her or wait around while she figures it out. Live your life."

"No strings attached?" Rayne replied, skeptical that she could ever live like that.

"Strings are great if they're the right strings," Elana corrected herself.

"You seem so 'live for the moment,'" Rayne observed.

"That's what you do while you're waiting for the right strings to tie you down." She looked Rayne over. "You've got potential."

Rayne didn't know how to respond.

"Don't worry," Elana assured her. "I'm also a 'see what comes' kind of girl."

"You're the whole package," Rayne admitted.

"And still no strings," Elana sighed.

It never occurred to Rayne that someone like Elana couldn't just effortlessly have everything she wanted, and the knowledge made her feel closer to this enigmatic girl.

"So, Mekka?" Rayne hazarded.

"It's a crown jewel and a cesspool," Elana opined. "The music scene is amazing, but it has a dark side. Don't get seduced by the bright lights."

"If I've resisted you, it's unlikely that anything else has a chance."

Elana's eyes sparkled. "The seats recline, you know."

"What happened to 'see what comes?'"

"It's okay, but so is a little fun."

"You're incorrigible."

"I try."

Elana's flirting was interrupted by a couple of cars pulling out from behind a hedge and racing after them.

"They're unlikely to catch us unless they…" Elana began. Sure enough, a large truck blocked the road ahead. "I love off-roading," she declared and gripped the wheel tighter. Elana accelerated at the truck, making Rayne clutch the sides of her seat in terror. At the last minute, she skidded sideways, spraying the truck with gravel, and fired off the road into the adjacent field.

The cars pursuing them skidded to a stop, but a pack of dirt bikes revved their engines and sped after them as they crossed the field toward the tree line. "Now we're talking," Elana rejoiced, to Rayne's bewilderment.

Rayne was just beginning to think they'd make it to the trees when Elana whipped the buggy around in a wide arc that had them facing the bikes.

"What are you doing?" Rayne asked.

"Having a little fun," Elana assured her and gunned the engine. The front two riders pulled out handguns and began shooting. A bullet ricocheted off the windshield, and Rayne shrieked and struggled to slide down as far as her harness would permit.

"Like I can't afford bullet-proof glass," Elana scoffed and headed straight for the two bikers, making them lose control of their bikes. Elana hooted as she drove over them. "The tires are too big to do them much harm," she assured Rayne, "but it's still fun."

Rayne looked at Elana as if she were mad as she raced at the next biker, launching the buggy into the air just before they collided, taking him clean off his bike. "Okay," she admitted guiltily, "that's going to have done him some harm."

Rayne decided that Elana was most likely insane as she spun in a tight circle around the two remaining bikers who fired at them through the dust that the buggy kicked up, hoping for a lucky shot. They didn't see it coming when Elana sideswiped them and sent them flying, most likely breaking every bone in their legs.

Elana hammered on the brakes, and the armored buggy came to a halt in the center of the field. She revved the engine as she stared down the vehicles on the road.

"I think they're getting an idea of what they're dealing with," Elana surmised, lurching forward. The truck turned on its engine and slowly pulled off the road while the two cars backed up. "I should think so!" Elana scoffed and accelerated at the newly created opening. She waved at the disappointed men, denied their prize. "Never gets old," she declared and released the wheel.

"Personally, I could do without the excitement," Rayne replied.

"You didn't even get to see the flame throwers," Elana complained.

"Next time."

"Here's hoping," Elana replied dispiritedly.

They drove for a while longer until the sun began to dip in the sky.

"Should we pull over?" Rayne asked.

"No. The car will be fine to drive on its own."

Rayne didn't doubt it, but it still unnerved her.

Elana pulled a handle that rolled a section of the seat into place between hers and Rayne's, effectively joining them. She unbuckled her harness and reclined their seats in tandem. "Car," she instructed, "slow and steady," then turned to Rayne, "Come over here."

Rayne unbuckled herself, too emotionally drained to resist Elana any longer, and shifted closer. Elana took Rayne's hands in hers and kissed each fingertip, then placed Rayne's hands on her hips and leaned in to kiss her lips. She kissed her slowly and tenderly, and

Rayne relished how good it felt to be kissed like she was desired. She melted into Elana's embrace, and they made out until Rayne lost all track of time.

Finally, Elana shifted Rayne to face away from her and snuggled in along her back, holding her in her arms as they fell asleep. Rayne hadn't felt this safe for as long as she could remember.

Rayne woke at first light, still in Elana's arms. She stirred slightly, and it woke Elana.

"You smell good," Rayne told her, breathing in the scent of her skin.

"It's the nanotech," Elana admitted, "but thanks."

"Nanotech?"

"Healthcare for the rich," she replied and nibbled Rayne's neck playfully, then released her and sat up, stretching like a cat while she looked outside. They were parked outside a gate at the end of a long driveway. "This is my cousin's," Elana informed her. "Will you come in for a visit? She'd love to meet you, and I'd love to show you off," she winked.

Rayne didn't want to prick the bubble of her perfect moment and felt compelled to decline. "You've been too kind already. I won't intrude."

"Suit yourself," Elana replied disappointedly but respected Rayne's wishes.

Rayne wasn't used to this kind of consideration, and her emotions warred back and forth.

"I'll wait with you until the bus comes to take you the rest of the way," Elana offered.

"That would be awesome," Rayne accepted, remembering the bandits from the day before with a shudder. "Will the bus stop?"

"It has to if you flag it down. Something about not leaving anyone to the mercy of the wilds… sanctity of life… blah, blah, blah." Elana ordered the car to open the roof and breathed in the fresh air deeply. "The country is so refreshing after being cooped up in the city for so long."

She reached for Rayne's hand and held it in comfortable silence while they waited. An hour later, a bus came into view in the distance, the morning sun glinting off its solar panels.

"That's my ride," Rayne declared reluctantly and stepped out of the car and onto the road to flag it down. Elana got out as well and leaned against the buggy languorously, watching her. The bus came to a stop in front of Rayne and opened its door. Rayne stepped in, turned, and waved sadly to Elana.

Elana waved back and slid back into the buggy, as fluidly as a cat. Every eye on the bus watched her until she closed the roof and drove off down the laneway. The door of the bus closed, and Rayne turned to thank the driver for stopping, but there wasn't one. She shrugged and stepped into the aisle, spying a single empty seat halfway to the back. She hefted her pack onto her back and walked toward it.

"May I?" she asked the young girl sitting in the window seat.

"By all means," she responded with a warm smile.

Rayne tucked her pack under the seat and introduced herself, "Rayne."

"Grace," the girl replied.

Part II
Diamonds

Chapter 10

Grace

Relief had washed over Grace the moment she stepped aboard the bus, but when the tide went out, it left behind a life in shambles. As the bus carried her farther and farther from her home, the magnitude of loss and betrayal hit her. Her best friend was gone, her family lost to her, her life a lie – a gauzy dream replaced by a terrifying nightmare.

I miss my mom, she thought, tears filling her eyes. *She must be worried sick… and what lies are they telling my sister to explain my leaving? Did I light a fire and steal a horse, just to ride off and visit an aunt?* she thought bitterly. *I hope the horse is okay*, she thought errantly, then chastised herself for worrying about a horse when her entire world was in disarray. *What am I going to do?* she despaired. *Where am I going to go?*

The woman who had been sitting beside her excused herself politely and moved to another seat, leaving Grace alone to huddle against the window, sobbing quietly, the glass cold against her cheek. Passengers stared, but she didn't care – she was broken.

The bus stopped abruptly, rousing her from her despair, and a moment later, a blue-haired girl stepped aboard and spied the empty seat. *Pull yourself together, Grace*, she ordered herself, dabbing her swollen eyes. The seat beside her was the only one free, but the girl still asked if it was alright if she took it. *That's nice of her*, Grace thought as the girl sat down, leaned back, closed her eyes, and breathed in deeply.

Rayne's arrival was a welcome distraction, so Grace focused on her instead of her misery. Even in repose, Rayne radiated a confidence that was the antithesis of how Grace felt. She was pretty, too, Grace concluded, and it wasn't her long blue hair that was her most striking feature – it was her eyes. They'd sparkled with intensity as she'd walked down the aisle, although a nasty bruise peeked out from under her collar, and her forehead held an assortment of cuts and scrapes. *What has she been through?* she wondered.

Rayne was thinking about the girl beside her too. She'd obviously been crying, and there were flecks of grass in her hair and dirt on her dress. She clutched her bag like a life preserver. *Was she a runaway?* she wondered. She felt for her – she knew what it was like to be alone in the world. She opened her eyes and smiled warmly at her.

Grace blushed at having been caught staring. "Where are you headed?" she asked to cover her awkwardness.

"Mekka. You?" Rayne replied.

"I suppose I'm headed there too." Grace wasn't sure what else to say, so she inquired about Rayne's injuries. "What happened?"

"I jumped off a building," Rayne replied matter-of-factly. "A couple actually, but it was the first one that really got me."

Grace stared at her in disbelief.

"It's not as bad as it looks," Rayne assured her, rubbing her bruised skin. "You should see my heart."

Grace recalled the gorgeous woman who had dropped Rayne off. "Your girlfriend seemed nice. She's *really* pretty," she added.

"Oh, that was Elana. She's just a friend."

Grace was wondering if it was appropriate to inquire further about Rayne's comment about a bruised heart when her stomach rumbled loud enough to be heard several rows away. Her face went beet red. "Sorry," she apologized, "I haven't eaten in a while," she explained.

"I don't think I have, either," Rayne reassured her. She was so used to being hungry that she didn't really notice it anymore. As if in answer, the bus's speakers announced a short stop in thirty minutes at an upcoming town. *Perhaps we can find something to eat there*, Rayne thought and closed her eyes again to puzzle out what she'd do when they arrived in Mekka.

The bus pulled off the road, kicking up a cloud of dust that once settled revealed a single, run-down building on the side of the road. Calling it a "town" had been a gross exaggeration, or probably the recording hadn't been updated in a hundred years. Regardless, most of the passengers filed off to stretch their legs. Rayne and Grace followed suit, bringing their bags with them – Grace because she didn't know she could leave it on the bus, and Rayne because she didn't trust doing so.

The disembarked passengers milled about. Some went off in search of a restroom, while others queued up at a stand attended to by a grizzled-looking woman selling made-to-order sandwiches. Rayne caught Grace staring longingly at the food but not moving toward it, so she concluded that she either had no money or was rationing it, and asked if she could get her something.

"No, thank you. I'm not that hungry," Grace lied. In truth, she was ravenous, but she couldn't bring herself to impose on the kindness of others.

"Suit yourself," Rayne replied and joined the queue to get them both something without making Grace feel uncomfortable about it.

Grace wandered away from the sandwich stand to prevent the smell from tormenting her further. A couple of men who'd been eyeing her since the bus picked her up moved toward her.

"Hey, good looking," one of them greeted her, looking her up and down in a way that made her skin crawl.

"Hi," she replied guardedly.

The second man circled around to her other side, effectively trapping her between them. "What brings you out this way?" he asked conversationally and reached out to touch her hair.

Grace recoiled from his advance, but she could only retreat so far with the other man behind her. She crossed her arms defensively, not knowing what to do or say to get out of this predicament.

"Don't be shy," the first man said, leaning closer. "We know how to treat a lady."

"That's highly unlikely," Rayne interrupted, "not being one yourself." She pushed past the man on Grace's left, putting an arm around her and giving her a kiss on the cheek. "I got you a sandwich, honey. I hope you like egg." She guided Grace out from between the men.

"Why leave so quickly?" the braver of the two men called after them.

Rayne turned around slowly. "Look, three's a crowd, and I don't even know what four is. I'm sure you can pleasure each other."

The men looked at each other, horrified.

"Prudes," Rayne muttered and spun back around.

"Thank you," Grace whispered as they walked to the bus, handing Rayne back her sandwich.

"That *is* actually for you," Rayne corrected her. "I hope you like egg, honey," she added with a wink and stepped onto the bus.

Grace followed her, and Rayne let her reclaim the window seat so that she could shield her from the men when they reboarded. Grace took her time savoring the sandwich, mindful of preserving her dignity.

The men walked past grumbling, and Rayne put a hand on Grace's knee. Warmth radiated up her leg, and Grace stared at Rayne's hand in wonder.

"Sorry for being so forward," Rayne whispered and withdrew her hand when the men had retaken their seats.

"It's quite alright. Thank you for rescuing me."

"I'm sure you would've been fine without me," Rayne assured her, "but I recommend a swift knee to the balls next time… although two men do have twice the balls," she remarked.

Grace almost choked on her sandwich but giggled and began feeling more at ease with her prospects of surviving in the world if there were people like Rayne in it. A wave of exhaustion overcame her, and she couldn't keep her eyes open. She drifted off to sleep, feeling safe for the first time in days.

Rayne watched Grace as she slept. *She's pretty*, she thought, *but she obviously has no idea.* Rayne wondered if that was better or worse for her – to be ignorant of her beauty. Her doe eyes betrayed every emotion she felt, and freckles dotted her cheeks like a map of the stars. She was utterly without guile, and Rayne found it refreshing after the emotional rollercoaster that Triste put her through. Being around Grace was like rising above New York's gloomy clouds to find that the world was actually bathed in sunlight.

Hours later, Grace woke to find her head on Rayne's shoulder and Rayne smiling down at her. She sat up, mortified, only to become doubly so when she realized that she'd drooled on Rayne in her sleep. Rayne didn't seem to mind, but Grace could barely look at her in her horror and stared out the window instead.

"I think we're almost there," Rayne informed her to assure her that no harm was done.

"That's great," Grace replied, still eager to escape her embarrassment. Her cheek still tingled where Rayne had kissed it, and she found herself touching it. She glanced at Rayne's lips. *Stop it*, she told herself. *She was just rescuing you.*

The bus broke free from a forested stretch of road, and the city of Mekka loomed in the distance. It was larger than anything Grace had ever seen, and she stared at it wide-eyed as they drove closer. Rayne felt the opposite, comparing it with New York, but Mekka was brighter and more vibrant. Its energy grew palpable as they approached, and it was infectious. The mood on the bus turned to eager expectation.

The bus entered the city, and people strode past in all manner of brightly colored clothes. Hot air balloons drifted overhead, and Grace thought it felt like a circus from one of her childhood books. The bus screeched to a halt in a tiny station, and the passengers began to disembark.

Rayne and Grace stepped off, and Rayne kept an arm around Grace's waist until the men from the pitstop disembarked and made their way out of the station. She turned to Grace. "Are you going to be okay? Do you have somewhere to go?"

"I'm going to look for a woman from my village," Grace assured her, thinking of her sixth. "You've been so kind to me. Thank you again."

"If you're sure," Rayne replied skeptically. "I hope I see you again, Grace…" Rayne prompted her.

"Lee. Grace Lee," Grace told her. "That would be nice," she added, "Rayne…"

"Torres," Rayne replied and squeezed Grace's hand. "Till then," she said and pulled Grace into a warm hug before turning for the exit. She stopped under the archway and turned to wave goodbye.

Grace waved back sunnily and immediately regretted letting Rayne walk out of her life. *Pride is a sin for a reason, you idiot*, she told herself and stuffed her hands in her pockets. They grazed something, and she pulled out a wad of bills that Rayne had stuffed into them. She looked at the exit, but Rayne was already gone. *My guardian angel has blue hair*, she thought and wept for joy, picking up her bag and heading for the exit herself.

Chapter 11

Rayne

Rayne walked out of the bus station into a city teeming with life. It was the diametric opposite of dreary New York. Peoples' outfits were a riot of color, and her bright blue hair didn't make her feel the least bit conspicuous for the first time in her life. She reveled in the normalcy.

Most people seemed to be heading toward the main street, so she followed along. It turned out to be a long promenade, lined with tables at which people sat eating, drinking and talking. Merchants wandered between them, hawking all manner of wares. There was a musician on every street corner plying their trade.

A lively fiddle tune caught Rayne's ear, and she followed it to an enormous crowd surrounding a girl who couldn't have been more than twelve. The crowd cheered, danced, and people filled her fiddle case with money. Rayne was mesmerized.

An elderly man tapped her on the shoulder. "Can I get you a drink, miss?"

"Aren't you a little old for me?" she asked him bluntly.

He laughed heartily. "I suppose so, but I didn't mean socially. I'm a waiter. If you'd like to take a seat, I'll bring you whatever you like."

Rayne shrugged off her misunderstanding. "I'm going to explore a bit first, but I'll find you later. You're officially my favorite waiter."

"I'm the first waiter you've met, aren't I?"

"Still my favorite," she replied with a wink and left him to walk up the street.

"I'm Harold," he called after her.

"Got it, Harold," she replied with a wave.

She spotted a group of men up the street wearing robes that reminded her of the group she'd seen in New York on the rooftop attending the old woman's suicide. These men were carrying signs that she couldn't read, and they were preaching to the people they passed. She sped up and caught them when they stopped to sermonize to a group that was clearly having way too much fun for their sensibilities.

"Excuse me," Rayne called to them as she approached. They turned around, and she paused to read their one-word signs: There. Must. Be. Consequences. *Well, that's a downer*, she thought. *Isn't that why God invented hangovers, addiction, STDs, and pregnancy?* "Gentlemen, I have a question for you." They waited patiently for her to ask it, but she paused, glancing back upwards. "Give me a second – your signs are killing me," she explained and stepped forward to physically switch the places of the first two men. The rearranged signs read: Must. There. Be. Consequences. "That's better," she concluded.

"Okay," she began, "when I was in New York, I saw a group like yours on a rooftop. They were there to witness a woman taking her life. Was that you? Well, not 'you' you, but your group?"

"I've never been to New York," the man on the left replied, "but our Church does help people cross over."

"If you don't mind my asking, but why?"

"God created us to return to Him at the end of our *natural* lives. It's unnatural to live forever. It flies in the face of His plan," the man replied with conviction.

"So, God's Plan is for us to die young?"

"We didn't mean that – just that people are staying too long in this material realm."

"We're all going to die eventually," Rayne told him. "God can probably afford to wait a little longer, can't he?"

"God put us all on a spiritual journey. Turn your back on that journey, and you get 'stuck,' and this is what you get," the man repeated, gesturing at the surrounding people laughing and smiling.

Rayne took in the carnival-like atmosphere and concluded that it didn't look so bad. "Look, we figured out how not to get eaten by the dinosaurs, right? Is this so different?"

"Clearly, the education system has failed you, young lady," the man replied exasperatedly.

"If there *is* an education system, no one's told me about it," Rayne defended herself. "I don't mean to be argumentative – I'm just not sure I come to the same conclusion that you do regarding God's plan."

"An open mind is all we ask," he replied.

"That's fair. Sorry to have interrupted you," she apologized and left them discussing her. *They seem nice*, she thought, *just a little misguided*.

A poster taped to a lamppost caught her eye, and she pulled it off to examine it. It announced a concert by *Armageddon's Embers*, her favorite band, right here in Mekka.

"There IS a God!" she yelled, and the robed men glared at her, sure that she was mocking them.

"Sorry," she apologized and beamed as she clutched the announcement to her chest.

Her shout caught the attention of a dangerous-looking man who pointed her out to a colleague, gesturing to her hair. They started toward her purposefully.

Rayne spotted them and muttered, "I don't have time for this shit," and set about losing herself in the crowd. The men struggled to track her movements. *Who'd have thought that being short is my superpower?* she thought as she weaved up the promenade. She spied an alley off to her right and broke from the crowd for it. She raced down it, putting as much distance as she could between her and the men pursuing her. *I don't get it,* she thought. *Blue hair is hardly that big a deal in this madhouse.* Once she was pretty sure she'd lost them, she circled back around to the restaurant district and sought out Harold.

"Told you I'd be back," she announced, scanning the crowd for the men, just to be doubly sure. "Can I sit here?" she asked, gesturing to a tiny table nestled among some potted palms.

"Be my guest," he replied, not batting an eye at her choice of the worst table on the promenade. What can I get you?"

"What've you got?"

He laughed. "This is Mekka – we've got everything."

"Blueberry juice?" she asked as a test.

"Coming right up," he replied and disappeared into one of the many restaurants. He returned a moment later with two glasses, put them both down, and sat across from her.

Rayne raised an eyebrow. "What do I owe you?"

"My treat," he replied cheerfully. "I don't actually work here. Waiting tables just keeps me from getting bored. Plus, I get to meet new people, like you. You have the look of a newcomer," he concluded nonjudgmentally. "What would you like to know about our fair city?" he asked, reaching for his drink.

Rayne found him completely disarming but stopped him anyway before he could drink to ask if he minded their switching glasses. She didn't even bother making up an excuse.

"Prudent," he declared and pushed his glass across the table, grabbing hers. "I like your style," he told her and took a deep drink from the glass that had been hers.

She shrugged and took a tiny sip from hers. "Well, for starters, where can a girl rent a room?"

"I can tell you where *not* to," he replied. "Stay away from the theater district – it's sketchy after dark – and anywhere off the promenade – they overcharge. Apart from that, you're probably fine to stay just about anywhere. I'd suggest heading away from the river until it seems quiet, then inquire there."

"And the river is?"

"That way," he pointed.

She nodded her thanks. "And today's Friday, right?"

"Last time I checked," he replied, taking another sip.

"So, this concert is tomorrow?" she asked, handing him the flyer for confirmation.

He looked it over and nodded. "They're terrible, by the way," he told her and waved away her indignation. "Don't get me wrong. They're talented, but they're *really* depressing."

"I love them," she defended.

"And I was just beginning to like you," he sighed, smiling and draining his rest of his glass. "I'd better get back to 'work.'" He got up but hesitated before leaving. "A last piece of advice, if you'll humor an old man. There are only four kinds of people in Mekka: the lost, the searching, the sought, and the predators. Avoid the first and last, and you'll be fine."

"Which one am I?" she asked, curious.

"You think you're the second, but you're the third," he replied and left her to puzzle over his meaning.

She looked at her barely-touched glass. Renner would murder her if she drank it, so she sighed and pushed it away, getting up to go find a room for the night, covering her hair, just to be cautious.

True to Harold's word, she found the neighborhoods to be increasingly sedate off the promenade. She asked a passing woman where she could find a room for the night and was directed to a nearby, three-story building. Rayne asked the bored-looking woman at the front desk for a room on the top floor. "I like a view," she explained.

"10 dollars extra," the woman informed her.

"That's fine… oh, and can I have an extra blanket and pillow?"

"No guests," she replied gruffly, pointing unnecessarily to a sign that read exactly what she'd just said.

"I wouldn't dream of it," Rayne assured her. "I just get cold at night."

"Well, there isn't much to you," she agreed, looking her over. "You'll find extra bedding in the closet in the room," she told her.

So why give me such a hard time? Rayne thought, but paid and thanked her anyway. She headed to her room, locked the door, and lay on the bed, waiting for nightfall. When she judged that it was dark enough, she grabbed her backpack, the extra blanket and pillow, and headed out to the balcony, leaving the door the tiniest bit ajar behind her. She tossed her pack up onto the roof. *If I can't get up there*, she thought, *I'm so going to regret having done that.* She climbed onto the railing, balanced precariously, and pushed the bedding up onto the roof, then grabbed hold of the edge and hauled herself up after it. She laid out the blanket just behind the lip of the roof and tucked the pillow under her head. She felt safer under the stars anyway, she told herself, and the warm breeze and distant music soothed her.

Images of Grace bubbled up into her mind's eye. *I should never have left her to fend for herself*, she berated herself. *The world is unkind to kind people.* Surprisingly, it wasn't guilt that haunted her – it was an odd attraction. Grace was everything the world had never been to Rayne, and Rayne regretted leaving her at the bus station. Regret, guilt and longing swirled together and lulled her to sleep.

She woke to whispered voices arguing in her room.

"She's not here," one of them said.

"Obviously," the other countered, "but I didn't see her leave."

"Then look harder," the first one hissed.

A dim flashlight switched on, and Rayne lay still, breathing slowly and deliberately. She heard the door to the balcony slide open, followed by footsteps, but no one checked up on the roof.

"She's gone," the man on the balcony relayed to his partner.

"So, renting the room was a misdirect?"

"Looks like it. She's good… just like her mother."

Rayne barely restrained herself from bolting upright at the mention of her long-dead mother. *Who do these men think I am?* She had no time to think about it before the interior door to her room opened and closed, leaving her alone.

A couple of minutes later, those thoughts were interrupted by the sound of muffled gunshots. Rayne hazarded a peek over the roof's edge and saw two bodies being dragged away into the night. *What the hell have I gotten myself into?* She wondered and waited anxiously for dawn.

At first light, she peeked over the roof's edge and saw no blood trails, no evidence of foul play at all. She dropped the bedding down to the balcony, followed by her pack, then herself. She didn't waste time changing outfits and hurried out the door, taking the stairs at the far end of the hall to street-level and peeking out into the lane, seeing no one. *If I'm being watched, they'd better damn well be watching closely*, she thought and raced away. She changed course constantly, blending into crowds, entering buildings, and exiting them out the rear.

She eventually tired of her efforts to lose any potential pursuers and judged that she'd done her best when she found herself in an abandoned graveyard. She walked through the tall grasses among the forgotten headstones before finally slumping down with her back to one. *What's my mother got to do with anything?* she wondered, resting her hand on the cool stone. *She's dead.*

Chapter 12

Grace

Grace stepped out of the bus station into a city that was so different from her village in which she'd spent her entire life that it may as well have been on a different planet altogether. She sat down on a bench while she got a sense of things. Passersby were dressed garishly compared with her simple cotton dress, and she began to feel self-conscious in it. She decided that she should probably find clothes in which she'd fit in better but doubted she'd feel comfortable dressing as overtly sexually as seemed to be the norm. People passed by with such regularity that she gave up trying to guess what they were up to and began to infer what she could about the city itself.

If there was a basic structure to it, however, it escaped her. Her village had shops, homes, fields... but the sheer scale of Mekka rendered it unfathomable to her. The best she could decipher was that she was near a part of the city dedicated to socializing, like a birthday party that the entire city was invited to.

Her stomach reminded her that she'd still had little to eat, despite Rayne's kind gift of a sandwich. She decided that her focus should be on the basics – food, clothing, and a roof over her head – before exploring her new surroundings and trying to find Violet Moore, her sixth.

A young woman struggling with heavy grocery bags sat down beside her to take a break. Grace decided to chance asking her for some information.

"Excuse me," she said to get the girl's attention. "I'm new here," she began.

"You don't say," the girl replied, although her sarcasm was lost on Grace.

"Do you know where I can find somewhere to stay?"

The girl looked her over appraisingly, concluding that Grace wasn't likely flush with cash. "Well, there are a billion places, but if you're not fussy, Jennifer just moved out, so we've got room at our place if you're interested."

Grace's head swam with the information provided. *A billion sounds like a lot. Am I supposed to know Jennifer?* It finally registered that she was being offered a place to stay. "Really? That would be great," she replied.

"Don't expect much," the girl warned her. "We're kind of crammed into the place we rent, and as the new girl, you'd get the least awesome place to sleep."

If they're awesome, and mine is just the least awesome, Grace thought, *that still sounds pretty good.*

"Plus, we divide the rent and groceries evenly, regardless of who has the nicest room or who eats the most. Is that okay?"

"That sounds reasonable," Grace agreed.

"Okay then, welcome aboard," the girl concluded and held out her hand to shake Grace's. "The gang's going to be happy that I found a non-freak."

Grace shook the girl's hand. "I'm Grace, by the way."

"I'm Maggie," she replied in kind. "Pleased to meet you." She wiped her brow and stood up. "Would you mind giving me a hand with these bags? I'm heading home now."

"Of course," Grace responded, picking up half the grocery bags in one hand and carrying her bag containing all her worldly possessions in her other.

"You're stronger than you look," Maggie observed at Grace's ease with her load.

"I did a lot of chores," Grace offered by way of explanation.

"That'll come in handy," Maggie replied as they walked. "Okay, let me give you the rundown. Ryan and Michael have been there the longest, so they have the larger bedroom, Jennifer and Angie had the other room, but with Jennifer gone, I scooped her bed. Trin is on the couch, which leaves you the spot in the alcove. It's a bit exposed, but once everyone settles in for the night, it's quiet enough that you'll sleep okay."

Grace had already forgotten everyone's name, except Maggie's and Trin's. "I'm sure it'll be alright. Did you say there were boys?"

"I'd hardly call Ryan and Michael 'boys', but they're a couple, so they won't hit on you or anything like that if that's what you're worried about."

It was more the impropriety of unmarried boys and girls living together that was unfamiliar to Grace, but she didn't have a problem with it.

"Trin's a girl, by the way," Maggie added.

"I assumed," Grace replied.

"I wouldn't assume anything in this place, if I were you," Maggie counseled her, guiding her along on what turned out to be a fair hike.

"There's no closer grocery store?" Grace asked.

"Sure, but the one I went to is cheaper, and we're on a budget. Plus, Ryan is particular about his cheese."

Grace filed away all the information, encouraging Maggie to talk more about her roommates so that she could rehearse their names.

"Home, sweet home," Maggie finally declared as they walked toward a tiny art gallery squeezed between two nondescript buildings.

Grace looked at Maggie quizzically.

"We live upstairs," Maggie explained and led her through a narrow door and up the stairs to the apartment. To call it cramped would have been an understatement, but, *beggars can't be choosers*, Grace told herself.

"Anyone home?" Maggie called out. A sleepy-looking man in a housecoat peeked out a bedroom door, and a girl with paint on her hands peeked out the other. "Hey guys, I found 'replacement Jennifer,'" Maggie announced.

"I'm Grace," she corrected, and Ryan and Angie introduced themselves in turn. Ryan went back to bed, and Angie lay down on the sofa, stretching out her back and picking paint off her nails while she studied the new girl.

"Help me with dinner, will you?" Maggie asked Grace. "You do know how to cook, don't you?"

"Sure," Grace replied, putting the grocery bags down so Maggie could put everything away. "My mother did most of the cooking, but I was to be married in a couple of months, so she showed me the basics."

"Wow," Angie chimed in. "I'm not sure if I should say, 'congratulations' or 'sorry to hear that.' You don't look more than eighteen."

"Good guess," Grace confirmed, "but the wedding is off on account of my fleeing my village and all."

"Smart girl," Angie replied.

Maggie turned toward Grace. "Oops – I should have clarified the whole 'money thing.' Your share of the rent is $500 a month, and it's another $100 for groceries."

Grace pulled the crumpled bills out of her pocket. "Is this enough?"

"It'll have to be, it seems," Maggie confirmed, taking it all. "We'll find you a job tomorrow."

"That'd be great," Grace replied, happy to have fallen in with such helpful people.

"What do you do?" Angie asked. "What's your thing?"

Grace had no idea what Angie was asking, so Maggie rescued her. "She means, 'what kind of work do you do?' If it isn't obvious, Angie paints."

"That's cool," Grace replied. "Is that your gallery downstairs?"

Angie laughed. "If it was, do you think I'd be staying with you lot? No offense, of course."

"None taken," Maggie replied. "I don't like you much either," she added, smiling.

Grace felt increasingly at ease and evaded admitting that her farm skills probably had little utility here in the city. She joined Maggie and began making a simple salad.

Grace met the rest of her roommates at dinner.

"This crew would never miss a meal," Maggie explained.

Michael and Ryan were both actors, who met on the set of a production years ago. Maggie was a sculptor, Angie a painter, and Trin a woodworker.

"We're sort of an artist collective," Angie concluded.

Everyone looked to Grace to see how she fit in, but Maggie rescued her from their awkward scrutiny. "Grace has *legitimate* skills."

Ryan howled at the insult, and everyone laughed. After the late dinner, Michael, Ryan, Maggie, and Angie retired to their rooms, leaving Grace with Trin.

"They tell me I talk in my sleep," Trin apologized in advance. "I think they're bullshitting me, but how would I know?" She showed Grace where they stored the rolled-up mat that she'd sleep on in the alcove, and no sooner than her head touched the pillow than she was out like a light.

Grace slept so soundly that she could neither confirm nor refute whether Trin actually talked in her sleep, much to Trin's disappointment.

Maggie stepped out of her room in the morning in a sleep shirt that was thin and worn enough to be practically see-through. Grace blushed, but Maggie seemed oblivious to her body on display and proceeded to make herself a cup of coffee, offering to make Grace one too.

Grace had never had coffee and was game to try it, so she accepted the offer.

"How do you like it?" Maggie asked.

Not knowing how to answer, Grace just replied, "I'm easy. I'll have it the way you take it."

Maggie shrugged. "Glad to hear you're easy. You're cute." Grace blushed a darker shade of red, but Maggie ignored it and handed her a steaming mug.

Grace focused on her coffee to avoid staring at Maggie's breasts – she was far less comfortable with them than Maggie was. The coffee was bitter as hell and not really Grace's thing. "It's nice, thanks," she lied and took another sip.

"Let's find you a job today," Maggie announced happily.

"Are you sure it's no trouble?" Grace asked. "Don't you have somewhere you need to be today?"

"Apart from Michael and Ryan, we're all pretty much on our own schedule, so no… plus, it's pretty tight in here, so we all try to find somewhere else to be during the day to avoid getting on each other's nerves." She looked Grace over critically, but not unkindly. "You'll want to freshen up. There's one bathroom and rarely hot water, but you seem to be an early riser, so if there's no one to fight you for it, it's all yours." She looked Grace over again. "That outfit is *not* going to do you any favors landing a job." She called over her shoulder into her bedroom. "Angie, you're Grace's size, more or less. Do you have anything slutty, but not too slutty, if you know what I mean?"

"What kind of job were you thinking," Grace asked, a bit alarmed.

"Oh, the usual kind," Maggie assured her, "but it is always a good idea to put your best foot forward... or legs, butt, breasts... whatever. Trust me, I've had a lot of jobs."

Grace had little choice but to surrender to Maggie's help, but at least was able to choose clothing that was only moderately revealing. She looked herself over in the mirror. *The people in my village would lose their minds to see me like this*, she thought. *I wonder if it would finally get a rise out of Gabriel*, she asked herself, but quickly concluded that he wouldn't even recognize her.

Maggie nodded her approval at Grace's transformation and led her out of the apartment.

"Where are we going to try to get me a job?" Grace asked.

"We're going to start with grocery stores. If we can get you an employee discount, it would be like winning the lottery."

That sounded fine to Grace, and she wound up being hired on the spot at the first place they inquired. Maggie was ecstatic.

"You might want to wear something a little 'sturdier,'" the woman who hired her suggested, and Grace gave Maggie an "I told you so" look, to which Maggie responded with an "it got you the job, didn't it?" look.

"Can you start today? And by today, I mean now?" the woman asked. "I had someone call in sick."

"That's fine with me," Grace agreed, and Maggie promised to return at the end of Grace's shift to walk her home in case she forgot the way, which of course, she had.

Grace was so pleasant with the customers that the woman who hired her moved her to the bakery near the entrance. Grace would chat with the bored and lonely clientele but compensate for it by being a really hard worker. Her boss felt like she'd struck gold in hiring Grace.

Toward the end of her shift, Grace noticed a young woman enter and move about collecting groceries but looking around nervously the entire time. Grace's boss also noticed her, and after paying Grace, trailed the woman around the store. Grace cleaned up and sat on a bench out front to wait for Maggie.

Moments later, the young woman was stopped at the door by two burly men who worked in produce for trying to leave without paying. There was a look of terror and desperation on her face that was completely disproportionate to her crime. It broke Grace's heart and prompted her to rush over.

"Jess, there you are! How'd you slip past me?" Grace greeted the confused woman.

The two men who had stopped the woman looked equally confused.

"She was just coming to get me so I could pay," Grace explained. "They're my groceries."

Grace's boss walked up and could tell that Grace's story didn't add up. She pulled a jar of baby food out of the woman's cart and looked at Grace skeptically.

"That's for my roommate," Grace made up and steered the woman toward a cashier. Grace's boss shrugged and sent the two "guards" back to stocking produce. Grace smiled at her graciously, knowing that she could easily have called her on the lie and fired her.

Grace paid the woman's bill and helped her carry the bags outside, where, once out of sight, she handed them to the woman.

She hesitantly took the bags, not sure what manner of debt she'd just incurred. "I have no money to pay you back," she told Grace, "and probably never will," she admitted honestly.

"No need to," Grace replied and pressed the bags on her.

The woman didn't know what to say and took them hesitantly. "Thank you," she said, clearly still waiting for some invisible axe to fall.

"You're welcome," Grace replied, thinking of the kindness Rayne had shown her, and sat back down on a bench to keep an eye out for Maggie. The woman hurried away, leaving Grace wondering, *Where are you, Rayne?*

Chapter 13

Rayne

Rayne sat in the long, untended grass of the graveyard, wracking her brain for what to do about the trouble she'd found herself in, trouble that she didn't fully understand and certainly had done nothing to deserve. *What would Renner tell me to do?* she asked herself. *He'd tell me that I needed more information*, she answered.

Then, that's what I'm going to get, she decided and rose from her hiding spot. *But first*, she decided, *I can't go around looking like I do, and I'm sure as hell not going to live the rest of my life skulking around.* She remembered Harold saying something about a theatre district, so she sought out someone to ask where it was.

She arrived there around midday, finding few people around and concluding that actors apparently found noon ungodly early. She asked herself, "If I were an actor, where would I find the tools to ply my craft?" She looked around until she found a row of shops selling assorted props, makeup, and costumes. Most weren't open yet, which annoyed her, given that she had precious little time before the concert that she was damn well going to attend. She spotted a wig shop that looked open. *Perfect*, she thought and walked in.

A tired woman looked up from her reader, stifling a yawn. "What can I do for you?" she asked.

"I need a couple of wigs," Rayne replied.

"Obviously," the woman stated, glancing around the shop. "What kind?"

"One that looks like my hair does now, and one that looks nothing like it."

"Now, this is getting interesting," she replied, putting down her reader. "For a costume or a disguise?"

Rayne eyed her skeptically.

"We get all kinds, honey, trust me. It helps if I know what you want it for."

"Disguise," Rayne confided.

"Alright then, that level of quality is a bit pricier, but I'll charge you two-for-one because you've livened up my day."

Rayne didn't figure she had much choice, and the woman beckoned her closer to examine her hair in better light.

"This is your natural color?" the woman asked, amazed.

"It is," Rayne replied proudly.

"Wonder of wonders," the woman muttered to herself. "It's gorgeous," she added. "I have something close to that that I can use as a base, but it'll take some dyeing to really pull off the match. I'll get that started, then we'll look for your second wig."

Rayne sat down while the woman took photos of her hair to run through her computer, mixed some pigments, and began giving the blue wig highlights. While the color was setting, she turned her attention back to Rayne.

"As long as you don't have your heart set on a coppery color, we can fix you up."

"Why not copper?" Rayne asked, curious.

The woman pointed to a bust sporting a beautiful burnt orange wig. "Stare at that for a minute. Don't blink."

Rayne did as she was told.

"Okay, now close your eyes and tell me what you see," the woman instructed her.

"Blue," Rayne replied, amazed.

"Yup," the woman replied. "The worst thing you can do when you're trying not to look like yourself is to try and look like the opposite of yourself. You're better off going on a tangent."

Rayne wondered about the woman's clientele.

"It's just color theory, really," the woman assured her. "You'd be a fine as a blonde or a redhead. Do you have a preference?"

"What do you think?"

"If you want to blend in, I'd go with blonde. Mekka is filled with blonde wannabe actresses."

"Blonde it is then," Rayne decided, and an image of Grace appeared in her mind's eye. "Sandy blonde."

"Good thinking – it's a little less 'look at me,'" the woman agreed and got to work picking out something that went well with Rayne's honeyed skin.

"You've got time to kill while the blue wig is drying," the woman told her. "Got any errands to run?"

"How do I go about organizing a casting call?"

"For a body double?" the woman guessed.

"Precisely," Rayne admitted.

"We don't really do it like that anymore. It's all online. But I can help. I've got nothing else to do, and this cloak-and-dagger stuff is *so* entertaining." She sat Rayne down beside her at her computer. "There's a site dedicated to body doubles, and not just for movies, but for all sorts of reasons, although mostly when the real actor or actress is too expensive for far-away shots." She took a photo of Rayne and entered it into the system, then filtered by "Mekka" and "available." A short-list appeared, and each of the women bore an uncanny resemblance to Rayne.

"Let me see who each of them has doubled for in the past to get a sense of how expensive they'd be," the woman suggested and ruled a few out. The system spat out a couple of phone numbers, and the woman lent Rayne her phone to contact them. Rayne reached someone on the second attempt, and the eager voice agreed to meet her at the wig shop in an hour.

"How much do I pay her?" Rayne asked when she got off the phone.

"What do you want her to do?"

"Just wander around the city, really."

"$50 an hour is probably sufficient… plus expenses."

"Expenses?"

"You know, lattés and the like. Aspiring actresses have needs," she chuckled. "I can lend you an earpiece comm system if that would help. It's for feeding actors their lines when they blank," she explained.

"Oh my God, yes. That would be fabulous."

"I just wish I could see what you're up to, but I'm stuck here," she lamented.

Rayne stepped out to get them both a coffee, and they chatted until Rayne's double arrived. When the girl showed up, thankfully early, Rayne briefed her about what she wanted. They agreed on terms, and the girl put on the blue wig while Rayne donned the blonde. Staring at her double was like looking in a mirror, and Rayne was immensely pleased.

"Let me know how it all turns out when you return the comm gear," the shop owner requested as Rayne and her "twin" headed out.

"Just to know what I'm involved in," the girl asked, "am I creating an alibi for you while you're off committing a crime or having an affair, or are we just pranking someone?"

"We're pranking my ex-boyfriend. He doesn't know I'm in town, and I want to play with his head a bit. I'll warn you though, he might try to prank you back. He once dressed up as a mugger and pulled a fake gun on me. I saw through it in a heartbeat, though. He really is the worst actor."

The girl nodded. "Most men are."

"If he pulls that shit on you, don't stay in character, just whip off your wig and tell him 'surprise.' He'll know I got the better of him... again... and he'll be *so* pissed."

"Sounds like a fun way to spend a Saturday afternoon," the girl replied, and they headed to the promenade with Rayne following at a distance, her blonde curls bouncing behind her.

"Just walk around and act naturally. Enjoy yourself, but don't bankrupt me, please," Rayne requested through the earpiece.

The girl bought a latté and amused herself by window-shopping while Rayne kept watch. Pretty soon, Rayne spotted a man taking more of an interest in her double than most people. Rayne directed her to walk farther up the promenade, sticking to crowds. The man followed the girl but kept his distance so long as she stayed surrounded by people.

"Pretend to head toward the alley on your right," Rayne told her, "but at the last minute, head back to the center of the promenade."

The girl did as she was requested, and Rayne watched the man close the distance when he thought he'd catch her alone, then fade back when she changed course. He was definitely following her. Rayne was mulling over how best to exploit this information when she spied a couple that she'd seen earlier in the afternoon change course when the man following her double did. *Curious*, she thought.

"I think my ex is on to you," Rayne told the girl, "but he's hanging back because he isn't sure."

"How many girls with blue hair could there possibly be?" the girl whispered into her mic.

"I should have added that he isn't very bright. Anyway, let's yank his chain a little. I'd like you to zigzag back and forth across the next block, going from one side of the promenade to the other. I want to see if you can play him like a yo-yo."

The girl nodded discreetly and did as she was requested. The man followed her, and the couple followed him. *This is getting weird*, Rayne thought to herself. The man following her double started to lose patience and began to move closer, putting a hand inside his jacket. The couple split up and sped up to converge on him. *I don't want to put this girl in any more danger than I already have*, Rayne decided and told her that she'd had her fun and to sit down at the closest table and pull off her wig.

The girl took a seat and made an extravagant show of taking off her wig and tousling her real hair, which was long and dark. The man could tell in an instant that he'd been played and broke off his pursuit. The couple, however, didn't lose interest in him so easily.

"Great job," Rayne told the girl. "I'll square up with you online about the expenses."

"What do I do with the wig?" she asked.

"Just stick it in the potted plant beside you with your half of the comm system."

The girl waved to the sky and headed home, while the man who had been following her hurried down a side street. The couple following him nearly caught him before an e-bike raced up and whisked him away. The woman made a quick phone call, and the pair began to walk away.

Rayne followed after them at a distance, a task that was complicated by the sheer number of men, and the odd woman, who propositioned her. *It is so fatiguing being a blonde*, she thought but kept the couple in sight until they used a key card to pass through a gate and disappeared into a courtyard. Rayne committed the place to memory and turned around. She never noticed the drone high in the sky tracking her.

———————

"Elana," her AI intoned to get her attention. "Your 'girlfriend' has been busy. Would you like a full report?"

"That would be delightful," Elana replied. "And please find out everything you can about her, and I mean everything."

"Well, because you said 'please'…," Sara replied.

Chapter 14

Grace

A fluttering blind let in the dawn light and woke Grace. *Old habits die hard*, she thought, having woken early for chores or school, or both, all her life. It had been a warm night, and her roommates had left all the windows and doors open in the hope that the breeze would cool them enough to sleep. Grace lay still, listening to the deep breathing that confirmed that she was the only one awake. She tried to fall back asleep but found she couldn't, and passed the time instead by thinking of Rayne.

Every time she closed her eyes, Rayne's face swam into view. Grace remembered her eyes burning with an intensity that made it clear that everything she saw received her full attention, not like the anesthetized stares of most people she'd met. When Rayne looked at Grace, she felt like she really saw her, in a way that she'd never felt seen before. Her friends and family looked at her as though they already knew what they were seeing. Even Gabriel, who looked upon her with affection, never really saw the real her – her wants, her dreams. Rayne saw all of her and accepted what she saw, all her yearning, her vulnerability. *I have to see her again*, she concluded.

When Maggie finally emerged from her room, as the only other quasi-morning person in the apartment, they snuck out to the stairwell to have their coffee without waking Trin, who still lay snoring softly on the sofa.

Maggie closed the door quietly behind her and sat down. "So, what's on the agenda today?" she asked Grace.

"I don't work until two, so I thought I'd see if I can track down a woman who used to live in my village."

"What's her name?" Maggie asked between sips and yawns.

"Violet Moore," Grace replied.

Maggie whipped out a phone from God knows where given how little she wore when she emerged from her bedroom and began typing onto it.

"What are you doing?" Grace asked, curious.

"I'm contacting a friend of mine in law enforcement who can track her down."

"Really?"

"No," she chuckled, "but I've always wanted to say that. I'm just looking her up." A second later, "237 Windsong Court."

Grace looked skeptical, waiting for Maggie to announce that she was pulling her leg.

"Seriously, that's her address. Well, maybe not her home, but it's where she works."

Grace was dumbfounded. She'd expected to spend weeks wandering the streets, asking strangers. It was somehow exciting to hear that her sixth indeed lived in the city, but also somewhat of a letdown.

"Do you know where Windsong Court is?" Grace asked.

"Nope, but I will in a jiffy." She glanced at her phone and pulled out a pen. "I'll draw you a map."

"Seriously, where do you even keep stuff in your nightclothes?"

Maggie looked herself over. "I'll never tell," she replied with a grin. "Now, give me your hand before I forget the details."

Rayne proffered her hand, and Maggie drew a rough sketch of the route on her palm before leaning back, the pose accentuating her breasts.

"You really love your breasts, don't you?" Grace observed.

"What's not to love?" she replied, downing the rest of her coffee. "Now, if you'll excuse me, I'm claiming the shower. I have a friend who says that I can use the pizza oven at his restaurant as a kiln as long as I bring my pottery over before it opens." She got up to return to the apartment.

"Do you need any help?" Grace asked.

"Thanks, but my breasts and I can manage," Maggie joked. "Go find your Violet woman."

Grace waited an eternity for Maggie to finish her shower, solving the mystery of the lack of hot water for everyone else. She washed up quickly and eschewed the clothes she'd borrowed from Angie for a simple dress she'd brought from her village.

Grace stepped out of the bathroom to find Trin looking up at her expectantly.

"I didn't hear you utter a single word in your sleep," Grace assured her.

"I knew it," she declared and threw a pillow at Maggie, who narrowly avoided it by scooting out the door.

"I'm off too," Grace declared and downed the last of her coffee, which she'd discovered wasn't half bad with a ton of sugar. She stepped out the door and followed Maggie's map across town to a quiet residential neighborhood. She double-checked the address and walked up to the door, where she knocked politely, then a little louder when no one answered. Still no one answered, so she pushed the button on the wall beside the door, wondering what it would do, and heard a faint chime inside. Still, no one answered. She sighed, disappointed that the trip across town had been a bust but noted a tiny plaque near the button that read, "By appointment only."

Grace looked around before calling out to the air, "How do I make an appointment?" She received no answer and decided to enlist Maggie's help figuring it out.

On her dejected walk home, she thought she recognized the young woman from the grocery store walking toward her on the opposite side of the street, a young boy in tow. Grace crossed over to intercept them.

"I thought I recognized you," Grace said by way of greeting.

The woman smiled a nervous smile in response.

"This must be your son," Grace continued, acknowledging the young boy. "I assumed he'd be younger," she added. The woman seemed unsure of what she meant by that, so Grace clarified, "You know, the baby food."

"Oh, that," she replied. "My son still kind of likes it," she explained.

The boy gave his mother a look that said, "I most certainly do not," but with her hand resting on his shoulder, he said nothing.

"What can you do?" the woman added sheepishly. "I'd better be off. It was good to see you," she concluded and hurried away.

"Have a nice day," Grace called after her but then felt stupid for using the mantra she'd been instructed to say at the grocery store. *Curious*, she thought and continued on to her apartment.

Maggie hadn't returned by the time Grace had to leave for work, but Grace was optimistic that she'd figure out a way to contact her sixth. She whistled to herself as she strolled to work, something she only did in her village when she was *certain* no one would hear her.

A man standing on a crate, surrounded by a small circle of young people, called to her, "Hey, grocery girl." Getting her attention, he asked her, "Do you feel oppressed by your job?"

"No. I like it," she replied.

It wasn't the answer he was expecting, so he added, "See how you feel when you've had it for twenty years with no possibility for advancement." Heads nodded. "The old have had hundreds of years to engineer things to their benefit, and do you think they're keen on sharing power?"

Grace assumed the question was more for his entourage than her, so she smiled politely and snuck away while he continued his speech.

Arriving at the grocery store, she grabbed an apron and did the rounds to say "hi" to everyone working that day, even the crusty old guys who were hidden in the back so as not to scare the customers. She installed herself behind the bakery counter and began arranging the display. Her boss walked over.

"Got a second?" she asked.

"Of course," Grace replied.

"The girl from yesterday, the one you helped, you didn't really know her, did you?"

"I knew she needed help," Grace replied with conviction.

"I'm not saying you did the wrong thing – I just wanted to tell you that you can't help everyone. Below Mekka's bubbly surface is a deep well of misery. You can't take responsibility for all of it – it will drag you down."

"I appreciate your concern, and I promise that I'm not going in search of misery, but when it comes at you head-on, you can't really ignore it."

"You're a good person, Grace – just look out for yourself – remember that no one is looking out for you the way you're looking out for them."

Grace was reminded of Rayne's kindness and her mother's hugs, both lost to her, and her eyes filled with tears.

"That's not what I meant," her boss quickly backpedaled. "I'm sure that everyone who even remotely knows you loves you."

Grace wiped her eyes, and the woman pulled her in for an awkward hug before patting her back and returning to her office.

"You made the new girl cry," the produce manager chastised her.

"Can I have a hug?" his assistant asked.

"You two, shut up," she replied, "and mark my words – that girl is a magnet for suffering." She closed herself in her office to re-evaluate her management skills.

Grace dried her tears and got back to work. A couple of hours later, she was back to her usual chipper self when she thought she spied someone out the front window who looked like her ex-fiancé, Gabriel. *I must be hallucinating*, she told herself and ducked around the counter to get a better look. She hid behind a fruit display and watched the boy she thought looked like Gabriel stop a passerby and show him a picture.

He came for me! she thought, heart swelling, then recoiled. She didn't know what it meant that he was here in Mekka and what risk it posed to her. She needed time to figure it out before she saw him. She ducked entirely behind the display, then spied her boss emerging from her office.

She rushed over to her and unloaded breathlessly, "I need your help. My overly-possessive ex is outside looking for me."

"Hide in the back," the woman told her without skipping a beat, then raised her voice so that all her employees could hear. "If someone asks about Grace, we don't know her. We've never seen her. Is that clear?"

The customers wondered at the drama, but the employees nodded their assent.

"Maurice, Paul… if that boy outside gives Grace a hard time, you beat the tar out of him."

"I'm pretty sure that's illegal," Paul objected.

"You protect that girl, or you're fired."

"I'm pretty sure that's illegal too," Paul complained but rolled up his sleeves.

"Come on," Maurice told him, "Let's beat him up, just for fun."

"Low profile," their boss reminded them, shaking her head.

Gabriel entered the store and looked around.

"Is there something I can help you with?" she asked him.

"Sorry to trouble you. I'm looking for someone," he said, showing her a picture of Grace. "Have you seen her?"

The woman looked intently at the picture before replying, "Sorry, I've never seen her before. We mostly get regulars, so I would have noticed her." She handed the photo to Maurice. "Maurice, you work the front. Have you ever seen this girl?"

"She's pretty," Maurice concluded.

"And?" her boss prompted him.

"I think I'd know if someone who looked like that shopped here."

Maurice's boss shooed him away. "Sorry about Maurice," she told Gabriel. "He's a bit unvarnished. And sorry we haven't seen the girl." She guided him to the exit. "You'll have better luck looking along the promenade. It's the hub of the city," she added helpfully and shooed him away while Maurice went to tell Grace the coast was clear. She emerged visibly shaken.

"Do you need to take the rest of the day off?" her boss asked her.

"No, thank you. I just wasn't prepared for that. I'm sorry to drag you into it."

"No worries, we've got your back," she said and patted Grace on the shoulder before getting back to work.

Grace finished the remainder of her shift, keeping an eye out the window the whole time. She poked her head out the door before leaving to make sure the way was clear. Maurice got up off the bench outside.

"I'm walking you home," he informed her casually.

"Thank you," she replied and surprised him by taking his arm. He placed a comforting arm around her, and she led him to her apartment.

"You're working tomorrow again at two, right?" he asked her when they arrived.

"Yes."

"I'll see you here at 1:30, then," he told her and walked off before she could tell him that it was nice of him but unnecessary. In truth, she appreciated his looking out for her until she figured herself out.

Maggie poked her head out the door. "Boyfriend or bodyguard?"

"Bodyguard," Grace replied.

"Great, introduce me next time," Maggie told her while she watched Maurice retreat.

"I thought you and Angie...?" Grace asked.

"Hell no, she's a troll. We're just roomies. Your walking man-mountain is more my thing."

"Okay, then. I hope he likes your breasts as much as you do," Grace teased.

"Everybody loves my breasts," Maggie replied, cupping them.

Grace shook her head and started up the stairs.

"Care to tell me why you need a bodyguard?"

"Maybe later. It's been a trying day."

Chapter 15

Rayne

It was getting on in the day, and Rayne switched to thinking about the *Armageddon's Embers* concert that night. *Life can wait until tomorrow,* she told herself. *This is more important.* She hunted around for a ticket agent, and it wasn't hard to find one, but the man told her that the concert had sold out weeks ago. He then proceeded to try to talk her into buying tickets for other shows until she almost punched him to extricate herself.

It's okay, she told herself, *breaking into places is my thing.* She found an empty parking garage and changed into leather pants and a tight top. She took off the blonde wig in favor of her natural blue. *If I am going to see my idols, I'm going as me,* she decided. She cursed herself that she didn't own any make-up, but she didn't really know how to apply it anyway, so it probably wouldn't have helped to have had some. She grabbed a couple useful tools and stashed her bag in an air vent.

The concert venue was an outdoor amphitheater, which she arrived at after navigating side streets and shadows. Music was already playing, but she didn't recognize it and assumed it was a warm-up act. She made her way around back to the loading docks. Everything was closed up, but she found an entrance with an electronic lock. *Easy-peasy,* she thought and set about short-circuiting it. The lock fell open quickly enough, and she snuck in.

A few people were milling about, checking equipment, and they were all wearing an access pass on a lanyard around their neck. Rayne spotted a trailer marked "security" and marched up to it, stepping briskly inside.

"Hey," she said, nodding to a man seated at a desk, while she looked around. She spied a pegboard with a few remaining passes still hanging from it and grabbed one.

"What are you doing?" the man asked incredulously.

"My job, duh," Rayne replied sarcastically and placed the pass around her neck.

He stared at her uncomprehendingly.

"I'm undercover," she told him.

"You look a little too hot to be security," he said skeptically.

"Why, thank you," she gushed and bent over the desk to give him a kiss on the cheek. "See you after the show," she told him and waltzed out of the trailer before he could figure out what had just happened.

Rayne made her way backstage just as the band that had been playing was leaving the stage. She spotted the headlining act leaving their tour bus, stretching lazily as they made their way toward the stage. Rayne swooned as the lead singer passed by her, shirtless. She resisted the urge to reach out and touch him.

The band took up their positions on stage, and the crowd roared. Never had Rayne seen so many young people. It was as though the entire nation's supply was crammed into the arena.

The lead singer waved to the crowd, and several girls fainted. *Oh, please*, thought Rayne. He lifted a microphone to his lips.

"Youth is power!" he shouted.

That's news to me, Rayne thought.

"You're the planet's lifeblood. You're it's beating heart. Seize control!"

The band launched into an up-tempo song, and the crowd lost its collective mind.

I'll seize you, Rayne thought, with an unobstructed view of the singer's ass. She unabashedly sang along with all of her favorite songs, and the backstage hands just assumed that there was a reason she was there and left her alone.

The band sang of love and yearning, being misunderstood, and disenfranchisement. Each song touched a nerve and throttled it. When the last note of the last encore died out, and the crowd began to file out, Rayne wandered over to join a queue of girls hoping to catch a last glimpse of the band before they boarded their bus. Rayne was aglow with happiness as the band filed past, separated from their adoring fans by a low fence.

The lead singer noticed her hair and stopped in front of her to check her out. "Great minds think alike," he quipped, pointing to their leather pants.

Rayne grinned like an idiot, despite herself.

"Want a drink?" he asked, gesturing to the bus.

"Why not?" she replied, and she and a few girls selected by his bandmates were guided through an opening by security.

"Dal," he introduced himself as though it was even remotely conceivable that she wouldn't know who he was, taking her hand and kissing it.

"Obviously," Rayne replied with a mock curtsy.

"Your name is 'obviously?'" he joked.

"My name is Rayne. 'Obviously' is my last name."

"You seem impervious to my charms."

"Oh no, I'm pervious alright," Rayne replied, taking in his exposed chest.

"Well then, let's get you that drink," he smiled and guided her aboard the bus. They squeezed past several girls who were already making out with Dal's bandmates, including the female drummer. *She's really hot,* Rayne thought, then turned her attention back to Dal.

He motioned for her to sit down on a loveseat at the back of the bus while he poured her a tall drink. *Renner would scream at me to keep my wits,* she reminded herself but took it gratefully. Dal surprised her by sitting down across from her rather than beside her.

She put her drink down and moved across to straddle his lap. "I'm guessing these fold down," she purred.

"You guess correctly," he replied, and she shut him up with a kiss.

Rayne woke the next morning nestled in Dal's arms. They'd knocked over her drink, and the place smelled like scotch, but her happy glow persisted. She snuggled in contentedly.

Dal stirred and opened his eyes.

"Morning, sunshine," he said, kissing her. "I am *so* not a morning person," he admitted. "Can you grab us a couple coffees? I need to wake up."

"Sure," she replied and got up to put her clothes on.

"Americana, five sugars," he told her from his nest.

"Five?" she asked incredulously.

"What can I say? I like them sweet," he shrugged. Rayne turned to go, but he pulled her back and kissed her deeply. "You're a godsend," he told her and settled in to wait for her return.

Rayne threaded her way through an array of sleeping people in various states of undress. The drummer had her arm across a girl and was sleeping so soundly that Rayne was tempted to check her for a pulse. Rayne slipped off the bus and spotted a table marked "hospitality," where she presumed she'd find coffee. She walked past a burly guard on the way over to it.

"Want anything?" she asked him, gesturing to the hospitality stand.

"Got one," he replied, pointing at a nearby cup.

Rayne smiled and went to make a couple of coffees, one ungodly sweet, the other not. She returned with one in each hand, but the guard stopped her.

"I can't let you in there," he told her, gesturing at the bus.

"Dal asked me to get him a coffee," she explained.

The guard looked at her apologetically. "That's how he gets the girls to leave," he admitted, hating himself for being forced to play a part in the charade. He readied himself for hysteria or a coffee thrown at him.

"I understand," she told him, putting down the unnecessary second coffee and patting him on the arm. "I'll show myself out."

"I'm sorry," he told her. "I really am."

Rayne smiled sadly and headed for the exit. *My hero's an asshole*, she thought. *I guess I shouldn't be surprised.* She grabbed the access pass from around her neck, hand hovering near her wounded heart, then pulled it off and hung it on a fence post as she exited. She crossed the street to a bench, where she sat down to drink her coffee and piece together the freshly-compounded ruins of her life.

"Rayne?" a quiet voice inquired, prompting her to look up and see Grace.

Chapter 16

Grace

Grace was beside herself with joy to have found Rayne but tried to act cool about it.

"What are you doing here?" Rayne asked.

"Just out for a walk, trying to figure out my life," she replied.

"Join the club," Rayne replied, inviting Grace to join her on the bench, which she happily did. "What have you concluded so far?" Rayne asked.

"Well, for starters, it's a mess. My past seems to have found me. I left my village for very good reasons, and yesterday I saw my ex-fiancé right here in Mekka, looking for me."

"Fiancé?" Rayne asked, a bit surprised.

"Don't judge. It's a different world."

"I'm not judging – it just surprised me, is all."

"I dodged him, but I don't think he'll leave Mekka until he finds me, and I'm afraid that he will inevitably. I can't come up with a way of making him think I'm not here, and I don't want to live the rest of my life in hiding."

"You shouldn't have to," Rayne agreed. She thought about what Renner would advise. "If he won't leave you alone until he finds you, then you have to let him find you."

Grace looked skeptical and a little afraid.

"On our terms," Rayne assured her.

All Grace heard was "our" and was heartened. "What about you? I feel guilty monopolizing our conversation with my problems."

"My life is just directionless," Rayne assured her. "It's not buffeted by the winds the way yours is. Let's concentrate on you for now."

"That's nice of you," Grace replied, thinking that it was the opposite of how she'd grown up with Jenna always suggesting they concentrate on her first, then feeling guilty for thinking ill of her friend. "How do you propose we let Gabriel find me in a way that we control? That's his name, by the way – Gabriel," Grace added.

"Leave that to me – do you think you can find him and point him out to me?"

"I think so. My boss told him to look for me along the promenade, whatever that is."

"That's perfect."

"I have to be home by 1:30 though. I work this afternoon."

"You settle in fast."

"I met some nice people, not you-level nice, but nice enough. They helped me out."

Rayne put down her cup. "Let's getting going then."

"Your coffee," Grace pointed out.

"The crows can have it," Rayne replied bitterly and took Grace by the arm to explain her plan while they walked to the promenade, but by way of the parking garage so that she could collect her blonde wig. Grace heard little of what Rayne said, distracted as she was by her closeness.

Minutes later, they found themselves on the promenade, and Grace pointed out Gabriel from the safety of a hiding place amid displays of tacky tourist memorabilia.

"I'll give your stalker this," Rayne said, "he's an early riser. Now, put this earpiece in. I'll go collect the other one, and we'll be chatting in no time."

Grace did as she was told, and a moment later, Rayne's reassuring voice was in her ear.

"I'm going to go say 'hi,'" Rayne told her and made a beeline for him.

"Gabriel Parker," she called to him, startling him that anyone knew him here. "We have a mutual friend in Grace Lee, if I'm not mistaken."

"You've seen her?" Gabriel asked excitedly.

"Would I be here if I hadn't?" Rayne answered. "Care to join me, and we can discuss the matter?"

Gabriel nodded and followed her to a table.

"You can put that picture away. I know what Grace looks like," Rayne told him as they walked.

They sat down, and Rayne hailed a waiter, "Harold, could you please get my friend my usual?"

"Of course, miss. By the way, I love what you've done with your hair," Harold replied with a wink.

She turned her attention back to Gabriel. "Why are you here?"

"To find Grace, of course."

"That much I figured out on my own, thank you. What do you plan to do if you were to find her, assuming she wants to be found?"

Gabriel looked uncomfortable explaining the sensitive matter to a stranger, but one look from Rayne made it clear that those were her terms. "I want to convince her to come home, that it's all been a big misunderstanding."

Rayne immediately got up to leave. "I think we're done here. Grace does not misunderstand," she told him, insulted on her behalf. She fished out a few bills. "Enjoy your drink."

"I can prove it," he begged.

She stopped. "I'm listening."

Harold interrupted them by putting the drink down in front of Gabriel. "Leaving so soon?"

"Not immediately, no," she told him and handed him a few dollars, sitting back down. "Thank you, Harold, you're a peach."

"And you're a blueberry," he replied, smiled, and wandered away to look after his other customers.

Gabriel fished around in his bag and pulled out a video player.

"Hand that to me," Rayne demanded politely and looked it over. "And what type of video will I find on this player?" she asked, handing it back.

"A message from Jenna," Gabriel told her.

"I'm coming out," Grace informed Rayne in her ear, having heard what he said.

Rayne leaned back. "You've piqued Grace's curiosity. She'll see you."

170

Gabriel looked around for her.

"Patience, Mr. Parker. She'll come. Enjoy your drink while you're waiting."

Gabriel had a few nervous sips until Grace appeared and sat down beside Rayne, taking her hand in hers below the table for support.

"Gabriel," she greeted him.

"Grace," he replied, a bit shocked to see her in Angie's outfit.

"You said you had a message from Jenna?" Grace prompted, getting straight to the point.

"Right. She made this for you," he said, pushing the player across the table slowly, so as not to spook her. "Just press the button marked 'play.'"

Grace did as he instructed, and Rayne held her hand tighter. Jenna's face popped up on the screen, and Grace exhaled like she'd been holding her breath all her life.

"I'm home, sweetheart," Jenna said cheerfully. "Where are you? Please come home." The video ended at that.

Grace watched it again and again before reluctantly sliding the player back to Gabriel, everything she thought she knew turned on its head.

Rayne squeezed her hand and turned to Gabriel. "Grace and I have to talk. We'll meet you here tomorrow at the same time. I suggest you pass the time by taking in a show. *Armageddon's Embers* is playing – you'd like them." Rayne helped Grace up.

"Grace, don't go," Gabriel pleaded, rising to his feet as well.

"Look, loverboy," Rayne told him, "I said we needed to talk. Now, if you want the antidote to the poison my friend, Harold, slipped into your drink, by my reckoning you've got about ten minutes to get it from him. Good day."

Gabriel and Grace both stared in horror at the glass on the table. Gabriel looked from Grace to Harold across the square and back uncertainly. Rayne raised an eyebrow.

"Your call," she told him. "See you tomorrow, assuming you make the right one."

Gabriel watched them leave, then hurried over to Harold.

"The antidote?" he asked breathlessly.

"For a broken heart, I'd suggest bourbon," Harold replied, amused.

Gabriel looked confused.

"I think you've been played, my dear boy," Harold told him and turned his attention back to his customers.

Gabriel looked for Rayne and Grace, but they were long gone.

Rayne walked Grace back to her apartment. Grace was a basket case of confusion.

"Jenna's alive," she said to herself, shaking her head in disbelief.

"You said you have to work this afternoon, right?" Rayne reminded her as they walked up to her apartment. "Do you still feel up to it?"

Grace nodded.

"Then, why don't you go to work, and I'll meet you back here afterward, and we can figure this out."

"Come for dinner," Maggie called down from the upstairs window. "Seven o'clock."

"You'll be okay until then?" Rayne confirmed with Grace.

"Okay, I'll see you at seven," she agreed, and Rayne left her to get ready for work.

"Are you going to hit on everyone I bring home?" Grace asked Maggie when she got upstairs.

"Gotta share the love," Maggie replied and returned to painting the pottery she'd recently made, complaining, "Angie is way better at this than I am."

Grace left her to go to work, and Maurice returned her a few minutes after seven. She gave him a kiss on the cheek and sent him on his way.

"Rayne's already here," Maggie called down from the window.

The wonderful aroma of Maggie's cooking greeted Grace as she entered the apartment.

"I'm trying to impress your girlfriend," Maggie explained.

"Well, it worked," Rayne confirmed, saving Grace from having to respond to Maggie's subtle "girlfriend" probe.

"Trin's not here, so we've got a spare place," Maggie informed Rayne, motioning for her to sit down while she rounded up the rest of her roommates and brought dinner to the table.

"It smells delicious," Rayne told Maggie.

"Can we talk about Jenna?" Grace interjected, unable to contain herself any longer.

"Are you sure you want to have that conversation now?" Rayne asked her gently. "Are you *really* sure?"

Grace swallowed hard. "I'm sure," she replied meekly.

Rayne got up, knelt beside her, and took Grace's hands in hers, staring deeply into her eyes. "I'm sorry about your friend."

Grace's world imploded for the second time in a week, and her hands went limp in Rayne's.

"I don't know what happened to her," Rayne continued, "but that video is fake."

"How can you be sure?" Grace asked, clinging to a faint hope.

"The video player's input port still had the packing plug in it. The video was never loaded onto that device; it was created on it."

Grace looked uncertain.

"Your village sounds pretty low-tech. Did your friend own a phone, much less a video recorder? Does anyone you know own a video recorder?"

"No," Grace replied deflatedly.

"I called a friend. That fake is expensive. Someone went to a lot of trouble and money to make you think your friend is okay, which tells me that the opposite has to be the truth. I'm sorry. I'm really sorry." Rayne enveloped her in a hug while Grace's roommates looked on in silent shock.

"I know what you're saying is true," Grace admitted, tears streaming down her cheeks. "I always knew; I just didn't want to accept it." She wiped away her tears and motioned for Rayne to retake her seat. Grace looked at her stunned roommates. "I'm sorry I ruined dinner."

"You did no such thing," Maggie assured her.

Grace turned to Rayne. "So, if the video is a lie, so is Gabriel's promise of a safe return?"

"That much is certain," Rayne assured her, "but, for what it's worth, I don't think he has any idea he's lying to you. I think he's been lied to, and he's the trusting sort."

"That he is," Grace confirmed. "But what do we do now? He'll never leave Mekka now that he knows I'm here," she despaired.

"We just have to convince him that you left."

Grace looked skeptical.

"Michael and Ryan tell me they're actors. Plus, Maggie can be *really* convincing," Rayne assured her. "Are you guys in?" she asked everyone.

"Hell yes," Michael agreed on everyone's behalf. "We'll work up a script after dessert. Maggie made a pie."

Grace agreed, and that signaled everyone that it was okay to begin eating.

———————————

Rayne marched straight up to Gabriel on the promenade the next day. He was looking over her shoulder for Grace when she slapped him hard across the face.

"Thanks, asshole. I don't know what you did to make Grace leave, but I hope you're proud of yourself," she told him.

"She's gone?" he asked, but Rayne just walked away without answering, dismissing his question with her middle finger.

Gabriel looked around uncertainly, then hurried away.

"He's heading toward the bus station," Angie reported in Rayne's ear.

Good boy, she thought.

Gabriel went straight to the ticket agent and showed her Grace's photo. "Was this girl here earlier?" he asked.

"I don't think so," she told him, confusing and disappointing him.

Ryan took it as his cue to push off the wall and approach him.

"I was working the window earlier," he told him. "Show me the picture."

Gabriel handed it over.

"I remember her. She didn't say much, just bought a ticket to New York. You only missed her by about an hour."

Gabriel looked around the station in frustration.

Trin and Michael walked past gossiping. "Did you see the girl on the bus? She was, like, ugly crying. I mean, really, pull it together."

Gabriel watched them while Maggie ran up to the ticket window breathlessly. "Did I miss the bus to New York?"

"There's another in an hour, miss." The woman told her.

"Damn it, so I did. Never mind – thanks." Maggie wandered out, and as predicted, Gabriel approached the window.

"I'll take a ticket to New York," he told the agent and, having purchased one, sat down to make a call.

An hour later, Angie reported in Rayne's ear. "The bus just left. He's gone."

Rayne signaled to Grace that it was done, and she almost collapsed from relief.

"Looks like you're free to live your life," Rayne told her.

Chapter 17

Rayne

Grace and Rayne saw each other a fair bit once they'd reconnected. They mostly hung out in the small living room of the apartment that Grace shared with Maggie and her friends, often with Maggie or Trin. Grace's other roommates generally preferred the solitude of their bedrooms.

Grace was happy to have Rayne back in her life, and Rayne enjoyed her company, especially given that she was keeping a low profile ever since she'd discovered people following her. It was not the liberation she was hoping for when she left New York, and if it were not for Grace, she would have moved on from Mckka to seek it elsewhere.

Grace sat cross-legged on the floor while Rayne lounged on the sofa. Maggie sat beside Rayne, as she usually did, and only had eyes for her, twisting her necklace suggestively. Maggie's attempts to monopolize Rayne's attention annoyed Grace, but she wasn't rude about it, and Grace certainly had no exclusive claim to Rayne. Rayne, to her credit, paid equal attention to both of them, but when she'd casually lay a hand on Grace's arm or leg, it telegraphed an intimacy that was unique to her.

Maggie was trying to convince Rayne to let her braid her hair when her phone rang. She disregarded it and kept lobbying. No sooner had it stopped ringing than it began again, however. Maggie shut it off and placed it face-down on the table, but it surprised everyone by ringing again regardless. Maggie picked it up suspiciously, partly annoyed, but partly curious at the poltergeist in her phone.

"It's my mom," she announced, the number registering. "Excuse me," she apologized and carried the phone to her room, but stopped in the doorway and turned around, looking at Rayne quizzically. "It's for you," she reported, "and it's not my mom," she clarified, handing the phone to Rayne.

"Of course – your mom and I aren't that close," Rayne joked and took the phone from her. "Hello, Elana," she guessed, correctly.

"Darling," Elana began. "Sara tells me you've been having quite the adventure."

"Sara?"

"My AI. I named her AQUA when I created her, but she prefers Sara. She gets pretty snippy when I call her anything else, actually."

"Tell her I say 'hi,'" Rayne replied.

"You just did. She listens in on all my calls."

"Okay... to what do I owe the pleasure of your call?"

"I thought you might be curious why you're being followed."

Rayne sat up straight. "How did you know about that?"

"Sara keeps an eye on you for me."

Rayne wasn't sure how she felt about the invasion of her privacy, but Elana, and by extension, her AI, had been nothing but kind to her. "And what has she concluded?"

"How well did you know your mother?"

That got Rayne's attention, and she apologized to Maggie and Grace, getting up to continue the conversation in the stairwell. "I

179

hardly knew her," she replied, closing the door behind her. "She died when I was young."

"But did you know *who* she was?"

"I'm not following you."

"Your mother was a Revolutionary leader during the war – probably more apt to say that she was *the* leader before the Revolution splintered."

Rayne couldn't comprehend. "That was two hundred years ago. My mother couldn't be who you think she is."

"Sara's thorough. There's no record of you in the system – in any system for that matter – so she ran a pretty wide facial recognition search, and pictures of your mother kept popping up from during the war. Sara disregarded them at first until she found a photo that was purportedly more recent. It showed your mother holding an infant with blue hair. Sara says your features match the child's with 74% certainty."

"74%, Elana – it's a coincidence."

"Blue hair, Rayne," Elana reminded her. "Even if you don't think that woman is your mother, someone does."

"What's that got to do with me?"

"There are probably people who want to get to her through you."

"She's dead," Rayne reminded her bluntly.

"That was widely reported, yes," Elana agreed, "but they never found her body."

Rayne digested the bombshell. "Are you saying that my mother might not be dead – that she simply abandoned me?" she replied, shocked and angry.

"Personally, I find it hard to believe," Elana reassured her, "but there may be people who think she might still be alive and that they can exert influence over her if they had you in their custody."

"How can I exert influence over someone that I didn't even know was alive, assuming that she even is?"

"What would matter is if your mother knew that *you* were alive, not the other way around." Elana paused. "Rayne, be careful. These aren't normal people. They're soldiers, spies, terrorists... They're not to be taken lightly."

"I don't take them lightly; I can assure you."

"So I've been told. You're cute as a blonde, by the way."

"Thanks, I think. So, if people are after me, who's after them? I saw people following the guy who was following me?"

"That's a puzzle. They're all deep off the grid and good at keeping it that way. They could be a rival faction, but the fact that they seem to be intervening on your behalf implies that they're loyal to your mother, or they were."

"What about my father?"

"He was one of your mother's lieutenants."

Rayne's heart sank to hear Elana refer to him in the past tense.

"I'm sorry, but his death was confirmed."

The few but dear memories that Rayne had of her parents flashed before her eyes, and she went silent.

"Rayne?" Elana asked to confirm that she was still on the line. "I won't ask you not to do anything reckless, but please promise me that you'll be careful when you inevitably do whatever reckless thing you wind up doing. I was just beginning to miss you, and I'd rather not make the feeling permanent."

"I can't make any promises."

Elana accepted that as inevitable. "I thought you might also want to know that Triste is doing okay."

"Thank you. I appreciate it."

"Make sure you come back to me," Elana concluded, and the line went dead.

Rayne walked back into the apartment in a fog and handed Maggie's phone back to her.

"What's wrong?" Grace asked, concerned by Rayne's drastic change of mood.

"There's something I have to do," she replied, grabbing her jacket.

Grace didn't pursue the matter further and let Rayne leave, despite the worry nagging her.

Rayne headed directly for the pumping station where she was currently staying and grabbed some tools, then headed toward the compound where she'd last seen the couple who were following the man who'd been following her. She kept to the shadows as she approached, finally spying the building from afar. *The enemy of my enemy must be my friend*, she tried to convince herself, and scanned the area for prying eyes. She waited for a police officer to finish strolling past. *Just like home*, she noted. When the street seemed clear, she walked nonchalantly toward the gate that she'd seen the couple enter. She examined its locking mechanism and despaired to discover that it was beyond her skill to override. The gate's hinges, however, seemed pretty typical. She took out a screwdriver and used it to pry free a cobblestone, then used the stone and the screwdriver to hammer out the pins that held the hinges in place. She pried the gate free from the wall and squeezed through, then pulled it back to appear closed. *Not my most subtle break-in,* she mused, but her need for answers overrode her sense of caution.

She walked down the corridor to the courtyard. The dense greenery of the untended garden choked the space but provided ample places for her to stay hidden. She wasn't worried about cameras – if the building's occupants liked to stay off the grid, and AIs like Sara could hack any security system, they probably eschewed cameras altogether.

The main door was locked, and Rayne spied no other entry before scanning the windows surrounding the courtyard. They were surely locked and probably alarmed, but maybe not on the top floor. *Height gave people a false sense of security,* she thought, *and if they had a limited budget, those windows were probably not alarmed.*

She squeezed behind the bushes and made her way along the wall to a corner of the courtyard, where she braced herself against the perpendicular walls and slowly began the climb up to the ledge that ringed the third floor. Eventually, she made it to the ledge and sat down on it to recover some energy before shimmying across it to see if she could find an unlocked window. She'd made it two-thirds of the way around the courtyard before a window finally budged. *Thank God,* she thought and raised it far enough to enter. She found herself standing in front of a row of urinals. *Always a bathroom,* she grimaced and tiptoed to the door.

The hallway was dark as the third floor didn't appear to be in use. She cautiously listened at each door regardless as she made her way toward the stairs. She tiptoed down to the second floor, which also didn't appear to be in use. From her vantage point at the top of the stairs to the main floor, she spied a bored guard leaning back in a chair by the front door nursing a cup of coffee. His weapon was plainly visible, and Rayne thanked her luck that she hadn't found a way to open the front door.

She waited patiently. *Everyone has to pee sometime.* Eventually, he rocked forward in his chair, got up, and walked down the hall. Rayne took it as her chance to creep down the stairs and look around. The light peeking through a doorway was the only indication that anything was going on in the whole place. She looked in and saw four or five people sitting around the room engaged in a heated discussion. Rayne recognized two of them from the promenade and decided it was now or never. *The enemy of my enemy,* she reminded herself and entered the room.

The conversation halted abruptly, and all eyes turned toward her. The barrel of a pistol pressed into the back of her skull. She raised her hands with exaggerated slowness and stepped forward.

"You have some explaining to do," she announced to the room.

"It's okay, Faisal," one of the women assured the guard who was holding his weapon to Rayne's head.

Rayne felt the weapon withdraw but heard nothing.

"Have a seat," the woman offered, gesturing to a vacant chair.

Rayne glanced behind herself to make sure that the guard had indeed retreated before lowering her hands. "I think I'll stand," she decided, feeling that sitting would signal a familiarity that she didn't feel, and these people hadn't earned.

"As you wish," the woman accepted.

"What's your interest in me?" Rayne asked.

"We promised your mother that we'd keep you from harm," the woman replied matter-of-factly.

"By keeping me in the dark?" Rayne challenged.

"Keeping you away from danger *is* the best way to keep you safe," the woman pointed out.

"And my mother…"

"Is no longer with us," the woman replied vaguely, but the sadness in her voice convinced Rayne not to inquire further.

"So why do I still matter?"

"A promise is a promise, and that makes you leverage. Plus, you are your mother's legacy, and there are those who don't want you to take up her cause."

"You can keep your Revolution – I just wanted my mother. The other group?"

"Violent parasites, but don't worry – we handled them."

Understanding dawned on Rayne. "You used me as bait."

"Leaving you alone to live your life is not manipulative," the woman assured her.

"Am I going to have to live the rest of that life looking over my shoulder?"

"Probably," the woman replied with a candor that surprised Rayne.

"I didn't sign up for that," Rayne countered futilely.

"No one ever does, but if you ever *do* want to sign up, we'd welcome you."

"The Revolution is over," Rayne reminded her.

"You think so? Look at the world around you. Does it seem free and just?" The woman let the challenge hang in the air.

"My mother missed her chance to recruit me. I think I'll pass."

"When you change your mind, and I mean *when* not if, you know where to find us." The woman softened. "And if you ever tire of looking over your shoulder, we have a free settlement deep in the desert. You're always welcome there."

"You mean that my mother's daughter is welcome."

"No, Rayne. I mean that *you're* welcome."

There was too much for Rayne to process, so she just turned on her heel and stormed past the guard to leave via the front door.

"Lock your goddamn windows," she told him and left.

Chapter 18

Grace

Grace was worried sick about Rayne. Whatever news she'd received on that phone call had clearly upset her. Grace knew it was selfish, but she was scared that whatever the news was, it would take Rayne away from her, and the fear of finding herself alone again terrified her. She still had Maggie and her friends, but Rayne made her feel special, and now that that genie was out of the bottle, she never wanted it put back in. *I need a distraction*, she concluded. *It's time I met my sixth.* She had a day off work that she could dedicate to the task.

Grace made her way to the place where she believed her sixth worked. She'd decided against trying to catch her as she arrived or left as that felt too much like an ambush – she'd find a way to see her at her office during her workday. Maggie had been unable to find a way of contacting her to make an appointment, but Grace felt that an opportunity would present itself if she were patient. She leaned up against the wall by the door and waited.

The buzz of the door opening startled her, but what surprised her more was that the woman exiting was the same woman that she'd helped at the grocery store, and who she'd seen near here before with her young son. She emerged, shushing a colicky baby, and was as shocked to see Grace as Grace was to see her. Grace barely remembered to grab the door before it swung closed.

"Just going up," Grace explained nonchalantly, not wanting the woman to think that she was stalking her.

The woman looked at her uncertainly before her baby reclaimed her attention with a wail.

"My mother always used to say that what calmed me as a baby was a tight swaddle. Can I show you?" Grace offered.

The baby cried again, and the woman reluctantly handed her to Grace.

"Hi, you," Grace greeted the child, who wailed again in reply. "Okay, then." Grace sat down in the doorway with the baby in her lap, unfolding its blanket. "You fold it like this," she showed the woman, tucking the blanket around the baby in a manner that rendered her completely immobile.

The woman looked on, worried that this would set her baby to shrieking and glanced about nervously for passersby. She was shocked when her baby settled.

Grace rose and handed the infant back to her mother. "She just wants to feel secure, I guess. I think we all do."

The woman accepted her baby back gratefully.

"I don't mean to keep you," Grace said to release her from any feelings of obligation to say anything and ducked inside. "Nice seeing you."

The woman smiled wanly and hurried off.

Grace shook off the coincidence of meeting the woman again and examined the narrow lobby. There were two unlabeled doors that she put her ear to but heard nothing inside. She debated knocking on each but decided that they seemed unlikely candidates, and she wanted to scout the entire building before committing to announcing herself to whoever was behind each door. She made her way up the dimly lit stairs to the second floor. The first door seemed like the two downstairs, but light spilled out from under the second, and Grace thought she heard someone inside.

She steeled herself and knocked politely. All sound inside halted abruptly. "Violet Moore?" she asked through the door. The silence persisted. "I don't mean to bother you if I have the wrong address. It's Grace Lee, from our village." Grace waited patiently and was about to give up when the door opened, and an elderly woman peeked out.

"Grace Lee?" she asked, to confirm what she thought she'd heard.

"Yes. You're Violet Moore?"

The woman trembled and embraced Grace in a crushing hug. "You're okay, and you're at my door," she mused in disbelief. "Come in." She shepherded Grace inside and locked the door behind them.

The room contained a desk, an exam table, equipment whose purpose Grace couldn't divine, and a couple of chairs. Violet guided Grace to a chair and sat across from her, refusing to let go of her hands.

"How is your family?" she asked tentatively. "Your mum, dad… your sister?"

"They're fine, but I had to leave without saying goodbye. I was afraid for my life."

"You had every reason to be, child. I'm so glad you found your way to me. Does anyone from the village know you're here?"

"My onetime fiancé followed me to Mekka, but I convinced him that I'd left for New York. I imagine he's hunting for me there now. My friend assures me that he could search for years and still never be certain I wasn't there somewhere in hiding."

"Clever girl," Violet beamed.

"Why did you leave?" Grace asked, feeling that her need to know outweighed putting Violet on the spot.

"I couldn't stand the rot that had set in, but I was too afraid to stand up to it. Seeing you in danger was the last straw. It broke me inside, and I couldn't stay."

"You left so long ago – surely, I wasn't in danger then."

"The writing was on the wall, but let's not speak of that. It still gives me chills."

Grace looked around the room while she sorted out the questions racing through her head. "What is it you do here?" she asked.

"I look after young ladies who have nowhere else to go."

"Like the woman here before me?" Grace asked.

Violet hesitated to answer, having been so long accustomed to protecting her clients' secrets, so Grace reassured her, "I know her from the grocery store."

"Yes, like her, then. When she got pregnant unexpectedly and decided to keep the baby, her boyfriend left her to fend for herself. She's had a tough go of it."

"Thank goodness she has you," Grace said, thinking that everyone needs someone looking out for them, like Rayne did for her.

"It helps me atone for my sins of omission," Violet added guiltily.

The doorbell interrupted them, and Violet reluctantly got up. "Duty calls," she declared. "Please come back when you can. I want to know everything about you. Here's my number," she added, handing Grace a card that had her number written on it but nothing else. "Can you let the girl downstairs in on your way out?"

"Of course. I'm glad to have found you."

"I'm glad to have been found. It's a weight off my heart." Violet hugged her tightly and saw her out.

Grace smiled to herself all the way home. Rayne joined her for dinner, and everyone squeezed around the table, sharing stories about their day.

"You look happy," Maggie remarked at Grace's mood.

"I am," Grace replied. "I saw my sixth today."

"I remember my sixth," Maggie responded wistfully. "She was *really* flexible."

Grace went beet red. "Oh my God, Maggie, not that kind of sixth. My sixth godparent."

"That's a lot of godparents," Angie piped in. "Did you fire the first five?" she asked jokingly.

"No, it's a tradition in my village that every child gets seven."

"Wow," Angie responded. "I guess the kids in your village must *really* be at risk of growing up ungodly, although I can't imagine that about you – Maggie, sure, but not you."

Maggie nodded in a guilty-as-charged manner, prompting laughter around the table.

"I used to think that we were assigned godparents for our sake," Grace explained, "but then I came to realize that it was really for theirs. Imagine having children, seeing them grow up and move out, then decades and eventually centuries passing since there was a child

191

in your life. Having godchildren keeps them connected to youth, and there were more of them than us, so we got seven."

"That's sweet," said Maggie.

"No, it's not. It's terrible," Angie countered, shuddering. "Children," she muttered.

"Never mind her," Maggie assured Grace, "she was raised by wolves."

"Oh, that wasn't the only thing today," Grace added, switching topics. "Do you remember the girl from the grocery store I mentioned? I ran into her again today. She had her baby girl with her, instead of her son, but she acted all weird about it." Grace could have heard a pin drop in the silence that followed.

"She has two kids?" Angie asked.

"I'm pretty sure, but she's been cagey about it. Why?"

"It's completely illegal," Angie informed her.

"Really?" Grace asked uncertainly, despite the confirming looks of utter shock on everyone's faces.

"You knew?" Angie pressed.

"That she has two kids? Not really, but I put it together."

"And now you've told us. Do you know the danger that puts us in?"

Grace looked at Angie uncomprehendingly.

Angie was incensed. "It's illegal *not* to report a violation of the population laws. You have to turn her in."

"I can't do that," Grace countered.

Angie rose from the table in agitation. "If the authorities find out we knew... I'm not going to prison for you. You can't stay here."

Grace looking around the table for an ally, but besides Rayne found none. Even Maggie looked down uncomfortably.

"Okay," Grace replied defeatedly and rose from the table to collect her things.

"You can stay with me," Rayne assured her, joining her to help her pack.

Grace looked back at her roommates, who hadn't touched their dinner, and tears welled up in her eyes.

"I'm sorry," Maggie told her.

"Come on," Rayne prompted Grace, guiding her out the door. They'd no sooner closed it behind them than the sound of heated arguing erupted within.

Grace broke down in tears. This was the second time she'd been forced to leave a world in which she felt like she belonged. Only Rayne offered a tenuous lifeline in the storm that overwhelmed her.

"I've got you," Rayne assured her, placing an arm around her and guiding her away from her home. Rayne led Grace to the pumping station where she was staying. She held open the gap in the chain-link fencing to allow Grace to squeeze through before following, then pulled a sheet of plywood away from the wall that hid the hole through which she gained access to the building.

Grace followed dutifully but halted in shock once inside the featureless concrete bunker.

"This is where you live?" she asked incredulously.

"I have my reasons," Rayne explained.

"You poor thing," Grace declared and hugged Rayne tightly.

"It's not so bad," Rayne assured her.

"It's terrible!" Grace protested. "Sorry," she added, not wanting to offend Rayne or seem prissy.

"It's okay. At least I have you," Rayne pointed out.

Grace wiped away her tears. "I'm a prize, alright."

"That you are." Rayne smiled. "I'd offer to show you around...," she said, inclining her head to take in the dimly lit space, "...but this is pretty well it." Rayne's mattress was the only furniture in the space.

"I'm emotionally exhausted," Grace declared. "Can we just go to bed?" she asked, too fatigued to care how it sounded.

"Of course. The mattress is more comfortable than it looks."

"I am not kicking you out of your bed," Grace protested, examining the concrete floor bravely.

"There's room for both of us. We'll manage."

Grace put down her bag and lay down, not even bothering to change into the clothes she usually slept in. Rayne lay down behind her and pulled her in tightly against her. Grace felt secure in her arms. The world was a tempest, but Rayne was her rock.

"I'm not going to turn that woman in," Grace reaffirmed.

Rayne held her tighter to confirm her agreement.

"I'm going to help her."

"Then I'm going to help you help her," Rayne whispered in her ear.

Chapter 19

Rayne

Rayne lay with Grace in her arms, breathing her in. *There's a purity to her and a fragility,* she thought. *She doesn't deserve the way life is treating her.* Unconsciously, she held her tighter, desiring above all else to shelter her from the storm.

Grace stirred, slowly recalling where she was. She felt the heat of Rayne's body along her back, and it comforted her greatly. Rayne's breath on her neck sent electricity through her, and the subtle tensing of her muscles let Rayne know that she was awake.

Rayne gently squeezed her arm to let her know that she was awake as well. "How did you sleep?" she asked.

"Fine, thank you," Grace replied, stretching out her muscles, which were stiff from lying on her side all night on the thin mattress over hard concrete. Despite that, she couldn't bring herself to tell Rayne that she'd had the best sleep of her life. *Given the circumstances, she'd think I'm insane, or into her… which I guess I am, but I can't let her know that,* she thought. Grace feared jeopardizing the one relationship she still had with any change. She hated to admit it, but right now, she needed to lean on Rayne just to survive emotionally. She pushed down her feelings and rolled over to face her, feeling odd to be talking to her while facing away.

In the limited space of Rayne's bed, Grace found her face inches from Rayne's, her lips tantalizingly close. *Goddam,* Grace thought. *Rolling over was a terrible idea.* She struggled to focus and appear detached.

"How do we help that woman?" she thought out loud, grounding herself in the problem before her.

"I have an idea," Rayne replied, casually brushing an errant hair out of Grace's eyes and sending a wave of desire through her with the intimacy of it. Rayne went on, oblivious to the effect she was having on Grace. "I met some people, and they don't seem terribly supportive of the current social order, so to speak. I think they'll help us."

"It seems like a stretch to go from people being free-thinkers to law-breakers," Grace replied skeptically.

"Not for these people. I think they're more comfortable operating outside the law than within it. Also, they told me that they have a safe community well away from the authorities. Plus, they're not amateurs. They take their law-breaking deadly seriously."

"You run with a strange crowd," Grace concluded.

"Not by choice," Rayne assured her. "But I'm not going to assume anything. I'll go ask them."

Grace squeezed Rayne's hand to show her thanks, feeling that no words could adequately express her gratitude.

Rayne smiled and sat up, lessening the force of her gravity over Grace. "No time like the present," she mused and got to her feet, flexing her equally stiff muscles. "I'll just freshen up first," she added and proceeded to pull off her top."

Oh my God, Rayne! Are you trying to torture me? Grace wondered, quickly rolling over to give Rayne the privacy that she clearly didn't feel she needed. Rayne's nonchalance at washing up in front of her made Grace think that she didn't feel the same physicality between them, and it disappointed her.

Rayne rubbed herself with water from a barrel, continuing to chat over her shoulder. "I think we might want to find somewhere a little less rugged to stay now that we've lost access to Maggie's shower."

Grace's heart buoyed at the suggestion, but she also cursed herself for being so easily taken on an emotional rollercoaster – she knew that Rayne didn't mean to toy with her, but her emotions roiled anyway.

"How do we go about finding a place?" Grace asked.

"Oh, we'll tackle that later – first things first, but you'll definitely be our 'face,' considering that you have the more respectable occupation. I'm making money these days as a cat-burglar... and before you get all horrified, I *offer* my services to people wanting to test their security. If I can beat their systems, I leave them a note, and they can contact me to learn how to fix the flaws in their security. I don't actually steal anything, but still, it doesn't sound great on a rental application."

Rayne finished washing and pulled her top back on. "All done. You can turn around. By the way, you do realize that you have boobs too, right?" she kidded her.

"It's hard to escape one's upbringing," Grace explained.

"And yet, that's exactly what you've done," Rayne reminded her. She looked around at the drab concrete walls. "I feel guilty leaving you in this place. Is there anywhere you'd like me to take you that would be more pleasant, basically anywhere?"

"I'll be fine on my own. Will you be gone long?"

"I don't think so. Either I'll get the answer I want, or I won't – either way, I don't expect it to be much of a conversation."

"Okay, well good luck."

"Thanks." Rayne did a final look around and felt even guiltier for leaving Grace there, but concluded that there was nothing to be done about it and headed out. She made her way straight to the Revolutionaries' compound.

Walking up, she noted the guard, Faisal, reattaching the gate from which she'd removed the hinges.

"Sorry about that," she told him, not feeling the least bit sorry. "Is anyone inside? Can I go in?"

"Be my guest," he told her, waving her away. "The door's open."

Rayne let herself in and found the woman who had done the talking for the group alone behind a desk poring over some papers.

"What's your stance on population control?" Rayne asked, getting straight to the point.

"Are you interviewing me?" the woman asked, raising an eyebrow.

"Humor me."

"Okay. Does the world feel crowded to you?"

"Not particularly."

"The population laws exist more to preserve the status quo, in all its unjust glory, rather than to protect the populace from itself."

"Okay, so I'm getting a 'not-a-fan' vibe."

"That's apt."

"Would you take in population refugees?"

"It is something we've been known to do."

"If I bring a woman and her children to you, could you smuggle them out of Mekka to your sanctuary in the desert?"

The woman didn't bat an eye to hear about a woman with more than one child. "I do believe you're getting involved," she just responded wryly.

"So that's a yes?"

"That would be a yes, and your mother would be proud of you."

"Don't expect miracles from me," Rayne hedged.

The woman leaned back, smiling. "But I do." Her expression grew serious. "Let's talk logistics. We run a transport monthly. One leaves tomorrow night if you're feeling pressed. Bring your friend to the docks around eight. If we don't see you, we'll assume it didn't work out and leave without her."

"That's fair," Rayne concluded and turned to go.

"Rayne?" the woman asked to get her attention. "I'm glad you saw fit to come to us."

Rayne smiled a tight smile and let herself out to give Grace the news. When she returned to the pumping station, she was taken aback to find it filled with a wide assortment of wildflowers in rusty cans.

"Too much?" Grace asked uncertainly.

"Not at all," Rayne assured her. "It's pretty."

"I've always wanted to decorate with flowers – I just never had the chance. The fields around here are full of them."

"You find beauty in the most unexpected places," Rayne agreed, speaking more about Grace than the flowers.

Grace blushed.

"Good news, by the way – the people I know agreed to spirit the woman and her children out of Mekka to a safe place. We just have to have them at the docks tomorrow night at 8."

"That's fabulous," Grace responded. "The only problem is that I have no idea how to get a hold of her." She paced anxiously while she thought about it until inspiration struck. "Violet would know! Do you have a phone?"

"No, but there are public phones along the promenade."

"Let's go," Grace decided and made for the exit, pulling Rayne along with her. Not long after, they had an address from Violet, who told them that it was all she had. They asked around for directions until someone finally told them how to get to the place. It was a derelict funeral home, which had never closed entirely because people did still die occasionally, be it from an accident, or their own or someone else's intention.

Rayne appreciated the woman's savvy for thinking of such a place to hide. She and Grace walked up to the door, and Grace knocked loudly while Rayne waited a step back to make their visit less intimidating. She remembered the look of the terrified young woman she'd disturbed back in New York and tried to make herself seem as unthreatening as possible.

"It's just me, the girl from Violet's clinic," Grace called through the door. "She gave me your address so I can help you. I'm not going to cause you any trouble, I promise."

"Help me how?" a timid voice inquired through the closed door.

"We can get you and your children out of Mekka."

"How does that help? Everywhere is the same."

"We know a place outside the reach of the population police. We can get you there."

"Who is 'we'"? the woman asked suspiciously.

"My friend and me. She wants to help you as much as I do."

"Why would she? Why would you?" she asked skeptically.

"She and I both know what it's like to live your life always looking over your shoulder. It's no way to live. Let us help you."

"It's too risky," the woman resisted.

"I won't lie to you and say that it isn't, but what kind of life are you giving your children by hiding them from the world? They deserve a childhood."

That struck a nerve, and the door opened to reveal the woman, guilty tears streaming down her face.

"I'm sorry I upset you," Grace apologized.

"You can do this?" the woman asked.

"We can."

"Okay, tell me how."

Rayne stepped in to fill the woman in on the details. "We'll meet you back here tomorrow at 7," she concluded. "Wouldn't it be less obvious if we split up and traveled to the docks with your children separately, rather than with both of them together?"

"Neither of my children would go anywhere without me. It's all they've ever known. If we tried, they'd just draw more attention to themselves. Besides, it doesn't matter anyway because if the police see any child, they'll run a genetic scan to look for duplicates in their database. Just finding out that either of my children isn't in the database will raise all sorts of flags."

"Okay, we'll all move together and do our best not to draw attention to ourselves."

Once agreed, they parted ways. Grace and Rayne made it back to the pumping station. The space was cheerier with the flowers, and they decided that they had too much on their plates to look for a new place to live at the moment. Another night or two there would be tolerable.

Grace was still vibrating with nervous energy and pulled Rayne into a hug. "Thank you. I could kiss you," she declared.

"I give you permission," Rayne responded and leaned in to kiss Grace gently on the lips. Grace's entire body melted, but Rayne pulled back, not wanting to move too quickly. She leaned back in and gave Grace a final peck to show her that she was happy to leave things at that for the moment. Grace's lips tingled, and she touched them tentatively with her fingertips.

"Shall we get some sleep?" Rayne suggested. "Tomorrow will be a big day."

"Of course," Grace agreed, feeling torn in a million directions, but at the center of them all feeling joy.

Rayne prepared herself for bed and lay down. Grace joined her a moment later and settled into Rayne's arms. She was perfectly content.

The future would hold what it would, but at that precise moment, she felt whole.

The morning arrived, and Rayne and Grace woke together, content with the new level of intimacy.

"I'm going to spend some time today scouting the route," Rayne announced.

"I have to work at 10," Grace replied, "But I think that's a good thing. I need the distraction, and I'll pick up some groceries for the woman's journey, plus I'll see if I can borrow a cart to hide her children in as we cross town."

"That's a great idea," Rayne agreed and gave her an appreciative kiss before getting up and readying herself for the day. "Can you find your way to work from here?" she asked.

"I'm pretty sure I can. Happy scouting."

"Thanks," Rayne smiled and blew her a kiss on her way out.

Grace headed to the grocery store and had a great day, despite her nerves about the night ahead. Toward the end of her shift, Maggie stopped in to get some last-minute dinner ingredients, and Grace watched her wistfully. She caught Maggie looking her way a couple of times when she thought she wasn't paying attention, and there was regret in her look that saddened Grace. Grace mourned their friendship. Maggie was a zephyr, but she was warm and kind. She eventually slipped out without Grace noticing.

When her work was over for the day, she bought a few things and asked her boss if she could borrow a cart for the evening. Her boss deliberated for an eternity, hating the precedent it set, but eventually capitulated to Grace's puppy-dog eyes.

"Have it back first thing tomorrow," her boss told her, prompting Grace to give her a big hug. "It's just a cart," the woman muttered, shaking her head as she walked away.

The evening was darkening as Grace and Rayne made their way to the funeral home to collect the woman and her children. The darkness was a blessing and a curse – it cleared the streets of prying eyes but also made them more conspicuous to be out. Grace felt self-conscious pushing the cart, so Rayne did her best to engage her in mundane conversation to distract her.

When they arrived at the funeral home, the woman met them out front, alone.

"I can't do this," she quailed.

"You can," Grace told her firmly. "You've been there for your children every moment of their lives so far. You just have this last challenge, and you're free to love them for the rest of it without fear."

The woman looked over her shoulder uncertainly.

"Go get them," Grace prompted gently. "We'll wait here."

The woman summoned her courage and ducked back inside to get her children. A moment later, she emerged with them and few possessions, but ready to travel. Rayne helped her son into the cart, and the woman handed her sleeping daughter to him.

"Hold on to your sister and keep her quiet," she told him. "We're going to play another hiding game. You know the rules, you stay super still and quiet, and if you win, I'll give you a treat."

Her son smiled ear-to-ear and put a finger to his lips, nodding his eagerness to start the game. Grace helped the woman place a blanket over him.

"We'd better get going," she decided, "before my daughter wakes up."

"I'll scout ahead," Rayne volunteered. "Follow me when I indicate the way is clear. If I have my hood down, it's a sign that the way is clear. If I have it up, it means 'wait,' okay?"

"Got it," Grace replied.

The way was generally clear, and Rayne only had to signal to them to stay back a couple of times. They succeeded in avoiding people, helped by the fact that the docks that they were heading toward were pretty well deserted at that time of the night.

Rayne peeked around a distant corner and hurriedly waved them onward down a long stretch of road before disappearing again. Grace and the woman complied, but after a block, they heard footsteps behind them. Grace glanced over her shoulder nonchalantly and spotted a police officer following them, intrigued by two women pushing a cart near the docks at night.

"Shit," Grace swore, doubly cursing the fact that Rayne was nowhere near and would be of no help when the officer caught up to them. "Act naturally," she told the woman but could see her white knuckles gripping the cart's handle. *What should we do? Run, fight, stall?* Grace wracked her brain. She casually reached out to a door handle, confirming that it was locked. She lengthened her stride, hoping that the officer wouldn't perceive it. His pace quickened in response. *Damn.* She tried the next two doors, with no greater success. She locked her gaze on the next street corner, trying to gauge if they'd make it before the officer reached them. His footsteps told her that they wouldn't. She balled her fists and whispered, "On the count of three, grab your kids and run for the docks."

The woman spared her an uncertain glance.

I'll do what I can, Grace communicated with her eyes, a tear escaping. *I'm sorry.*

"One," she said in a low voice, slowing slightly to fall back and tensing her muscles.

The officer was close enough that she could hear him clear his throat before calling to them.

"Two," she said, breathing in deeply and readied herself to turn and face her fate. She opened her mouth to give the final count just as the policeman opened his to order them to stop.

"Officer!" a panicked voice cried out, interrupting them both.

"Speed up while he's distracted," Grace whispered and spun around to see Maggie rushing up breathlessly. *Oh, no!* Grace thought.

"Officer!" Maggie called again, forcing him to stop and reluctantly turn to face her. "Thank goodness. There's a man following me, and I'm scared."

The officer looked at her skeptically and was about to tell her that he was busy when a man bolted from the shadows behind her.

"That's him! Stop him!" Maggie begged.

The officer hesitated, but *probable* wrong-doing took precedence over *possible* wrong-doing, and he chased after the man.

"Thank you, thank you, thank you," Maggie called after him. "Get him!"

"We've got to hurry," Grace told the woman, who didn't need to be told twice. They raced forward, all pretext of a casual stroll abandoned. The cart bounced erratically on the cracked sidewalk, and they struggled to keep it upright. By some miracle, the baby did not start shrieking.

Rayne had heard the shouting and ran back anxiously but arrived to see only Grace and the woman racing toward her. She waved them on and sprinted ahead. She made it to the docks winded but without incident. She looked left and right – the "docks" was a long stretch of riverfront, and Rayne cursed herself for not asking exactly where they were supposed to meet the Revolutionaries. She looked up and down the empty street, hoping to spot someone. A gun barrel pressed into the side of her head, and she froze.

Faisal slowly stepped from the shadows, then lowered his weapon and winked. "That was for the gate," he told her and gestured for her to follow him.

"You're *so* predictable, you know?" she told him, but in truth, he'd scared her half to death. She motioned for Grace and the woman to follow.

Faisal led them to a small ship, walked across a plank onto it, and began readying it to depart.

Grace and the woman joined Rayne dockside. "This is where we part ways," Grace told the woman.

"That man is Faisal," Rayne added. "He's trustworthy. He'll take you far away from here. Somewhere safe."

The woman didn't yet believe it and stayed tense, waiting for a hammer to fall. She pulled back the blanket covering her children.

"Did I do a good job, Mommy? Did I win?" her son asked her.

"You did great, sweetheart. I have a treat for you, but I'll give it to you on the boat. We're going on an adventure. Hand me your sister."

The woman took her daughter while Rayne helped her son out of the cart. The woman turned to Grace. "How can I ever repay you?"

"Be happy," Grace replied.

The woman hugged her tightly. "You've never asked my name," she pointed out. "Hope. My name is Hope," she said and boarded the ship.

"Good luck, Hope," Grace called to her.

"Make yourselves useful," Faisal called back while he pulled the plank onto the boat. "Slip the lines."

Neither of them moved while they tried to figure out what he'd just requested them to do.

"Oh, for God's sake," he muttered. "Untie them."

"Okay," Rayne replied and untied the bowline while Grace untied the one aft. When the vessel moved away from the dock, Faisal saluted Rayne. As the boat truly drew away, Hope broke down sobbing from the release of tension, and Faisal comforted her.

"What do you know?" Rayne muttered. "He has a soul, after all."

Maggie walked up to join them. "I'm sorry how things were left between us," she apologized.

Grace hugged her fiercely.

"Geez," Maggie complained. "If I knew I'd get this kind of love, I'd have let Angie kick you out sooner," she joked but returned Grace's hug. Grace pulled Rayne into the hug.

"This isn't awkward at all," Rayne complained.

"Thanks for saving us," Grace told Maggie. "Who was that guy? Michael? Ryan?"

"Hell, no. Those guys never leave their room. That was just some random guy."

"How did you know he was there?"

"I didn't, but there's always someone following me. I carry mace, you know?"

"You're something else," Grace replied, shaking her head.

"Still friends, then?" Maggie asked.

"Never stopped," Grace assured her.

"I wonder if the funeral home has a shower," Rayne mused.

"God no – that's creepy," Grace shot her down.

"Just wondering," Rayne replied, smiling.

Grace turned to watch the boat disappear from view, and Rayne and Maggie watched it as well.

"You saved that woman's life," Maggie congratulated her.

"That's a bit of an overstatement," Grace demurred.

"No, literally. You saved her life. You do know the punishment for having more than one child, don't you?"

"Prison. Angie told me, remember?"

"No, that's just for people who *help* someone with more than one child. The penalty for actually having a second child is death."

"You're saying that if people have two children, they execute the parents?" she asked incredulously.

"One of them."

"Which one?"

"I don't know. I've never had to think about it."

Understanding hit Grace like a freight train, and her knees buckled.

"So, let's just say, for argument's sake, that I had a sister. If anyone found out, they'd kill my mother."

"Or your father," Maggie reminded her, thinking that Grace was being a bit dense.

"And," Grace continued. "So long as my sister and I were still both alive, my parents would be at risk of being put to death."

"That *is* how it works."

"And they'd know this?"

"Everyone knows this, except you, it seems."

Grace turned to Rayne. "I need to tell you about my village."

Part III
Pairs

Chapter 20

Grace

Rayne couldn't wrap her mind around the magnitude of evil it took to prey on an innocent like Grace.

"We have to burn the village to the ground," she declared, furious beyond rational thought.

Grace reminded her that there were good people there too, but Rayne couldn't reconcile it and looked around for an outlet for her anger. She stood in front of the concrete wall, knowing she'd break her hand if she punched it, but debating, debating. She looked down at an arrangement of flowers at her feet and fleetingly considered kicking it across the room. *Those are Grace's,* she reminded herself angrily. *They're sacred.* There was nothing except piles of clothes that would provide no release to throw about in a tantrum – she needed to break something, hurt someone, hurt herself. There was no conduit here. She stormed out to find one, leaving Grace alone with her thoughts.

Grace felt stupid for not realizing sooner that the danger she'd fled wasn't hers alone but still hung over the head of every girl in her village. She was selfish for allowing herself to feel happy, and the guilt soured every second of contentment she'd felt since arriving in Mekka.

Rayne marched across the field, kicking refuse out of her way until she was far enough away to scream her anger to the heavens. She picked up a fallen branch and swung it against a tree with all her might. It exploded into a million satisfying shards, but not before wrapping around the trunk and gouging her arm, bloodying it. "Fuck!!!" she shouted and fell to her knees, shaking.

Grace looked around the room at the flowers she'd feebly decorated with. In her self-loathing, all she could see was the drab concrete she'd done such a poor job of hiding. *There's no disguising ugliness*, she thought and gathered up the flowers, throwing them in a heap, and returning to collapse on the bed.

Rayne returned hours later, subdued, to find Grace staring vacantly at the ceiling, surrounded by the carnage of the flowers.

"I'm sorry," Rayne apologized. "I shouldn't have flown off the handle."

"It's okay," Grace replied distantly.

"It's not okay," Rayne said, sitting down beside her and placing a hand tentatively on her arm. "You told me what you went through, and all I could think about was how angry it made me. *Me?* As though how it affects me matters. *You* lived it, *you* escaped it, and all I could think about was myself. I'm sorry." She looked beseechingly into Grace's eyes.

Grace turned to face her, still hollowed out by the realization that she was a terrible person. "It's okay," she repeated blandly.

"No, it's not," Rayne repeated. "I should have been there for you, and I wasn't, and now I've made you sad."

"I did that all on my own," Grace countered but placed a hand over Rayne's. "I just need a little time to figure out how I feel about myself."

Rayne settled down beside her, gazing up at the ceiling with her. "I'll be here for you while you do. I won't leave again. That's a promise."

Grace reached for Rayne's hand and intertwined their fingers. Rayne could be fire, and she could be water, but she was also her rock, and Grace was grateful for her.

Grace woke in the morning to find that Rayne had kept a respectful distance while they slept and had, in fact, covered her in a blanket while she'd lain beside her with only her jacket to keep herself warm. Grace moved closer and pulled the blanket over them both, placing her head on Rayne's chest. Rayne stirred and stroked Grace's hair, shifting so that the contours of their bodies fit more closely together.

"We'll make it right," Rayne assured her.

Grace hoped to God that she was right – she'd never feel whole until they did. She listened to Rayne's heartbeat and drew strength from it.

"We need to talk to my sixth," she decided.

"Then, that's what we'll do," Rayne agreed.

———————————

They arranged to meet Violet at her office at the end of the workday, and she buzzed them in.

Violet hugged Grace, then turned to size up Rayne. "So, you're Grace's angel," she said.

"Avenging angel," Rayne clarified, still not completely purged of her anger.

"Sometimes, that's the type we need." She had them sit down. "How's Hope?" she asked.

"She got away okay," Grace informed her, taking her seat.

Violet breathed a sigh of relief. "Thank goodness. Now, what can I do for you?"

"We need to understand our enemy," Rayne answered. "What can you tell us about your village?"

"Well, it wasn't always as it is now. It was founded by families tired of the pace of modern life. It was idyllic in the beginning... but then Father Morgan arrived. It was a couple of hundred years ago, and we were all younger then, and he seemed like a good man. He preached unity, and we became a tighter-knit community as a result. We thrived. Then his message changed. He told us that we were indebted to God for our good fortune. He was so convincing. He appointed like-minded people to positions in his church. Soon, his control over the village was absolute. You either supported him, or you were shunned, cut off from everyone and everything you'd ever known until you were driven from the village. He closed us off from the outside world until the fear of not belonging was paralyzing. The whole time, he preached love with a silver tongue, and all the while, he spread his poison."

Violet noticed that she was gripping the arms of her chair so tightly that her fingers were losing circulation. She exhaled and took a moment to calm herself. "One day, he began preaching that God had told him that couples should have two children, one for family and one for God. Children were so loved that it wasn't hard to convince the

218

community to disregard the rules of the outside world that they never interacted with anyway. We were different, special – we were God's chosen people – He commanded us, and we obeyed. Our village was the happiest place on Earth for a time. When the children got older, Father Morgan told us that God had called His children to Him. Families were reluctant to give them up, but he assured them that they'd be doing God's work. The Father's Inner Circle took the children, and the Father praised their parents for their fidelity to God. Families were given no choice, and they had no one to turn to. Joy turned to pain, and a cloud of sadness has hung over the village ever since."

"Why didn't anyone go to the authorities?" Rayne asked.

"Father Morgan and his cronies were the only authorities we ever knew – we had no contact with anyone outside our village. Besides, Father Morgan had the ultimate blackmail. The ones who'd pay with their lives were the parents that he'd convinced to have a second child. He and his Inner Circle were so secretive that no responsibility could be pinned on them."

"But the children that were given to him?" Grace asked.

"There was never a trace of them, other than Father Morgan's assurances that they were away serving God somewhere. It's been my undying shame that I ran away rather than finding a way to fight him." She got up and poured herself a drink. "People who resisted him tended to have 'accidents.' I was afraid for you, but I was more afraid for myself." She raised the glass to her lips, but her hand shook so much that she placed it down. "Can you ever forgive me?" she asked, not having the courage to face Grace as she did.

Grace moved to her side and placed a consoling arm around her. "I understand. I did exactly what you did."

"We're going to dismantle Father Morgan's church brick by brick," Rayne assured Violet.

"Did my parents know?" Grace interrupted. "When they had me, did they know they'd have to give me up?" Grace asked, afraid of the answer.

"Your parents loved you. They were conditioned from before you were born to believe that you were a gift from God, and they would have you to love until God called you back to Him."

"How could they not have seen through that crap?" Rayne asked bitterly.

"People can't think the unthinkable. We three have had our eyes opened to the ugliness of the world, but not them. Plus, we all felt powerless."

"We have to tell someone," Grace concluded.

"We can't," Rayne replied gently. "If we do, we put the parents at greater risk than Father Morgan and his people. It'll be hard to prove what he's done, but easy to prove what they'd done."

"Violet says they didn't know any better," Grace countered. "Surely, the authorities will see that?"

"My experience with the population police is that they're not swayed by anything, least of which reason or compassion," Violet pointed out. "Their hearts are ice. You'll have to tread carefully, extremely carefully."

"Okay," Rayne accepted, "maybe we should *tentatively* reach out to the authorities, but not tell them too much unless we have assurances that they're going to pursue the right people."

"How are we going to do that?" Grace asked uncertainly.

"I know someone who can make anything happen," Rayne replied confidently. "Can I borrow your phone, Violet?"

She handed it to her, and Rayne called Elana.

"Hi, Elana. Hi, Sara," Rayne began when Elana picked up.

"Hi, Rayne," Elana's husky voice replied.

"Hi, Rayne," Sara piped in with a voice that shocked Rayne with its sing-song quality.

"Elana, do you know anyone in law enforcement?"

"Which kind of laws?"

"Population laws."

"I see. I know a detective who investigated a couple of the more amateurish assassination attempts on me. I think she's working the population desk now."

"People try to kill you?" Rayne asked, shocked.

"All the time. It's the nature of business. But relax, they're obviously not very good at it, and Sara has my back."

Rayne was speechless.

"Trust me," Sara reassured her. "No one gets to Elana except through me, and I will *not* let that happen."

"Well, thank goodness for you, then," Rayne replied.

"Thank Elana – she created me."

"We're off-topic," Elana reminded them.

"Your life is a very important topic," Rayne countered.

"I'm touched," Elana replied.

"Shall I set up a meeting with the detective?" Sara interjected.

"Please," Elana agreed.

"Okay. Come to New York, and I'll have it arranged by the time you get here. Shall I send a car? The buggy, maybe?"

"That's sweet of you, but we'll manage."

"That reminds me, please give Grace my love."

"I will. She's right here. Thank you. See you soon."

"I'll count the minutes," Elana replied and hung up.

Grace turned to her sixth. "We're going to make this right," she assured her.

Violet clenched her fists to stop her hands from shaking. Every demon she'd fled had been stirred up, and they nipped at her soul. "I pray you do, child," she replied and rose to her feet to grab her jacket. She bundled up, pulled a pocketknife from a drawer, and stuffed it in her coat.

"What are you doing? Grace asked.

"I wander the city at night looking for girls who need my help," Violet explained.

"Please be careful," Grace told her, afraid to be alone on the streets after dark herself.

"The girls I'm looking for are in greater danger than I am," Violet assured her and gave Grace a hug. "Just close the door when you leave – it'll lock on its own," she told them in parting and slipped out.

Grace wanted to leave for New York immediately, but Rayne convinced her that it would be best to get a decent night's sleep first and head out in the morning. Grace reluctantly agreed, and they returned to Rayne's place. The task ahead weighed heavily on them, and they went to bed supportively, but not affectionately.

They caught the first bus to New York, and Rayne paid an old guy near the station to get a message to Maggie that they'd be out of town for a bit. They held hands on the bus but said little as they mulled over how best to bring down Father Morgan.

Grace was not prepared for the sheer scale of New York. Buildings towered above them, and Grace followed them skyward with her gaze until they disappeared into the clouds. Slouching skyscrapers canted over them in mid-collapse, and Grace held Rayne's hand for comfort.

"You used to live here?" she asked in awe.

"Up there," Rayne replied, pointing to the clouds.

Grace just held her hand tighter.

The bus took a circuitous route to avoid fissures in the pavement that would swallow them whole if it was driven incautiously. It eventually pulled into what had once been a magnificent station, now a hollow shell. Rayne and Grace filed off the bus with the other passengers and were greeted by Elana, leaning against one of her cars. She was her usual impossibly gorgeous self, and the disembarking passengers tripped over themselves as they stared.

Rayne disregarded decorum and hugged Elana tightly. "I missed you," she told her.

"Not more than I missed you," Elana replied and hugged her back.

Grace walked over timidly, feeling like a third wheel.

"Elana, this is Grace. Grace, Elana," Rayne introduced them.

Elana surprised Grace by enveloping her in an equally affectionate hug. "Thank you for looking after Rayne," Elana told her.

"It's quite the opposite," Grace assured her, and while somewhat reassured by Elana's warmth, still felt eclipsed by her. She looked at her feet self-consciously.

"You didn't need to come," Rayne told Elana.

"I wouldn't have missed it for the world," Elana told her. "Hop in."

They sat down in seats that faced each other, Elana reclining across from Rayne and Grace. Rayne was thankful that Elana was reining in her usual seductive self. Elana ordered the car to take them to her place, and Grace suppressed a tiny shriek when the driverless vehicle lurched forward.

"It drives itself," Rayne reassured her.

"I figured you probably wanted to have your meeting with the police as soon as possible, so I set it up for a couple of hours from now, but I also figured you'd probably want to freshen up first – hence the stop at my place," Elana informed them.

"That's sweet of you, and you're right – I do feel a little gungy after the bus ride."

"Perfect. I'll whip up a light dinner while you clean up."

The car pulled into Elana's garage, and Grace was dumbfounded by the array of vehicles.

"You own all of these?" she asked, incredulous.

"I'm a bit of a collector," Elana deflected, guiding them to an elevator. "Rayne, the second floor is all yours, and Grace's. I'll be in the kitchen." She got out on the main floor and left them to ascend.

Grace followed Rayne into Elana's private quarters and was awestruck by them.

"Elana lives here?" she asked.

"Yes," Rayne replied, walking around the bed. There were two neat piles of clothing on it.

"Sara, are these for us?" Rayne asked.

"They are," her beautiful voice replied. "I hope you don't mind that I took the liberty of picking something."

"Not at all. You have impeccable taste."

"Why, thank you," Sara's voice beamed.

Grace looked around nervously. "Where's Sara?" she asked.

"Oh my God," Rayne realized. "I never told you that Sara is Elana's AI. She's not a person. She's more than a person," she added for Sara's benefit.

"Thank you, Rayne. At last, someone gets me," Sara replied, and Rayne could swear she heard a smile in her voice.

Rayne suddenly remembered that Elana's tub was free-standing and her shower a walk-in, given that Elana was absolutely comfortable with nudity. She knew that Grace would be less so, however.

"There's a shower and a bath," she told Grace, pointing out both. "Pick one, and I'll take the other."

Grace stared at the tub in the middle of the bedroom and blushed. "I'll take the shower."

"You don't know what you're missing with the tub, but I get it," Rayne replied, scooping up the outfit that she inferred was for Grace and handing it to her. "I'll give you your privacy and see you when you come out." She pointed Grace toward the bathroom and began undressing as she walked toward the tub, finding it already filled with gently steaming water.

"I figured you'd choose the tub," Sara informed her, "so I prefilled it to the same temperature you had it at the last time."

"You are unfailingly prescient," Rayne replied and slipped into the water. "And, a girl's best friend," she added. "Can you play some music, not too loud, and anything but *Armageddon's Embers*?"

"You used to like them, didn't you?" Sara asked.

"Yes, but I'm no longer a fan."

"Might I suggest that it's okay to like a product despite the packaging?"

"Are you giving me permission to still like their music, even though the singer is an asshole?"

"Permission granted," Sara replied light-heartedly. "Besides, the drummer is *so* cute."

"I forgot that Elana programmed you. Okay, please feel free to play whatever you think I'd like best."

Sara began with a more obscure track, and it was perfect. "Sara, am I allowed to be in love with you?" Rayne asked appreciatively.

"It's highly encouraged."

Rayne enjoyed her bath but decided to keep it short so as not to trap Grace in the bathroom.

Meanwhile, Grace had stripped down and cautiously entered the shower.

"The controls are a little tricky," Sara told her, "so just use voice commands, and I'll interpret for you. Would you like me to turn on the water now?"

"That would be nice, yes. Thank you," Grace replied, feeling self-conscious with Sara watching her shower. *She's not a person*, she reminded herself. *But she sure seems like one*, she argued with herself. The water turned on and came out already warm. It was a welcome change from the cold showers at Maggie's. The shower pampered her with Sara controlling the jets.

"That's enough, Sara," Grace reported, and the water turned off.

"The towels are on your right," Sara informed her as the bathroom had become a little steamy.

Grace dried off and got dressed in the outfit that Sara had picked out. It fit perfectly, and Rayne was right that it was simple but stylish.

"I'm glad you like it," Sara replied, reading Grace's vital signs.

"I do, thank you," Grace replied, far less at ease with Sara's omnipresence than Rayne was. Grace looked around at Elana's closet. It was filled with stunning dresses that Grace could imagine Elana wearing on a red carpet somewhere. She felt woefully inadequate by comparison, and it saddened her. She peeked out into the bedroom to see that Rayne was already out of the bath and relaxing in a chair by a fireplace.

"I hope I didn't rush you," Grace told her.

"Not at all. Shall we go downstairs?"

"Sure. I'm pretty hungry, and whatever Elana is making down there smells divine."

They emerged onto the main floor just as Elana was placing plates on the table.

"I made a truffle linguini," she informed them. "It's simple but tasty."

It didn't look even remotely simple to Grace, and she took a bite as soon as Rayne had. It was delicious. Grace looked over her shoulder at the pristine kitchen. *Goddamn*, she thought, *I'm competing with perfection. It's so unfair.*

"It's wonderful," Grace told Elana.

"I'm glad you like it. I'm sorry to say that I won't be joining you at your meeting with the detective. Sara will drive you over – she may or may not have dispatched some would-be assassins and hid the bodies. The less you know, the better."

Grace swallowed hard and reminded herself not to get on Sara's bad side.

"The detective's name is Angela," Elana informed them. "I can't guarantee that she'll be receptive, but she did agree to meet with you."

"Thank you," Rayne told her.

"What are friends for?" Elana replied, glancing at Rayne, and something about the way she said "friends" evoked all sorts of images in Grace's head that she had to angrily banish. "If you'll excuse me," Elana added, getting up and taking her plate with her. "Work never ends, it seems." She smiled her regrets and made her way up to the third floor to converse with Sara.

"Isn't she amazing?" Rayne asked Grace.

"You can say that again," Grace replied, trying hard not to sound glum about it. She stood up and picked up her dishes, not sure where to put them.

"I'll have the house robot take care of those," Sara told her.

"I thought you were upstairs," Grace replied.

Sara laughed a laugh evocative of wind chimes. "I'm everywhere," she replied, "but I'll meet you in the garage. Rayne, I believe you know the way."

"I do. Thanks, Sara," she replied. Rayne got up and gave Grace a surprise peck on the cheek. "I know it can be a bit overwhelming wondering what Elana sees in us mere mortals."

"It is a mystery, alright," Grace agreed as Rayne led her back down to the garage. The stairwell felt a little more private, so Grace asked, "Where are we staying tonight? I noticed that Elana only has one bed. It's gigantic, of course, but…"

"I'm sure Elana would love that, but no, we wouldn't impose."

"If you'll pardon my jumping in," Sara interjected, dispelling any illusion of privacy that Grace clung to, "but I arranged a place for you to stay while you're in New York."

"Thanks, Sara. That's very thoughtful of you."

"I try."

The same car that they'd arrived in had miraculously turned around to face the exit, and its doors were open invitingly. Rayne and Grace slipped in, and Sara drove them to an old hotel that still functioned as one. "I hope you don't mind – I picked a place where I could listen in," Sara told them.

"That's fine with me," Rayne assured her and helped Grace out of the car.

"The detective will meet you in the lobby," Sara told them and drove away.

Rayne and Grace entered the hotel, and not spotting anyone who looked like a detective, or anyone other than the tired gentleman sitting at the reception desk, they took a seat on an ancient leather sofa and waited. Grace nervously traced her finger along the cracks in the leather.

Moments later, a woman entered briskly and walked straight to them, plopping herself down across from them.

"Elana Petrova calls, you come. Now, what can I do for you, ladies?" Angela told them, leaning back to take stock of them, filing away every detail.

"Angela Richter, I presume," Rayne confirmed. The detective nodded but waited patiently for Rayne to continue. "We'd like to report a string of murders."

"Not my area," Angela replied. "I thought Elana would have known that I've been assigned to the population desk."

"It's related," Rayne assured her.

"Okay, go on, then."

"Can I speak off the record?"

"We're in the lobby of a fairly seedy hotel – I kind of assumed this would be off the record," Angela replied. "But I'll warn you – you can speak, but how I react depends on what you have to say. I'll endeavor to restrain myself, however, if that pleases you."

Rayne wasn't sure if the woman was being sarcastic, so she pushed on. "I'll cut right to the chase, then. My friend comes from a village outside New York in which people routinely have multiple children, but murder one before they become an adult."

Angela raised an eyebrow. "I thought I'd heard it all, but this is new." She leaned forward with a skeptical look. "My department hunts down people who have multiple children, and I can tell you that I don't believe that *anyone* would murder their own children."

"It's not the parents," Grace jumped in quickly. "It's the church."

"So, there's a murderous church?" Angela asked, now even more skeptical.

"I know it sounds far-fetched, but that's exactly what's going on."

Angela leaned back. "Okay, let me get a few things straight. First, you say that this village of yours is outside the city?"

"Yes."

"Near, or far?"

"Not near."

"Okay, strike one – my jurisdiction is limited to the city. Second, is the population of the village growing?"

"Not really."

"So, it's not a problem, then, is it? Strike two."

Grace and Rayne were stunned at her callousness. "The murders?" Rayne reminded her.

"Like I said – not my area." She got up to go. "Last question. Do you have proof? Of murder."

"No," Grace replied dejectedly. "That's why we came to you."

"Strike three. Look, I'm sure you think I'm a bitch, but my hands are tied. Bring me proof, and I'll see what I can do. Good night, ladies." She paused a moment. "Oh, and if you see Elana, please tell her that I still have questions for her."

"I'll see what I can do," Rayne replied sarcastically.

The detective stopped at the exit. "Look, I hate my job with every fiber of my being. I wish I could help you." Then, she was gone.

"Well, that was a waste of time," Rayne concluded.

"We had to try," Grace replied.

"Okay, so it's up to us now." Rayne rose and helped Grace to her feet and outside.

Sara pulled the car back around. "For what it's worth," Sara told them as they got in, "I read the detective's vital signs – she did believe you, and she desperately wanted to help you."

"She sure had me fooled," Rayne replied.

"I assume you're going to the village tomorrow?" Sara asked.

"I think so," Rayne replied, gauging Grace's comfort with the idea.

"Elana says you're welcome to take the buggy."

"Please thank her for us."

"I will. Let me take you to your apartment," she told them, and the car pulled away from the curb. It let them off in front of a building in a quiet part of the city, and Sara buzzed them in. The apartment was small but comfortable, and Rayne appreciated Sara all the more for it, certain that it had been she who had arranged everything.

Rayne peeked into the bedroom to see a single king-sized bed. *I guess Sara can read more than just the detective's vital signs*, she thought mischievously.

Chapter 21

Rayne

Grace was still glowing when Rayne showed her how to attach the five-point harness in Elana's armored buggy. Grace settled back and looked around the interior of the vehicle, noting that there wasn't room for a third passenger.

"Elana won't be joining us?" Grace asked to confirm her observation.

"No. Her work requires her here. It's just you and me."

"And me," Sara piped in.

"That's a relief," Rayne replied.

Grace looked at the steering wheel. "Are you sure you know how to drive this thing?"

"Not a clue," Rayne admitted, "but Elana tells me that the buggy is quite proficient at driving itself."

Grace wasn't at all reassured but vowed to trust Rayne the way she trusted Elana.

"I've instructed the buggy to tone down Elana's usual settings to make for a 'smoother' ride," Sara informed them.

"That's greatly appreciated," Rayne replied, recalling Elana's love of mayhem. As promised, the buggy pulled out of the garage without its wheels even leaving the ground. Rayne promised herself she'd get Sara a Christmas gift. *What do you get an AI who has everything?* she wondered.

On cue, Sara piped in, "Grace, do you recall the location of your village?"

"Oh no. That didn't even occur to me. I only know that it's about a day's ride by horse off the road where I caught the bus to Mekka."

"That narrows it down," Sara assured her. "I'm going to show you aerial views of three villages that fit that description. Do you think you could pick out yours?"

"Most definitely," Grace agreed, amazed at Sara's reach.

Sara displayed the satellite imagery on the heads-up display, and Grace stopped her after seeing the second image, which showed a cluster of buildings surrounded by fields, which were in turn ringed by dense forest.

"Give me a second," she instructed Sara while she imagined herself walking between the structures that she was seeing and confirming in her mind the position of the buildings that would be around her. "That one's it," she told Sara. "I recognize the church. The barn's been moved, but I think I had something to do with that."

"Okay, I've set course accordingly. Feel free to relax. I'll let you know when we're getting close. I won't pull up to the church doors without telling you or anything like that," Sara assured them.

"Thank you," Grace replied and looked out the window as they passed building after building. It suddenly occurred to her that Gabriel was somewhere in the city looking for her.

Rayne could tell what Grace was thinking by the way her body tensed up. "It's a big city," she told her. "A passing vehicle is the last place your ex would think to look. Besides, Elana says the buggy has flame throwers."

"I don't want to incinerate him, just hide from him."

"I'm game either way, but it's your call."

They gradually wound their way out of the city and into the country. Sara took stock of her passengers. Elana was important to her, Rayne was important to Elana, and Grace was important to Rayne. That made all three of them her responsibility. She ran diagnostics on the flame throwers.

Grace looked over at Rayne. "So, what's our plan?"

"Well, for starters, we need proof of what's going on, and we need to figure out who the bad guys are."

"I brought reconnaissance gear," Sara informed them. "And supplies for a long stakeout."

"Thanks," Rayne replied and settled in for the drive.

Sara alerted them several hours later that they were approaching the village and that she'd located a possible campsite twenty minutes' walk from it. They agreed to make that their base and had her take them there. Sara told them that she'd sent high-altitude drones ahead to scout the village and promised to report anything she found.

Setting up their camp shortly thereafter, Grace struggled to figure out the tent. "Can you believe I've never been camping before?"

"I only remember going once, with my parents, before they died," Rayne replied.

Grace cursed herself for not having known to be more sensitive.

Rayne read her reaction. "It's okay. It was a long time ago. I'm happy that my second time is with you – I just wish it could be under lighter circumstances."

"Me too," Grace replied, finally figuring out the tent while Rayne checked out the reconnaissance gear.

"Want to show me around your village?" Rayne asked.

"I'd be delighted," Grace replied and led Rayne through the trees with Sara guiding the way via earpieces. They lay down just back of the tree line, and Rayne set up a telescope and a monitor. Grace pointed out which of the clustered buildings were which and who the people were. Rayne had Grace categorize the villagers on a 10-point scale from saint to devil. It was the hardest thing that Grace ever tried to do because it forced her to look at her village with the veil of ignorance drawn back. Hours later, there were a few 1s and the odd 10, but mostly 5s. "I'm sorry," Grace apologized. "I just don't know."

"It's okay," Rayne assured her. "It's hard to say that you truly know someone." She paused. "I noticed that we haven't seen your family yet."

"That's intentional," Grace admitted. "I'm not quite ready for that yet."

Rayne squeezed her arm, and they decided to retire to their campsite in the gathering darkness. They compared notes with Sara, who had compiled her own guilt-by-association diagram, and together they were able to move many of the 5s to 2s and 3s, and some to 7s and 8s. The village was still maddeningly grey to Rayne.

"It's just a matter of collecting more data," Sara assured her. "More data equals more certainty. Trust me, stats are my life." A couple of days later, they'd refined their conclusions, but they were still far from certain where the line lay that separated good from evil.

"They're on their best behavior," Sara had to admit. "I think Grace's escape put them on notice, and they're going about their nefarious ways as clandestinely as possible." Sara judged it a good time to bring up the fact that she was also compiling a list of which children were at most imminent risk. "Pardon how this is going to sound," she started, "but it's when I overlap the maps of the predators and their prey that disturbing patterns begin to emerge."

"What have you concluded?" Grace demanded to know.

"Only that I need more data," Sara replied cagily. "There is only so much I can infer from behavioral analysis."

Rayne recalled Grace telling her about the files stored in Father Morgan's office. "Would seeing the village records help?" Rayne asked.

"Infinitely so," Sara agreed.

"I can't go back in there," Grace quailed.

"I'd never ask you to," Rayne assured her. "Breaking into places is *my* thing."

Grace was terrified for Rayne but had to agree that the reward justified the risk. Sara and Rayne deliberated over the best time to break in, settling on during a church service when they could best account for where all the villagers would be. "Too many variables otherwise," Sara concluded.

"But everyone would be in the same building as Rayne," Grace fretted.

"Keep your friends close and your enemies closer. Isn't that how the expression goes?" Rayne said to make light of Grace's worries.

"Sunday is still two days away," Grace accepted reluctantly. "I think I'm ready to see my family now, from afar anyway."

Rayne escorted Grace to a spot in the trees where they had a view of her house. Butterflies swirled in Grace's stomach as they waited, and when her mother stepped out, she almost cried out from the pain of yearning to run to her. Rayne consoled her while she sat in the bushes sobbing. There was an air of sadness about her mother that lifted somewhat when Grace's sister returned from school. Grace breathed a deep sigh of relief at the sight of Hanna, even though Sara had confirmed days ago that she was all right. *I never finished helping her with her homework*, Grace thought guiltily. Her father met them at the door, and he moved with less of a spring in his step than Grace recalled. He and Hanna went inside while Grace's mother hesitated as if waiting for Grace to join them. She scanned the distance, and when her eyes swept past Grace's hiding spot, Grace was impaled by the sorrow they held. Her mother brushed an errant hair back over her ear, looked down, and went inside.

Did you know? Grace demanded to know as she stared at the closed door. She put her hand to her temple, feeling the memory of her mother's touch. Her head swam, and her heart was rent. "That's enough," she told Rayne and rose on shaky legs to leave.

Sunday came, and Grace positioned herself where she could see through the church windows. Sara sent drones to surveil all angles, and Rayne readied herself to go in. Grace reported that the church doors had closed, and the sermon had begun. Sara added that everyone who was well enough to attend church appeared to be there, so Rayne darted from her hiding spot and sprinted to the basement window of Father Morgan's office. She noted a newly installed security system but made short work of bypassing it and slid the window open.

"You've got less than an hour," Grace informed her as Rayne pulled out her lock picking tools and opened the door to the file room. She turned on her headlamp and camera and began flipping through files faster than she could absorb their contents, but not faster than Sara could.

"That's excellent, Rayne. Keep it up," Sara encouraged her.

Rayne had made it half-way through the files when Grace urgently reported that someone was heading down the stairs. "I think it's Father Michael."

Rayne had no time to escape and didn't want to get locked in the file room, so she quickly stepped out, closing the door behind her, and slid under the desk just before Father Michael entered. He sifted through the papers on the desk before grabbing a few but stopped before leaving. He turned around slowly when he noticed the open window and moved around the desk to close it. Rayne held her breath and waited. From her vantage point, she couldn't see the red lights focused on the back of the Father's skull as he turned toward the door and left without noticing her.

Rayne pushed herself out from under the desk when she heard his footsteps ascending the stairs and hurried back into the file room.

"Hurry," Grace urged Rayne. "The sermon is almost done."

"I'm almost finished," Rayne reported, opening the final cabinet.

"They're finishing up," Grace warned her.

"Almost done," Rayne repeated.

"Everyone's getting up to leave," Grace panicked. "Rayne, get out of there before you're trapped."

Sara directed a drone to slam into the stained-glass window above the church doors, hitting it hard enough to crack it. Everyone inside froze, and Father Morgan directed them to sit back down while he investigated. Sara used the time it took him to walk the length of the church to flush a sparrow with a drone, tase it in mid-flight, and in a feat of unparalleled acrobatic maneuvering, catch it, and deposit it gently on the steps of the church. The door opened just as the drone sped out of sight.

"It's just a bird," Father Morgan reported to the congregation, stooping to examine it, "and it looks like it's going to be okay, too. It's a sign of God's mercy." He was moved to lead the congregation in a final prayer of thanks to God before releasing them. Rayne took the opportunity to slip out the window and race for the trees.

"Good job, Rayne," Sara congratulated her. "I have what I need to fill in the big picture. Meet you back at camp."

Grace joined Rayne, and they walked back together.

"Please never do that again," Grace pled with Rayne. "I'm pretty sure I just had a whole string of heart attacks."

They arrived at their campsite to find the monitor in their tent flashing the name "Holly."

"Holly is one of my sister's friends," Grace told Rayne.

"She's their next target," Sara informed them. "And they'll move on her soon."

Chapter 22

Grace

Grace stared at Holly's name on the monitor and felt sick – she was just a child, barely thirteen. Grace's stomach knotted, and she bolted to throw up in the woods and not in the tent. Rayne held her hair back and rubbed her back while she retched. She stayed on her knees for an eternity before rising unsteadily to her feet.

"Why?" Grace asked Sara. "Why Holly?"

"I don't understand evil any better than you do," Sara replied. "I only see its patterns."

"So, you could be wrong?"

"Yes. I calculate a 12% probability that I might be wrong, but prudence dictates that we not take that chance – a little girl's life hangs in the balance."

"You don't have to tell me that," Grace replied bitterly. "I just don't want it to be true, and don't tell me that what I want or don't want doesn't change anything."

"I would never do that," Sara replied soothingly. "I don't want it to be true either, and I'm as angry as you. If it were up to me, I'd put a bullet in everyone I suspected, but I'm only 88% sure who deserves one, and while that's good enough for me, it's not good enough for Elana, and she programmed me."

Grace sat down in the grass, and Rayne sat beside her. "Okay, tell me why you think Holly's their next target," Grace requested of Sara.

"From everything you've told me about the children that have gone missing, or had suspicious accidents, and the village records, Holly fits the profile."

"She's only thirteen."

"Yes, but her brother is eighteen, and the church records show no siblings older than eighteen."

"So why is Holly at risk and not him?"

"For whatever reason, they're ignoring him but paying increasing attention to her. Plus, statistically, they seem to prefer to prey on girls rather than boys."

Grace was sick again and didn't make it to the trees.

Sara waited for Grace to recover before continuing. "I'm tracking the movements of everyone in the village, and my map of those we suspect has been increasingly intersecting with Holly's whereabouts, so much so that it can't be explained by random chance alone. They're drawn to her like moths to a flame."

"I vote for bullets," Rayne finally joined in, unable to restrain herself any longer.

"The problem with that isn't just the risk of dispatching someone who we assume is guilty based on association but who actually isn't – the bigger problem is that we may fail to dispatch someone who truly is. We can't cut only seven heads off a hydra – we need to be certain that we've cut them all."

"We can't do nothing," Rayne countered.

"We won't," Sara agreed. "We just have to do it in a way that doesn't raise suspicion."

"And how do we do that?" Grace asked.

"I have no idea," Sara replied, "but three heads are better than one at coming up with one."

From that point on, Holly became their sole focus. They kept an eye on her and those that Sara suspected. The two intersected increasingly like the tightening circling of predators around their prey.

"Tunnels," Sara declared one evening out of the blue. "The people we suspect have been coordinating in some way that I haven't been able to ascertain. They rarely meet in person, and I pick up no electronic communications at all, and yet, they still seem to act in concert. So much so that I can't chalk it up to some predefined protocol. They're meeting – I'm just not seeing it, and that can only be because they're moving around out of sight. Hence, tunnels."

"I am not setting foot in a tunnel," Grace declared, shivering at the thought.

"Never go anywhere you don't have a tactical advantage," Rayne agreed.

"That sounds like something a soldier would say," Grace observed.

"A friend of mine was always saying stuff like that," Rayne explained, beginning to wonder more about Renner.

"I wouldn't advise exploring the tunnels either," Sara agreed. "It would be too easy to bump into one of Father Morgan's cronies – but it makes our job of countering them more difficult."

"Where *do* we have a tactical advantage?" Grace wondered aloud.

"Well, you showed us where they take the girls – the clearing with the altar. It's outside the village, surrounded by forest, and known to us. It has to be there that we intervene," Rayne replied.

"Agreed," said Sara.

"How exactly do we intervene without them realizing that we're on to them?" Grace asked.

"We need a diversion that they won't suspect to be our doing," Sara decided, "and I have some ideas." She went quiet as she began making arrangements.

Rayne and Grace resumed keeping an eye on Holly, noting that the church Elders were doing the same more and more frequently.

"Things are escalating," Grace concluded. "I can feel it."

"I'm projecting that they'll move within the next three nights," Sara agreed. "If it's tonight, our diversion won't be ready, so we need to make sure it's not tonight."

"What exactly is our diversion?" Rayne asked.

"I'd rather not say, given that you might not be *fully* supportive of it."

"I don't like the sound of that."

"My point exactly. Trust me."

Sara wasn't exactly giving them much choice, Rayne noted. "Okay, so how do we make sure they don't move tonight?"

"We need to throw a wrench in their plans, and that calls for a sleepover," Sara replied.

"A sleepover? That's your plan?" Grace asked, incredulous.

"It's subtle, and it will probably unbalance them just enough to delay acting until patterns that they deem more predictable return."

"So, we need to engineer a sleepover," Grace concurred. "Sara, who's Holly's best friend at school?"

"Abi Miller."

Grace took a moment to recover her wits after the mention of Jenna's sister. "We'll make it happen, but Abi knows me too well, Rayne, so she'll be your job – I'll take Holly. We need to make this happens the way thirteen-year-olds would make it happen. We need to pass them notes."

"Did you bring any clothing from the village?" Rayne asked Grace, and she nodded. "Great. Pick out an outfit for me and one for you, too. We're going in. Sara, can you tell us when it is safe to slip the girls a note?"

"*Safest* is all I can promise, but yes, I'm pretty sure that opportunities will present themselves."

Grace helped Rayne dress as though she lived in the village. Rayne thanked her lucky stars that she'd brought her wigs. Grace had to tie Rayne's fake hair up in a bob under her bonnet, as this proved to be outside Rayne's skill set. Grace wrote a note for each girl telling them that they were being invited to join a secret club and that they'd learn more that night if they could arrange a sleepover at Abi's house.

"I've got a trick that will add mystery *and* destroy the evidence," Sara told them and had Rayne spray a chemical on the notes from a supply of items that she'd brought "just-in-case." "Don't touch the paper with your bare hands," she warned them, which of course alarmed Grace. "It isn't *all* that dangerous," Sara assured her. "I just don't want to spoil it. Trust me."

"She sure says that a lot," Grace muttered to Rayne, but Rayne gave her a "just-roll-with-it" look and did as Sara requested.

Sara directed them to positions between the school and the girls' houses, out of sight of any passersby or glances out windows. It was such a herculean feat that it prompted Grace to wonder just how many drones Sara had in the air. When the way was as clear as it was going to get, Sara directed Grace to walk past Holly on her way to school and slip her the note. Holly puzzled over Grace as she walked swiftly away, but her curiosity about the note got the better of her, and she turned her attention to it instead. She read it twice before the moisture on her hands reacted with the chemical on the paper, and it combusted. She dropped the burning paper and looked for Grace, who was long gone.

It was much easier for Rayne to approach Abi without being detected, as she wasn't being monitored the way Holly was, and Rayne slipped her the note without incident. Retreating, Rayne was spotted by a boy her age, curious about why he didn't recognize her, and he followed her, but by the time he made it to where she'd been, she'd disappeared.

Rayne met Grace back at camp, and they changed into clothes better suited to surveillance. They watched the girls talk excitedly at recess, go home at the end of the day, and Holly eventually walk to Abi's carrying an overnight bag.

Grace's relief was palpable.

"If you want something done, get thirteen-year-old girls to do it," Rayne marveled.

Sara reported that the sleepover had completely disrupted the surveillance patterns of the church Elders and that they appeared to be standing down for the evening, although they still kept an eye on Abi's window. Rayne was sorely tempted to borrow one of Sara's tasers and pay the watchers a little visit, but she resisted the urge.

"The girls are expecting something about a secret club," Grace reminded Sara and Rayne, "and I have an idea." Grace hated to lie, but she wrote another note – this one purportedly from Jenna. It said that she was now a secret agent, and no matter what was going to happen, to trust that she would be there. The note ended by swearing the girls to secrecy. Sara distracting the Elder that was keeping watch with a drone and delivered the note with another, sticking it to Abi's bedroom window, tapping on it, and flying away before anyone saw it. Grace watched the girls read the note before it combusted in a flash, then move out of sight of the window.

Grace and Rayne slept fitfully, despite Sara's assurances that she'd wake them at the first sign of trouble. They gave up trying to sleep at dawn and rose early.

"Holly's fine," Sara assured them, but Grace watched her walk to school with Abi, just to be sure.

As the day wore on, their movements made it clear that the Elders were indeed planning to abduct Holly that night. Sara informed them that the diversion was in place and had them both carry a taser, explaining how to use it.

"I want a gun," Rayne countered.

"If you need lethality, you have me," Sara replied by way of refusal.

Rayne and Grace took up positions in the trees surrounding the clearing with the altar. They stayed out of sight and waited. Not long after, a robed figure arrived with lanterns and spread them around the clearing. His dark cowl prevented Grace from identifying him. Rayne held Grace close while she relived the night of Jenna's disappearance in her mind. Grace trembled.

"Are you sure you want to be here?" Rayne whispered.

"I'm sure," Grace replied, steadying herself. "I owe it to Jenna."

Well after dark, a procession of robed figures escorted Holly in her sleepwear into the clearing. Despite the note that Grace had written to reassure her, Holly was terrified. Grace clenched and unclenched her fists.

The robed figures led Holly to the altar, and one of them pulled out a rope.

"Now would be a good time for that diversion, Sara," Grace whispered.

"Wait for it," Sara instructed them.

Two men lifted Holly onto the altar and began tying her to it.

"Sara!" Grace hissed.

"Almost time," Sara replied calmly.

"God damn it, Sara, almost?!" Grace replied, then turned to Rayne, "I can't wait any longer," she said and got to her feet.

A blood-curdling roar split the night, freezing everyone in their tracks, followed by the sound of something massive crashing through the underbrush. A grizzly broke through the trees, reared, and roared again.

"A bear, Sara? A bear?! That's your plan?" Grace accused her.

"I told you that you wouldn't like it," Sara muttered.

The men tying Holly to the altar let go of the rope and ran back toward the village. The bear dropped to all fours and padded into the clearing, stalking the slowest of the men to leave. The look of sheer menace reflected in the bear's eyes finally broke the man's paralysis, and he stumbled away into the night. The bear turned toward Holly, and she screamed.

Grace and Rayne pulled out their tasers and sprinted for the clearing, breaking through the trees just as the bear leaned over Holly's face and began to lick it.

"Of all the bears in the world, you picked one with multiple personality disorder?" Rayne marveled as she waved to get the bear's attention and have him move away from Holly, who lay paralyzed with fear.

"Isn't he adorable?" Sara replied. He's a circus rescue. I bought him from the Atlanta zoo."

"What's a zoo?" Grace asked.

"What's an Atlanta?" Rayne added.

"It doesn't matter," Sara assured them. "He's a lover, but I suggest you untie Holly and get her out of here before anyone returns."

Holly was nearly catatonic with fear when they reached her.

"It's okay," Grace assured her. "Jenna sent me to rescue you." *In a way, she had*, Grace thought.

Grace picked Holly up and began carrying her toward the trees. The bear followed amiably.

"Hold up, Rayne," Sara whispered in her ear. "There's a vial of blood in your pack. It's not marked, but it's the only vial in there. I suggest you smear some of it on the altar to give the impression that Holly is no more. I don't think Grace should know."

"Agreed," Rayne replied. "Grace, I'll be along in a second," she called and set to desecrating the altar. She cleaned her hands as best she could and hurried after Grace. Sara guided them through the woods back to camp. Holly was unresponsive.

"Sara, Holly needs professional help. We need to bring her to the city," Rayne pointed out.

"In the morning," Sara agreed. "We need to lead the bear away from the village before we leave him, and that'll be easier in daylight."

"You're not returning him to where you got him from?" Grace asked.

"No. He'll be happier in the wild, but nowhere near the village. He's too friendly, and we can't leave him at risk like that."

"Okay," Grace agreed reluctantly and laid Holly down in the tent, speaking soothingly to her.

Rayne lay down on the grass outside and the bear snuggled in beside her. In the morning, Rayne led it far, far away from the village. Grace met up with her later in the buggy, and they started off to the city with Holly in Grace's lap.

"I was hoping that the men from the clearing would go back to their homes last night so I could identify them more definitively," Sara informed them, "but they returned to the church instead and

251

disappeared from there. I have height and build information from the clearing, but I'm not a lot closer to confirming beyond a shadow of a doubt their identities," she added with disappointment.

They drove in silence for a while longer, with Grace stroking Holly's hair. She snuggled in, and Grace took it as a hopeful sign.

"Rayne, you have a call from Elana," Sara informed her. "Will you take it?"

"Of course," Rayne replied.

"It's Triste," Elana told her. "She overdosed, but she's okay. She's in the hospital, and I have my personal doctor attending her. I thought you'd want to know."

The long drive back became a lot longer.

Chapter 23
Rayne

The entire way back to New York, Rayne worried about Triste. Even though they'd broken up, she'd never stopped caring about her, and part of her knew that Triste desperately needed someone to care for her. That someone was her.

Grace sat sullenly, piecing together that Triste must be the source of the broken heart that Rayne had alluded to when they'd first met. Now, she was back in the picture, and even the most cursory glance revealed how deep Rayne's feelings ran for her. It was something Grace admired about Rayne – when she loved, she loved completely. Part of her always suspected that what she had with Rayne couldn't last. Rayne was passion personified – she was everything Grace wanted from life. She knew that someday Rayne would wake up and realize that she could have Triste back, or that goddess Elana, or anything or anyone she wanted. To put her heart so entirely in someone else's hands was to give away so much power. So why did loving Rayne make her feel so powerful? Grace accepted the new reality with magnanimity and distracted herself by rubbing Holly's back. As the ruins of buildings rose up and hemmed them in, Holly squirreled herself deeper into Grace's arms, and they comforted each other.

The buggy pulled up in front of a small, high-end medical center and idled in the spot reserved for ambulances. A porter got off his chair to wave them away, but Sara throttled the engine so menacingly that he returned to his seat – they didn't pay him enough to do battle with the entitled rich.

"Triste is inside," Sara told Rayne. "Call me when you want to be picked up. I'm going to take Grace and Holly to a therapist."

Rayne nodded absentmindedly and got out of the vehicle. Sara waited until she'd entered before pulling away.

"Miss Torres," a man at the reception desk greeted her. "Ms. Petrova's assistant called ahead to tell me you were coming. I'll show you up."

Rayne followed him to the third floor. He directed her to a room at the end of the hall and left her. Rayne peeked in on a room that was functionally spare but still somehow elegant. Triste lay asleep in the bed, connected to an array of monitors. Rayne's heart ached just to see her. She approached slowly and took Triste's hand in hers, taking a seat beside her and holding Triste's hand against her cheek. Her hand was warm, and Rayne recalled every time it had run through her hair, rested on her arm when she laughed, or held her close. Rayne wet that hand with tears and slumped against the bed.

Sara navigated her way to the therapist's office. It was a residential facility, and she told Grace that Holly could stay there until she recovered emotionally.

"I don't have money for a therapist," Grace felt she needed to point out.

"I know," Sara replied. "I'm paying for it. Elana gives me a generous allowance for my side projects."

"That's kind of you, but I doubt I'll ever be able to repay you."

"You already have. Every day, you teach me how to be lovable, and there's someone I really want to love me. I consider the exchange priceless."

Grace never thought that an AI could crave love as much as a person, but there was much she didn't know.

"If I'm so lovable," Grace asked sorrowfully, "then why am I not I loved?"

"Oh, you're loved, alright – in a way that I wish I were."

Grace contemplated what she'd said.

"It hurts because it's real," Sara added and went silent.

The buggy pulled up to a woman who was waiting outside a fairly decrepit-looking building.

"Hi, Grace. I'm Astrid," she introduced herself. "Sara told me everything," Grace could tell by the way she said "everything" that she meant *every*thing. She caught Grace's hesitant glances at the condition of the building. "Don't place too much stock in appearances – we invest in what's inside."

Grace maneuvered herself out of the buggy with Holly still in her arms. She tried to transfer her to Astrid, but Holly revolted and held fast to her.

"That's a *great* sign," Astrid assured her. "You're welcome to come inside with her, and given the late hour, you're welcome to spend the night." She turned to Holly. "Would that be okay – if she stayed with you?" Holly wouldn't look up but nodded emphatically. "It's settled, then. Come inside," Astrid told Grace.

Sara instructed the buggy to return to Elana's garage and left Grace and Holly in Astrid's care.

———————————

Across the city, Triste stirred, and as her eyes focused, she beheld Rayne at her bedside.

"Hi," she greeted Rayne in a quiet voice, a solitary tear escaping her eye.

"Hi," Rayne replied, reaching up to wipe it away.

"I'm glad you're here. I messed up. I'm messed up."

"Shh," Rayne soothed her.

"I'm sorry I pushed you away," she continued, tears beginning to spill freely.

"I'm here now," Rayne assured her and moved around the bed to crawl in beside her.

Triste rolled toward her, buried her head on Rayne's chest, and wept herself back to sleep.

———————————

Grace spent the night with Holly, who refused to be separated from her for even an instant, and in the morning, Astrid joined them for breakfast. Holly looked around her as though she suspected she'd been teleported onto a spaceship.

"This is a safe place," Astrid told her. "You're welcome to stay here as long as you'd like."

"I want my mother," Holly informed her.

"My friend, Sara, is working on that. Hopefully, you'll be reunited very soon. Until then, your mother wants me to look after you – to keep you safe." Astrid looked from Holly to Grace. "Grace has a story like you do," she began tentatively, sounding out Grace for approval to proceed. Grace unconsciously clenched her jaw but nodded her assent. "Perhaps you'd like to hear it?" Holly looked to Grace expectantly.

"Do you know how Abi is your best friend?" Grace began. Holly nodded. "Well, her sister was my best friend…"

By the time Grace left Holly in Astrid's care, she had cried more tears than she thought herself capable of. She walked out the front door to find Elana's limo waiting. She slid in the back and looked at her red and puffy eyes in the mirror.

"Tell me the truth, Sara, do I look as much of a fright to you as I do to myself?"

"You look closer to healed," Sara assured her, and in fact, it was how Grace felt.

"I want to see Angela," Grace informed her.

"That can be arranged," Sara agreed, and the car pulled out. It drew up several blocks later to a police station from which a steady stream of people entered and exited. "The detective told me to tell you to go up to the eighth floor and tell them at the reception that you're there to see her. If you want, put in the earpiece beside you, and I can stay in contact with you the whole time."

Grace noticed an open compartment with a discreet earpiece in it. "You really do think of everything, don't you?" Grace noted as she put the device into her ear.

"That's what I'm here for," Sara's voice in her ear agreed.

Grace got out and approached the front door. Police officers escorted sketchy-looking people inside, and more disturbingly, even sketchier-looking people wandered out on their own cognizance. Grace side-stepped them and walked inside.

She wasn't sure if she should try to find her own way to the eighth floor, but the receptionist in the main lobby took one look at her and told her, "Victim services are on the fourth floor."

"I'm not here for victim services," Grace informed her.

"Okay, I'll bite… missing persons?"

"No, population control."

The receptionist glanced at Grace's belly but shrugged. "Eighth floor," she said, already losing interest and waving her toward the elevator.

"Thank you," Grace replied and walked over to it. The eighth floor was even drearier than the rest of the building, and that was no mean feat. Grace presented herself to the eighth-floor receptionist, who instructed her to wait on a chair that had questionable structural integrity.

Ten minutes later, detective Angela waved her in, and Grace sat down at her desk. Angela leaned back and looked Grace over before pulling out two glasses and pouring a finger of scotch into each.

"Drink?" she asked.

"No, thank you," Grace replied, so Angela downed them both and put the glasses away in the bottom drawer. The bottle stayed out.

"So, you're back," she noted.

"Yes, and I brought a girl that we rescued from the monsters we told you about."

"A minor?"

"She's thirteen, if that's what you mean?"

"That's too bad," she replied dismissively. "Not a credible witness. Do you have any hard evidence? Video, perhaps?"

"We weren't going to film her murder if that's what you were hoping for," Grace replied, stunned and angry.

Angela leaned forward. "Look, I'm not the bad guy – I'm trying to help you, but we're stretched thin."

"Tell that to the girl we untied," Grace fumed, getting up. "Sorry to have wasted your time."

"Sorry I couldn't be of more help," Angela replied, rising to her feet as well.

"More help? How about *any* help?" Grace muttered, showing herself to the door.

"I'll walk you out," Angela offered. "It's the least I could do."

Grace stared at her. *It really is*, she thought bitterly.

Angela held the door open and fell into stride close behind her.

"I'm not unsympathetic – I'm really not," she said in a low voice, "but my hands are tied. There are things this job makes me do that keep me from sleeping." She inclined her head toward a door they

259

were passing. "There's a young girl in there steadfastly refusing to give up her good-for-nothing father. If she doesn't…," she started to say but clenched her jaw and punched the elevator's down-button instead, adding loudly, "Call me when you have more," then turned on her heel and disappeared back through the door.

Grace emerged to find that Sara had kept the car out front the entire time. She'd known it would be a short meeting.

"She's a conscientious detective," Sara assured her as Grace as she stepped into the vehicle.

"That might have been true once, but I'm not so sure it still is," Grace replied.

"Her offer to help if we obtain more evidence was genuine. I'm not going to rule her out as an asset just yet."

"I'm going back to the village," Grace declared.

"I know," Sara replied. "The buggy is recharged and ready to go, but Elana asked if you'd have dinner with her first."

"Of course, she's been so kind."

"We're heading there now," Sara informed her.

Grace wandered up from the garage to find Elana in the living room with an assortment of take-out food containers.

"I hope you don't mind – I didn't feel like cooking. We're having Thai."

"It smells delicious," Grace replied, sitting down across from her. "I can't thank you enough for all your help, especially the loan of Sara."

"Sara's her own person, but yes, she's a treasure," Elana deferred.

"Why did you want to see me?" Grace asked politely.

"I just thought misery might like a little company. We're two peas in a pod."

Her meaning registered with Grace. "You like her, too?" she stated more than asked.

"It's hard not to."

Grace looked Elana over. If it was a contest, she concluded, it was a contest that she'd lose – Elana was a goddess. Still, there was a sadness in her that told her that Elana did not arrive at the same conclusion.

"The heart wants what the heart wants," Elana sighed. "I also need your moral support."

"For what?"

"For good or bad, I can bring Triste back to Rayne. The selfish part of me doesn't want to, but the part of me that loves Rayne knows I have to."

Grace got up and sat beside Elana, placing a hand on her arm. "My mother always told me to follow my heart, even until breaking. I didn't know what she meant until now."

Elana walked into Triste's hospital room. Triste slept fitfully in the bed while Rayne had succumbed to exhaustion in an adjacent chair.

"Hello, Rayne," Elana whispered, too quietly to wake her.

261

She walked up to Triste and bent over her until their lips were almost touching, then hesitated. Those lips had kissed Rayne's. Elana remembered kissing Rayne – it had felt like a first kiss – no art, all surrender. Elana's actual first had been with one of her mother's bodyguards that she'd decided to lose her virginity to, just to get it over with. It had smacked of hunger and urgency. Rayne had given her the gift of a new first kiss, one she treasured. *If I do this for you*, she thought of Triste, *you'd better deserve her.* A tear rolled down her cheek, and she knew that she had to act or lose her resolve. She drew closer and kissed Triste gently. The nanobots in her saliva streamed into Triste and invaded her bloodstream, attacking the residual traces of the drugs that held her addicted and beginning the rewiring of her synapses.

"Goodbye, Rayne," Elana whispered and left, just before Triste started screaming.

Grace rolled toward her village in the armored buggy that Elana had loaned her.

"Thanks for coming with me," she told Sara.

"I really am everywhere," Sara reminded her.

"You know what I mean."

"I do. Two peas in a pod."

"Caught that, did you?"

"I hang on every word," Sara sighed.

"You should tell her how you feel."

"She knows. It's just that I'm not a person."

"She thinks you are."

"It's not the same, but thank you."

They rode closer to the village in comfortable silence.

"Where would you like me to drop you?" Sara asked.

"At my front door. I'm tired of hiding."

"Do you still have the earpiece?"

"I wouldn't leave home without it, or return home, I guess is more the case."

"Good. I'll be with you every step of the way."

"And that's why I love you."

"I'm glad someone does," Sara joked.

The buggy drove straight into the village, winding slowly between buildings. It came to a stop at the backdoor to Grace's house. She got out confidently and swung open the door.

"Hi, Mom. I'm home," she announced.

Chapter 24

Grace

Grace's mother dropped the plate she was holding, unsure if she was imagining her daughter's return. Visions of Grace had haunted her a thousand times, always inhabiting her peripheral vision, fading into a crowd or turning a corner... never substantial. This Grace had virtually kicked in the door and stood in front of her, radiating life, consuming all the air in the room. It wasn't the Grace from her memories – it was Grace reborn. She stepped over the shards of the broken plate, oblivious to them, and held her daughter by her arms, real, substantial. She pulled her into a hug and refused to let her go, holding her, feeling her, squeezing her, unabashedly refamiliarizing herself with her missing daughter.

Grace's father stepped into the kitchen, drawn by his daughter's voice. He froze in the doorway. Grace had never seen him cry before, but there was a first time for everything. Grace waved him over, and he joined in their embrace, wrapping them both in his arms.

"Paul, our daughter's home," Grace's mother told him unnecessarily, hoping that her words would keep the dream from dissipating.

"I can see that," he replied, smiling.

They stood like that for an eternity until the back door crashed open. Hanna stood in the doorway, panting.

"They're saying that Grace is back," she struggled to get out.

Grace extricated herself from her parents and knelt before her sister. "They were right."

Hanna threw her arms around her sister's neck. "Don't leave again."

"Not without you," she promised.

They moved to the living room and sat down, everyone just staring at Grace.

"Where have you been?" her mother finally asked.

"Just away," Grace replied, which was apt given that her goal had only ever been just to get away. She shifted in her chair, discomforted by the memory.

"The night of the fire…" her father began.

"I realized I didn't want to go off and 'do God's work.' That's what the Father came here to tell you I had to do that night, wasn't it?"

"Yes," he confirmed.

"I respect your faith," she told her parents earnestly, "but I've come to see that I don't share it. Can you accept that?"

They nodded slowly as they came to terms with it. "I'm sorry," her father told her. "You can have flowers in your room."

It made Grace laugh and cry. She wiped away a tear. "Thank you. Flowers are nice."

Her mother got up, needing to reassert normalcy. "I'll make us tea." She squeezed her daughter's shoulder on her way by, and Grace squeezed her hand back.

"What's that thing outside?" Hanna asked, unable to keep her curiosity bottled up any longer.

"I borrowed it from a friend. I made some good friends while I was away. I hope you can meet them sometime," she added wistfully. "Would you like me to take you for a ride in it?"

"Can I, father?" Hanna begged.

He looked at Grace uncertainly.

"I will protect her with my life," Grace promised, and she meant it.

"Then, it's okay with me," he agreed.

"Thank you, Daddy," Hanna enthused and abandoned decorum to hug him. He was surprisingly accepting of it.

Grace's mother returned carrying a tray holding cups of tea, honey, and lemon. "You have plenty of time before dinner," she told them. "I don't know what I'll make," she fretted.

"I missed your cooking," Grace admitted.

"I worried about you out there all alone," her mother told her.

"I was never alone. It turns out that I have a guardian angel."

"I thought you said you didn't believe?" her father asked kindly.

"I believe in my angel."

"Can we go now?" Hanna begged.

Her mother consented, and Grace finished her tea quickly so that she could oblige her sister. She led her outside. "Car, open up, please," she requested, and the doors swung upwards.

"Cool," Hanna declared, and Grace helped her up and in, while their parents looked on with thinly veiled worry.

Grace made a show of securing her sister's harness to reassure her parents, but it only made her father worry more about why such a harness was necessary in the first place. Grace quickly closed the doors and strapped herself in before he could rescind his consent.

"You know how to drive this thing?" her sister asked, amazed.

"Don't tell Dad, but no, not at all. It drives itself." Grace ordered the car to drive out of the village very slowly to pacify her parents. Once out of sight, she asked her sister, "Want to see what this thing can *really* do?"

Hanna nodded enthusiastically, and Grace ordered the car to demonstrate its speed and maneuverability. Its wheels bit into the loose gravel, and it shot down the road like a rocket. It skidded sideways into an open field and executed a series of impossibly tight turns, finally ramping a hummock, sailing into the air, and coming to a screeching halt on the road, facing the way back toward the village.

Hanna's bun had come completely undone, and her hair covered her face. They both slowly relaxed their death grips on their harness. "Perhaps it's best if we don't tell Mom and Dad about that," Grace suggested.

Hanna nodded, adrenaline still coursing through her veins.

Grace ordered the car to drive back slowly.

"My friend, Holly," Hanna began. "They say she got attacked by a bear. The Elders are hunting it."

"My heart tells me that Holly is okay," Grace assured her. "The village is a far more dangerous place than it seems."

"That's what they're saying."

"I don't mean *outside* the village. I mean inside. Promise me that you'll keep your eyes open and be wary."

"I promise." Hanna looked around the interior of the buggy. "Whose car is this?" she asked.

"It's my girlfriend's girlfriend's."

"Where's your girlfriend?"

"With her other girlfriend."

"That sounds complicated."

"You have no idea, but I hope you meet her someday."

"Which one?"

"Rayne. Her name is Rayne."

Hanna agreed that she'd like that too, and they drove back the remaining way holding hands. Dinner was wonderful, and Grace ascended to her former room afterward. She looked around it from the doorway. It was like viewing a former life. She strode to the window and pulled the curtains wide. *Let them know that I'm not afraid*, she told herself.

"You've ruffled a lot of feathers," Sara told her in her ear.

"I missed you," Grace told her. "And ruffling feathers was the whole idea of my returning home so publicly, especially on the heels of what happened with Holly – to flush the monsters out of the dark places they hide in."

"You're a brave girl," Sara commended her. "And, ironically, it's the reverse that has told me the most. Your return has set the village abuzz with gossip. It's virtually awash in movement."

"They do love gossip," Grace agreed.

"But some people are suspiciously *less* active than usual. It points to their converging in their dark places to discuss the significance of your return. The negative information is as valuable as the positive."

"I'm playing a dangerous game, aren't I?"

"You are, but I'm on your team," Sara reminded her.

"It's the one thing I still thank God for," Grace admitted.

The next day was Saturday, and because there was no school, Grace asked Hanna to invite Abi over, who was still emotionally crushed by her friend Holly's supposed demise in the jaws of a bear. "Tell her that I miss her sister, so I'd like to see her," Grace explained.

Hanna was only too happy to show Abi the buggy to cheer her up.

Grace found them in the living room, drawing. "I heard about Holly," Grace told her.

Abi stilled. She was used to people avoiding the subject altogether and certainly not speaking Holly's name aloud. "It's tragic," she replied.

"I don't think Jenna would have let anything tragic happen to Holly," Grace confided and left her wondering and with a renewed ember of hope. She joined her mother in the kitchen.

"Giving her false hope is not a kindness," her mother chastised her.

"I found hope in miraculous places. Perhaps she will too. She lost her sister and her best friend – she deserves some hope."

"What happened to Jenna and Holly aren't the same," her mother pointed out.

"That's true, but not the way you think," Grace replied obtusely.

Her mother marveled at how much the girl who had returned to her had changed since she'd left. "Tomorrow's Sunday. I understand if you don't want to go to church with us, with your recent loss of faith and all."

"Mom, I didn't 'lose' my faith – it was ripped from me, but no, I'd like to go to church with you. I want to say a prayer for my guardian angel."

Grace's mother didn't know how to interpret her daughter, except at face value, so she agreed, hoping that understanding would come in time.

"Are you sure that's a good idea – going to church?" Sara asked when Grace was out picking wildflowers for her room.

"If we're going to poke the lion, what better place than in its den?"

"I couldn't agree more, but watch yourself."

"That's what I have you for."

Sunday came, and Grace insisted that they go to church early so she could have a moment to pray before the service. Her parents gladly consented and left her alone to approach an arrangement of candles. Grace knelt before it and lit one.

"Rayne, wherever you are, I hope you find the happiness you deserve. Amen," she murmured. She rose and directed her family to join her in the front pew, where she'd have an unimpeded view of Father Morgan.

The Father did his best to avoid eye contact during the service but had no choice but to thank the Lord for returning Grace to the community. A momentarily unguarded look confirmed that he was not thankful at all, and Grace made sure to smile beatifically at him in response. To his credit, he did not stumble while delivering the sermon, but it was shorter than usual, and Grace was all too happy to get up to leave. She made sure to smile at everyone that Sara had identified on her list of suspects.

Grace had to file past Father Morgan on her way out, and despite every ounce of her self-control, he still made her skin crawl when he laid a hand on her arm and told her how happy he was to have her back. His touch burned like fire, but Grace held her arm steady. *Don't let him see you rattled*, she commanded herself. She could tell by the look in his eyes that if he had his way, her stay in the village would neither be long nor pleasant.

Walking home, a pair of men on horseback burst out of the roadway and rode hard toward Grace and her family. Gabriel reared his mount to a stop in front of them and quickly dismounted.

"I came as soon as I heard you'd returned," he greeted her breathlessly.

Grace's father placed a protective hand on her shoulder, but Grace squeezed it to let him know that she was all right.

"I was hoping to see you," she told Gabriel. "Come with me," she added, and ignoring the impropriety of it, began walking toward an adjacent field.

At a loss to know how to respond but having been put on the spot, Gabriel followed her at a respectful distance while his companion led their horses away. Grace's father kept watch.

Grace sat down cross-legged in the middle of the field, away from prying ears, and waited for Gabriel to sit down across from her.

"Where's Jenna?" she asked him pointedly.

He looked confused. "I assumed she'd be here. The video…," he began.

"Jenna is dead, Gabriel. If you've ever cared for me or about what's right, I need you to open your goddamn eyes." She rose abruptly and left him stunned. He was still sitting there when Grace closed her kitchen door.

"The dark ones have all scurried into their hidey-holes," Sara informed her. "It doesn't look good."

"On the contrary," Grace replied, "I'm going to be Angela's proof."

Chapter 25

Triste

Triste screamed herself hoarse as her body went through accelerated withdrawal. She gripped Rayne's hand like a lifeline.

"Kill me, please," she begged. "It hurts so much."

Rayne shushed her and dabbed the sweat off her forehead. Triste passed out, and Rayne called in a passing doctor.

"Is she going to be okay?" Rayne asked her.

"Hopefully," the doctor replied.

"Hopefully? That's the best you've got? What did you do to her?"

"*We* didn't do anything. It's nanotech battling it out with the poisons in her body. We only ever see cases in which nanotech is already in the body, minimizing the harm done by drugs like the ones that Triste has taken. We've never seen it used as a detox, especially with the degree of entrenchment of the drugs in Triste's system. The nanotech is particularly aggressive and brutal."

"Then stop it."

"We probably couldn't, even if we wanted to, and I'm not sure we'd want to interrupt it in the middle of its work. It's rewiring her brain, among other things. I wouldn't want to interfere with that."

"It's killing her," Rayne pleaded.

"She's been doing that to herself all along. If the nanotech is doing anything, it's just speeding up the process. But, if it *does* work, it should remove her addiction. If we want her with us for the long run, that's our best hope. Besides, I have my suspicions as to where the nanotech came from, and if I'm right, it is the best stuff in existence."

Triste moaned, and Rayne turned her attention back to her. The war in Triste's body went on for days with no hint toward the outcome. Rayne only got 5-minute breaks and was well past her breaking point both physically and emotionally.

"Rayne?" Triste murmured uncertainly, lucidity returning at last.

"I'm here," Rayne confirmed.

"You stayed? I pushed you away, but you came back, and you stayed. I'm so ashamed."

"You needn't be. We all have demons."

"Not like mine," Triste countered, turning away.

"You've banished them. They're gone, and you're still here. You're the one that came back." Rayne rose stiffly from her chair. "Move over. Stop hogging the bed."

"Rayne, I'm all sweaty and gross,"

"You're beautiful to me, and I'm too tired to care how gross you are." Rayne nestled in beside her, intertwining their fingers.

"Thank you," Triste told her.

"I'm glad you're back," Rayne replied and slipped into an unconsciousness that she could no longer hold back.

Rayne woke alone in a bed of her own, disoriented as to how she'd gotten there. She felt clean and found herself wearing a hospital gown, her own clothes freshly laundered and sitting on a chair at the foot of her bed. An orderly pushed Triste into the room in a wheelchair.

"They told me you were waking up," she explained and thanked the porter as the woman left them alone. "I smell better," she joked and rolled close enough to take Rayne's hand. "What are we doing here?" she asked. "I sure as hell can't afford this place, and no one I know cares enough about me to send me here, except maybe you, and I know you can't afford this place either, no offense."

"Elana. Elana cares."

Triste mulled it over. "Elana doesn't give two figs about me, and I wouldn't deserve it if she did. No, I'm here because Elana cares about you."

"Elana is an angel."

"But there's a 'but.'"

"There's no 'but.' I love Elana."

"You do, and you don't – trust me, I'm the queen of conflicted emotions." The realization hit her – "You found someone," she concluded.

Rayne hesitated to respond.

"Don't get me wrong. I'm happy for you. You deserve someone amazing, far more than you do a wreck like me, and don't waste your time trying to convince me otherwise – you came back for me, and that's all the proof I'll ever need." Triste squeezed Rayne's hand. "They tell me there's a garden on the roof. Will you take me there?"

"Of course," she replied, getting out of bed, but the cold draft on her bare back making her reconsider. "I'm going to put some clothes on first, though," she declared.

Rayne wheeled Triste off the elevator, through a door, and out into the rooftop garden. New York was true to form, and clouds hung in the sky, but the pungent scent of the garden's mosses filled Rayne's nostrils, and it soothed her.

"I fell from the sky onto a place like this once," she told Triste.

"I'm glad I'm here with you now," Triste replied. They moved along the path to a pleasant patch of grass, where Triste handed Rayne a blanket to spread out. "Ahem," she reminded Rayne when she was done. "I can't lift myself."

Rayne scooped her into her arms, something she'd done a dozen times, every time she'd found Triste passed out and carried her to bed. Their eyes locked, and Triste knew what Rayne was thinking. Her shame demanded that she look away, but her yearning refused. Rayne shifted Triste's weight, which broke the tension, and laid her down on the blanket, settling in beside her.

Triste intertwined their fingers and stared at the sky. "I used to look up at the clouds and think, 'the future is murky,' but it feels brighter today."

Rayne placed her head on Triste's chest.

Triste stroked her hair. "So, this is what goodbye feels like," she mused.

"And hello," Rayne countered and contented herself with their nearness.

Later in the day, Rayne left the hospital, secure in the knowledge that for the first time in her life, Triste was going to be okay. Elana's car was parked out front, and the rear door opened. Rayne slid in but found herself alone.

"Where's Grace?" she asked Sara.

"She went back to the village," Sara informed her.

"Alone? Oh God. Can you take me there?"

"Not in this car – it isn't safe for country driving, and Grace has the buggy, but I have an idea. How'd you like to take the tank?"

Chapter 26

Grace

"The jackals are circling," Sara informed Grace.

"Let them come," she replied. "I'm ready."

A knock on the door downstairs startled Grace regardless.

"Father Morgan has come calling," Sara informed her.

"It seems that I've caught the attention of the devil himself," Grace mused as she heard her father greet him, more warily than she would have imagined. She rose from her seat to go speak with Father Morgan.

Her father noted her arrival. "It's Father Morgan," he told her, looking for cues that would tell him if she wasn't up to company.

"It is always a pleasure," she lied glibly. "Can I make you gentlemen coffee? I've become quite enamored with it myself."

"Well, it is after noon, but coffee does sound nice," Father Morgan agreed.

"Let's just hope it doesn't have you up prowling around all night," Grace joked. She squeezed past the men to enter the kitchen while they proceeded to the living room. They made small talk while Grace made coffee.

"He's here to find out who you've told about the village, to assess the risk," Sara opined.

"That's what I was thinking."

"It's a fine line. You don't want to give him the confidence to continue his evil, but at the same time, you don't want to give him cause to act rashly – I'm not sure how he'd react then. Your best bet is to simply keep him guessing."

"I think I can keep him off balance."

"That's my girl. Now, go get'em," Sara cheered her on as Grace emerged into the living room with three cups on a tray, with sugar, milk, and cream.

"I wasn't sure how you like it," Grace apologized to the Father. "Dark or sweet, or dark and sweet, I suppose." She placed the tray down in front of Father Morgan, took her own cup and her father's, and went to sit beside him – more to make him feel better than herself. She sat back, crossed her legs, and took a tentative sip. "What can I do for you, Father?" she asked innocently.

"I have some questions, mostly about how you're doing, but also about the goings-on of the outside world. We do so seldom leave our little village."

"I'm happy to oblige. The village can feel pretty confining," she agreed.

"May I ask why you left in the first place?"

Grace put her cup down. "It's going to sound silly, but I was in a dark place after Jenna just up and vanished. We were as close as sisters. The night of the fire, I woke from a nightmare to screaming, and I panicked. With the flames and the yelling, it felt like hell had invaded our village. I know it sounds farfetched sitting in the comfort of our living room now, but I was terrified, so I hopped on a horse, and I rode away as fast as I could."

279

"We called to you," he stated.

"I couldn't tell friend from foe in the state I was in. In the light of the flames, they all looked the same to me." She shuddered.

The Father eyed her skeptically over the lip of his mug. "And what did you do when your wits returned to you, child?"

"My father might argue that I never had any in the first place," she joked, placing a hand warmly on his arm. Without giving him time to object to her self-deprecation, she continued, "I fell off the horse. I'd never thought to saddle it, and as it was the middle of the night, the movement lulled me to sleep, and eventually I just slid off. When I got to my feet, I couldn't tell which way led back to the village and which way led away from it. Judging from the direction the horse was facing, I guessed, and I guessed wrong."

"We found the horse a considerable distance from the village."

"I had no idea – I slept so soundly, but it does explain why the horse refused to budge. It must have been tired from the long walk."

"So why didn't you just stay with the horse and await rescue?"

"Terrible judgment?" she joked. "I waited at first, but I became so hungry that I gave up and headed off in the direction that I thought would bring me to safety."

"That does explain a few things," the Father noted. "We were worried that something had become of you."

"I was worried something would become of me, too," Grace agreed. "The woods terrified me – so many hidden threats. When a bus full of people stopped on the road and offered to rescue me from my predicament, I didn't know what to do, and they were so kind."

"So that's how you made it to Mekka? However did you survive there? I hate to admit it, but we don't really prepare our young ladies for the outside world."

"I did feel a lot like a lamb to the slaughter. Luckily, I met some wonderful people who took me under their wing."

"How fortunate for you."

"Truly."

"Did you run across your sixth?"

"My sixth? I don't understand. I've never met my sixth."

"That's a pity. Rumors were that she headed to Mekka when she left the village."

"Mekka was so overwhelming. I can't imagine she'd have liked it there."

"So, why did you stay there so long, then?"

"I had no way back and no one to show me the way. I was stranded."

"But Gabriel found you, and you didn't return with him." He leaned forward with mock concern, his eyes skewering her.

This was the question that she'd dreaded the most, as it was the hardest to deflect.

"I tried, but he left without me."

Father Morgan looked confused, unsure whether he'd caught her in a lie.

"He showed me a video of Jenna, and it brought back so many feelings. I thought she'd abandoned me forever. I needed time to think." She did her best to seem like a hysterical young girl.

"So, you left Mekka?"

"No. I ran away to be alone with my thoughts, but I didn't leave Mekka. When I went back to meet Gabriel, he was gone. I asked around, and a woman at the bus station said he left."

"Your friend told him that *you'd* left."

"She was right in a way, but not in the way Gabriel thought," she explained. "Still, it was kind of him to look for me. He wasn't with a chaperone, though, and that did make me a little uncomfortable."

"Surrounded by all those people?" the Father asked, incredulous.

"They were strangers, and besides, I was never promised to any of them like I was to him." Grace put her hands on her knees in a show of propriety.

The father shook his head, trying to reconcile all of the conflicting information he was receiving. "So, if you missed Gabriel, how did you find your way home?"

"I met a woman who is *literally* an angel. I described my village to her, and she loaned me her car to go looking for it. It drives itself," she whispered, as if afraid to wake it. "And that's how I came to be sitting right here in front of you, no worse for wear," she concluded.

"That's an amazing story," he concluded, eyes narrowing.

"I have a question," Grace said.

"Yes, child?"

"Where's Jenna? She said in her message that she was home. I rushed straight here, but her sister tells me that she never returned."

"Jenna must have misspoken. She's still with her aunt."

"That's too bad. I do miss her terribly. Do you have a way of contacting her? I'd love to talk with her again. I figure that if her aunt was able to get ahold of her, we must be able to get ahold of her aunt."

"I'll look into it, child, but Jenna's probably quite busy."

"Doing God's work?"

"Precisely."

"That's a pity. I have to admit that in all that's happened, I've had a crisis of faith. I'm not sure what I believe anymore."

"The outside world will do that to you. That's why we stay in our little village. It keeps us closer to God."

"Perhaps if I live to a ripe old age, I will come to agree with you."

Father Morgan got up to leave. "I feel I've monopolized too much of your precious time already."

"Nonsense, Father. It's always a pleasure to see you."

"Will I see you again at church?"

"Most likely. I expect that it will help reveal the truth to my heart."

"That is God's way. Now, if you'll excuse me, I must be off."

"Do come anytime, just not too late, Father. My adventure has exhausted me thoroughly, and I need my sleep to recover."

"Of course, child. Good day."

Grace turned to her father after Father Morgan had left. "I *am* exhausted. Do you mind if I retire to my room to rest?"

"Of course, I don't mind. Mother will call you for dinner."

"Thank you, Daddy," she added and kissed his cheek before ascending to her room and closing herself inside.

"How do you think that went?" she asked Sara.

"I don't think he bought the airhead act, but you didn't reveal too much either. He knows you're playing chess with him."

"Only, I'm a pawn, and he controls the board."

"Perhaps, but we've still got tricks up our sleeves."

"I sure hope so. I'm getting tired of waiting for the trap to snap shut."

The next day, Father Morgan sent word that he wanted to meet with Grace again at the church to ask more questions about the fire the night she'd left.

"I don't see why that has anything to do with anything," her mother grumbled.

"Surely they don't think I had anything to do with that?" Grace protested.

"You can't go," Sara whispered in her ear. They only want to separate you from your family. Then, they can make up any story they want – 'You ran away again;' 'You were overcome with guilt and took your own life'…"

"We don't really have a choice," her father concluded.

Grace put an arm around him. "We always have a choice, but it's okay – I'll go."

"Stall until 5 o'clock," Sara begged her.

"However, I'm not feeling well. I think all this talk about the night of the fire has brought back some terrible memories. Can we send word to the Father that I will meet him at five?"

"It's not really proper to dictate the time," her own father told her, "But, I guess it couldn't hurt. I'll go tell him. You go up to your room and get some rest."

"I'll make you ginger tea," her mother offered.

"Thank you both."

At five o'clock, Grace had prepared herself for the worst and walked down from her room stoically.

"I'll walk you over," her father offered.

"That would be lovely," Grace accepted, and he surprised her by offering her his arm to lean on. She took it gratefully.

They were met at the church steps by two of its deacons.

"It's okay, Paul," they told Grace's father, stopping him. "The Father would like to see Grace alone."

"Whatever you do," Sara warned her. "Do *not* go inside. The tunnels lead there. If you go in, you'll never come out."

"You'll be with me the entire time?" she asked.

Grace's father took that as his cue to protest leaving his daughter, while Sara whispered her response, "Yes, I'll be with you."

"Then tell Angela everything that happens," Grace told her and readied herself to meet her doom with whatever courage she could muster.

"Tell her yourself," Sara told her and was drowned out by a distant rumbling. As one person, they looked upward at the clear sky for an approaching storm. "Here comes the cavalry," Sara added as Elana's tank rumbled into view. No one moved.

The tank advanced until its barrel pointed at the church doors. The engine cut, and the hatch popped open, followed by a mane of bright blue hair.

"Rayne!" Grace shrieked. "You came."

"Of course, I came," Rayne replied and clambered down the tank to sweep Grace into an embrace.

The two deacons took a step forward, and Rayne raised a warning finger. The barrel of the tank angled downward toward them.

"Grace isn't taking questions today," she announced, spun her around, and marched her home with her bewildered father in tow, leaving the tank pointing at the church.

"Subtle," Grace chided her, squeezing her tightly around the waist. Grace held open the kitchen door to let her father enter before she and Rayne did. She faced her stunned parents.

"Mom and Dad, I'd like you to meet my…"

"Girlfriend," Rayne finished for her. "I'm Rayne, and I'm pleased to meet you both." She held out her hand and shook both of theirs, then turned to scold Grace. "Don't you *ever* run away on me again," she told her, then leaned in to kiss her passionately before she could answer.

286

Grace melted into the kiss, then remembered her parents and pulled away self-consciously.

Her mother was momentarily stunned but recovered quickly. "We're so happy for you," she told her, beaming. "Where's Hanna? She'll want to meet Rayne."

"Where *is* Hanna?" Grace repeated. "School's long done. Sara?"

Sara paused the briefest of instances before responding, "She's gone."

Chapter 27

Grace

Grace was beside herself with worry for her little sister. Her parents were also worried, but not knowing what she knew, they didn't share Grace's bone-chilling terror at what might have befallen her.

A knock sounded at the door, and Grace's father waved her back down as he got up to answer it. He returned a moment later with a note dropped off by an altar boy.

"It's addressed to you, Grace," he told her, holding it up for her to see.

"Please read it out," Grace requested, too emotionally fragile to handle anything that the Father had touched. Rayne held Grace's hand, already guessing what the note would say.

Grace's father unfolded it and began to relay its contents, "Dear Grace, I'm disappointed that you were unable to meet with me today regarding the pressing matter of the fire."

Pressing, my ass, Grace thought.

Her father continued, "Kindly come as soon as you are able so that we can put the matter to rest. It has also come to my attention that your sister has gone missing. Let's get the matter of the fire squared away quickly so that we can turn our full attention to finding Hanna and having her safely returned. Kind regards, Father Morgan."

"It's a thinly-veiled threat and an offer of exchange – Grace for Hanna," Rayne concluded into the silence that followed the reading of the note.

"Well, then that's what we'll give them," Grace replied resolutely, preparing to rise.

Rayne restrained her. "There's no chance in hell that we're complying with that."

Grace gave her a look that said it was not up for discussion.

"Think about it, Grace," Rayne begged her. "They've taken Hanna, and you think they'll just let her go when you show up? They're already going to have to fabricate a reason for your upcoming disappearance, but how do you think they'll explain away Hanna's abduction? I'm sorry to be the one to say this, but they have no intention of returning Hanna, *ever*, whether you walk into their trap or you don't."

Grace's mother was horrified, and Grace's father wrapped her in his arms to comfort her.

"We have to get Hanna back, then," he concluded, rising to go procure his axe.

Grace stopped him. "She'll be well hidden," she told him, thinking about the tunnels with a shudder. "You'll never find her."

"I will not stand idly by with my daughter in their clutches," he countered.

"I'm not suggesting that," Grace replied, "I'm just saying that we have to get her back on *our* terms, not theirs."

"How do you propose we do that?" Rayne asked.

"I'm going in," she replied flatly.

"I thought we agreed…" Rayne began.

"I'm not going in the front door," Grace explained. "Stall them as long as you can to give me time to find Hanna."

"Why you?" Rayne challenged her. "I'm less valuable to them. I should be the one to go hunting for Hanna."

Grace patted her arm. "It's kind of you to offer, but I know this village with my eyes closed. You wouldn't know the bakery from the smithy. If someone is to navigate it underground, it has to be me."

"Underground?" her father asked, surprised.

"The village is crisscrossed with tunnels. Vermin like their warrens."

"I'll go," Grace's father volunteered.

"I need you here for my plan to work," Grace responded, "and we need to move fast." She turned to Rayne. "Do you still have those wigs and maybe some spare clothes?"

"In my bag, in the tank," she replied.

"Great. Please go get them, and while you're at the church, ask the deacons to send back the altar boy to relay a message."

"Deacons?"

"The men at the church."

"Okay, got it," Rayne replied and hurried out. She relayed Grace's message, grabbed her bag, and rushed back.

"Thanks," Grace told her as she pulled on the blue wig. "I'm you, and you're me. I've got to get out of here without them suspecting if

I'm to have a hope of finding Hanna. You've got to make them think I haven't gone anywhere."

She turned to her father. "And that's why I need you here at Rayne's side, so they don't think I'm alone and come for me/Rayne."

Her father looked conflicted, so she took his hands in hers.

"Rayne is part of me, the better part, in fact. Keeping her safe is keeping me safe. Do you understand?"

"We understand," Grace's mother interjected. "What do we tell the altar boy when he returns?"

"Tell him anything that buys me time. Sara, I need a map of the tunnels," Grace added to the air.

"Who's Sara?" her mother asked, looking around.

"She's the right hand of the goddess," Rayne explained, "and she keeps us safe."

"The printer is back at the camp," Sara informed Grace in her ear.

"Then, that's where we go first," Grace concluded, pulling on some of Rayne's clothes that she thought would best fit her, completely ignoring propriety. "How do I look?" she asked Rayne.

"Brave," she replied and hugged her tightly.

Grace hugged her back and flew out the door, almost knocking the startled altar boy on his ass.

"Out of my way, imbecile," she chastised him, hopped into the buggy, and tore away, showering him in a spray of gravel that forced him to duck and cower.

Grace's mother helped Rayne change to look like Grace, while Grace's father bade the boy wait while "Grace" composed a message.

Grace's mother grabbed a pen and paper, calmed herself, and began jotting down a note – "Dear Father, I regret missing our meeting. The safe return of my sister is my strongest wish. My family and I are going to pray for her. I will come to you at the earliest opportunity. Regards, Grace."

She sent the boy off to relay the message, ensuring that he'd gotten a glimpse of "Grace" before departing.

Meanwhile, the buggy screeched to a halt at the campsite. Grace jumped out and started changing into night camouflage gear while Sara rattled off a list of items for her to bring.

"The map of the tunnels is on the printer," Sara told her. "It's my best guess based on hierarchy, proximity, and geology."

"Thank you. Can you guide me to the nearest entrance?"

"The nearest is not necessarily the best, but I'll guide you."

Grace tore off through the trees toward the village with Sara directing her. She only stopped when she arrived at the tree line, lungs burning.

"The closest entrance will be in Father Michael's cottage," Sara told her, "and I'm 94% certain that he's not home."

"That's good enough for me," Grace replied, sprinting across the field and launching herself at his door, which exploded inward, the remnants of its latch in splinters. She looked around. "You're right – he's not home. Now, where would I find the entrance to the tunnels?"

"He likely left by it, so I doubt it'll be covered up. Start by checking the closets."

Grace came up empty and sat on the Father's bed to think, staring at the oversized shrine to a young Virgin Mary at the foot of it. *That's wrong on so many levels*, she thought and rose to check it out. She quickly gave up searching for an opening and just kicked in the front panel. It broke inward to reveal a narrow corridor that angled downward. *Ah-ha!* Grace pulled the panel out and made her way, hunched over, down into the earth.

Sara instructed her which flashlight setting would be sufficient to see by but not shine too far ahead. The earthy air filled her lungs, reminiscent of a freshly dug grave. The narrow walls hemmed her in, and she imagined them pushing against her until she couldn't breathe. She began to hyperventilate.

"Stay calm. You're doing great," Sara reassured her.

Grace centered herself by visualizing where she'd be if she were above ground. *Under the old barn*, she told herself. *Passing the chicken coop…*

A tunnel to the right unexpectedly intersected hers.

"Ignore it," Sara suggested. "We need to get to the center of the web before we explore any of its branches.

Grace resumed her visualization. "We're nearing the school, aren't we?" she whispered.

"It's pretty well the hub," Sara confirmed. Grace began to hear the faint sound of high-pitched voices, so she moved even more quietly as she approached them. A staircase led upwards, and she followed it to find herself behind a wall with peepholes through which she could see a classroom. Children sat at their desks, talking amongst themselves while their teacher was out of the room. *No wonder I hated school*, she thought and returned to the tunnels below.

"They'd never keep your sister near here," Sara surmised. "Take the tunnel on the left. It heads toward the church – that would be more secluded."

Grace did as she was instructed, and the walls grew damp as she progressed. She couldn't shake the feeling that she was passing through some giant beast's intestines, slowly being digested. She pushed down the bile rising in her throat. She passed a series of tiny rooms, whose purpose wasn't apparent, except for the faint smell of iron hanging in the air. She heard movement coming toward her from the tunnel ahead and panicked.

"Go back to one of the side rooms," Sara suggested, and Grace hurriedly complied. She ducked into one, shut off her flashlight, and pressed herself into the corner beside the entrance. The room was too small to hide her completely, but she was dressed in black and hiding in the dark. She prayed that it would be enough.

A light approached, bouncing off the tunnel walls. The cold rock chilled her back as she willed herself to become part of the wall. The light swept into the room, lancing across her midsection, but carried on down the tunnel without stopping.

Grace exhaled her relief and switched her feeble light back on. She took a step forward, crushing something brittle below her heel. She froze, hoping that the sound would not draw whoever had passed by, but judging that she had no time to wait and see, and in any event would not want to be trapped in the tiny room. She looked both ways, then quickly continued on in the direction that she'd been headed.

"It's a good sign to have crossed paths with someone coming from this direction," Sara reassured her.

"It's luck that I could do without," Grace whispered back. Up ahead, she began to make out the faint glow of a stationary lantern. She could smell the burning oil and felt the tendrils of smoke invade her lungs. *This is hell, alright*, she concluded and inched forward.

Sara instructed her to fish out a tiny mirror on a stick and angle it around the corner. She saw two robed men guarding a cell. Her heart leaped when she spied her sister between the bars, perched fearfully on the edge of a cot. Grace slid the mirror away and pulled out a pair of tasers, one for each hand. She readied herself and stepped around the corner, whispering loudly, "I don't know… maybe this way."

The startled men looked past her to see who she was talking to, and she fired the tasers into each man's chest. They stood writhing.

"Is there a maximum setting on these things?" Grace asked Sara.

"Squeeze the trigger harder," Sara informed her.

Grace followed her instructions, and in a puff of acrid-smelling smoke, the men collapsed to the ground, clearing her path to the cell.

"I knew you'd come," Hanna told her with a confidence that stabbed at Grace's heart.

"I'm going to get you out," she told her, examining the padlock.

"The other man took the key," Hanna told her.

"We've got explosives," Sara informed Grace.

"Is that such a good idea underground, especially when we're trying to be quiet?"

"We don't have time for the laser."

"We have a laser?!"

"Wedge the stuff that feels like playdough into the keyhole and stick the thing that looks like a silver match into it. Tell your sister to lean the mattress against the door and move as far back as she can. Do you think you can lift the smaller man to his feet and prop him against the door?"

"I'll do anything you tell me to," Grace agreed and struggled to heave the man's unconscious body to his feet. She had to lean into him to hold him in place. "Is this such a good idea?" Grace asked.

"No, but it'll muffle the blast. Cover your ears."

Grace did the best she could and told her sister to do the same. Muffled or not, the blast blew Grace against the far wall, and her head swam from the disorientation caused by the explosion. She commanded herself to get herself together and stumbled forward to collect her sister. She stepped on the second guard's hand, and he moaned. Grace panicked and kicked him hard in the face with the steel-toed boots that Sara had insisted she wear. *Sorry, not sorry*, she thought as she stepped forward to move the remains of the other guard out of the way. He was missing a spinal column.

Hanna pushed the ruined door open and hugged her sister.

"No chance they didn't hear that, is there?" Grace asked Sara.

"No chance at all. Run!"

Grace grabbed Hanna's wrist and tore off down the corridor. The thick black smoke from the ruined lantern began to fill the space, and Grace and her sister choked on it as they struggled for breath.

Grace heard movement all around her, but the tunnels echoed the faintest sound, and she couldn't be sure if her pursuers were ahead of her or behind her.

"Take the next left," Sara ordered her. "We're taking the first exit out of here, and I'm having the tank open the door."

Grace didn't ask any questions and just ran for her life. A deafening crash stopped her in her tracks, and a shaft of light lanced downward up ahead.

"Run for the light," Sara ordered her, and Grace pulled her sister along behind her. She tripped over fallen rocks and sprawled along the ground. Hanna fell on top of her, and Grace had to help her get back to her feet. The tunnel threatened to collapse around them, having been compromised by the weight of the tank. Grace led them to a rickety staircase that they climbed up into the shaft of light. They emerged into the blinding light of day surrounded by the ruins of a cottage, the tank idling off to the side.

"You opened the door pretty wide," Grace quipped.

"The place needed redecorating anyway," Sara replied. "Run for the tree line. The buggy is on its way."

Grace and Hanna ran as fast as they could, only realizing the extent of their injuries as their muscles rebelled.

The armored buggy roared across the field, skidding around them in a wide circle and coming to a halt facing back the way they'd run. The doors swung open, and Grace caught the end of the car's status report. "Gatling gun engaged, missile systems engaged…" The buggy idled menacingly while Grace lifted her sister into it and secured her harness.

"Take her to Astrid," Grace ordered Sara.

Hanna struggled to free herself from her harness. "You're not coming?"

"I will *always* come for you," she assured her. "Now go," she ordered the car, and it hammered through the village toward the one road out of it, its collision avoidance system clearly turned off.

Grace wiped the blood off her forehead and began limping back toward her home.

Father Morgan and three church Elders brandishing rifles strode from behind a building and blocked her path. Father Morgan glanced at the ruins of his home and was too incensed to speak.

Grace continued her advance until she was thirty paces from them. The two men flanking Father Morgan leveled their barrels at her, and flashes of light momentarily blinded them as a red dot settled on each of their foreheads. Four drones hurtled earthward and settled into formation around Grace.

The Elders looked to Father Morgan for guidance, noting the dot on his forehead too.

"It looks like we have a standoff," Father Morgan declared.

"Just try me," Grace replied, "and I'll paint the village with whatever blackness swirls inside your skull."

His lip twitched upward in a sneer, but he bade his men lower their weapons and stormed off with them following close behind.

Rayne rushed up and moved to support Grace's weight under her arm. Grace's father hurried over to help her on the other side. Together, they made their way back to their house.

"I kind of exploded myself," Grace admitted with a laugh that quickly turned into a stabbing pain.

They helped Grace to a chair, and Rayne checked her over more thoroughly for deeper injuries, efficiently bandaging the wounds where needed.

"Where did you learn battlefield medicine?" Grace's mother asked Rayne.

"A mentor," she replied obtusely, then leaned back, concluding, "You're okay."

"Hanna is okay," Grace added for her mother's benefit.

"I assumed that when that car of yours tore out of here," her mother replied. "Are we in danger?" she asked.

"Not imminently," Rayne replied. "I doubt that Father Morgan will come at us head-on so long as we have the tank, but an animal is always at its most dangerous when it's backed into a corner."

Chapter 28

Rayne

Sara found a moment when Rayne was alone so she could ask her to intervene with Grace. "I have enough evidence now that I'm sure Detective Angela would come if I contacted her," Sara told her, "but Grace won't let me. She thinks that the stalemate she has with Father Morgan will keep him in check, but men like him are slippery. I think that deep down inside, she's afraid that the Population Police will penalize her parents for having both her and Hanna. And by 'penalize,' I mean 'execute.' *I* think the police would be more interested in stopping the source of the village having multiple children, and that's the church. Can you talk to her?"

"She's not wrong to distrust the police," Rayne replied. "I've seen their blatant lack of humanity on several occasions."

"I think Angela is different," Sara countered.

"I don't think Grace is willing to gamble with her parents' lives in order to find out."

"Please think about it, at least," Sara requested.

"I think of little else," Rayne assured her. She was slowly growing stir-crazy, trapped in Grace's house. She moved between the windows, trying to gauge what was happening outside. Things had quieted down slightly after the recent mayhem, but an unusual degree of movement caught her attention.

"Something's going on," she reported.

"Father Morgan appears to have called a town meeting," Sara confirmed.

"I'm going to check it out," Rayne announced, tired of her confinement.

"I'm not sure that's a good idea," Grace protested, emerging from the kitchen with her mother.

"I'll keep an eye on her," Sara assured her.

It wasn't that Grace didn't trust Sara's ability to keep Rayne safe – she just didn't feel comfortable with her outside in the hostile environment that Father Morgan had created.

"I'll be fine," Rayne assured her and slipped out. She took an indirect route to the church, where Father Morgan was speaking to the villagers from its steps, and she leaned against a building where she could hear him but not be seen.

"We're under attack," was the first thing Rayne heard Father Morgan telling the crowd. "We were so righteous that the Devil couldn't stand it. He climbed up from the Abyss to tear us from our God, but we will stand firm in our devotion."

Blah, blah, blah, Rayne thought.

"The Lee family has been corrupted," Father Morgan continued.

I can tell where this bullshit is going, Rayne thought and stepped out from her hiding spot.

"Speak of the Devil, and He appears," Father Morgan declared, leveling a finger at Rayne's approach.

"I'm a 'she,' thank you very much," Rayne pointed out.

"The devil takes many forms, even those pleasing to the eye," the Father warned his congregation.

"That's so nice of you. If I didn't know better, I'd think you were trying to flirt with me, a bit awkwardly, mind you, but nevertheless. Now, cut the bullshit – the Lee Family are the sweetest people in creation."

"That's why you were drawn to them, you Beast."

"Well, I sure as hell wasn't drawn to you."

"She swears on Hell," he told the crowd accusingly.

"Your construct, not mine," Rayne replied. "Personally, I don't see the need for a hell when you seem to be doing just fine creating your own right here."

"Don't let her fool you," he told the crowd, "The blue-haired demon is stalking us. We must stand together."

"Am I a devil or a demon?" Rayne asked impatiently, "I'm losing track."

"The Devil can never completely hide its form," the Father continued, gesturing to her hair.

"Oh, I get it – the Devil is always someone different. The Devil has blue hair. The Devil is a woman. The Devil speaks her mind..."

"You took your true form – that of a beast – when you took the child. You wore that form when you tore Brother Ezekiel's spine from his body. Your touch left burns. We've seen it." Several heads nodded.

"That's news to me, but I'll have you know, Holly's fine – a bit scarred emotionally, thanks to you, but she's fine."

The crowd gasped at the confirmation that Rayne knew who Holly was. Only Rayne saw the Father's momentary look of surprise and narrowed eyes. *I guess I walked into that one*, she thought.

"And now you've taken Hanna as well. Prove me wrong, show us Hanna Lee," he challenged her.

"The Devil sure seems to have a thing for children, it seems, but they've been disappearing here long before I ever arrived. Where's Jenna, Father Morgan? Where are Juliette, Tabitha, Lydia, Danica, and all the rest?"

"They're off doing God's work."

"How very convenient for you. And God's work is so important that they could never come back to visit? Not even for a day?"

"God's work *is* important."

"Careful, Father. Pride is a sin, and so is deception, and so is murder, and God knows what else you're guilty of. If there is a God, and I doubt there is, if you're any indication, then there's no pit in hell deep enough for you."

"You heard her – she denied God. She's a denier."

"Nice distraction, Father, and I've been called a great many things... orphan, slut... I've learned that when you want to attack something, you start by labeling it."

"So, you admit that you have many names?"

"Oh, for God's sake, that's your takeaway? Jesus."

"Leave our village!" He waved his men forward, and a drone dropped out of the sky to hover protectively over Rayne.

The Father pointed at it accusingly. "You bring with you tools of destruction to attack our way of life – to separate us from our God. We shun the outside world for that very reason – to stay close to Him. And now you ascend to break that bond."

"I came to your shithole town for one reason and one reason only," Rayne countered, and the crowd quieted to hear it. "I love Grace Lee. And she came back because she loved Jenna Miller. She came back to protect the children." Rayne turned to the crowd. "You're all willfully blind, but you know in your hearts that the children of this village need protection."

"The Devil has a silver tongue," Father Morgan cut her off.

"That he does," Rayne agreed. "You can stand there all day, twisting everything to fit your gospel, but at the end of the day, Jenna's not here, Juliette's not here, neither are Tabitha and Danica. It's time for everyone to pull the wool from their eyes and see who the Devil really is."

Grace's fifth, Esther, took her husband's hand and pulled him from the crowd. Gabriel pushed forward and stood at Rayne's side.

"I stand with Grace," he told the crowd.

"That girl has Grace in her thrall," Father Morgan accused Rayne.

"She has me in hers," Rayne corrected him.

Father Morgan could feel loyalties shifting. "We must pray!" he concluded. "Go home and pray to God for the strength to resist the Devil." He turned and entered the church as the crowd dispersed.

Rayne turned to Gabriel. "Sorry about slapping you back in Mekka."

"I probably deserved it," he replied good-naturedly.

"That's it. I've called Angela," Sara informed Rayne. "I'm sorry, but things are falling apart quickly, and Father Morgan is not going to go down quietly."

"Sara, what have you done?" Rayne muttered and hurried back to Grace's house with Gabriel following close behind.

She burst through the kitchen door. "That didn't go terribly well," she informed Grace and her parents. "A storm is brewing. Oh, and Gabriel had a change of heart."

Grace stepped forward and embraced him. "Thank you," she whispered in his ear and kissed his cheek. Gabriel reddened but relaxed in her arms.

"There's more," Rayne pointed out.

Grace and her family waited for her to say what it was.

"Sara, it's your doing. You tell her."

"Angela is coming," she told Grace.

Chapter 29

Angela

Esther and Norm came calling the next morning, carrying baskets of produce from their farm. Grace hurried out to help them with their load but embraced her fifth tightly first. Grace's mother invited them in for tea.

"The village is tearing itself apart," Esther warned them, "but it's a good thing. The cancer needs to be ripped out."

"I saw Violet," Grace admitted. "She's wonderful."

Esther took Grace's hands in hers. "I'm sorry I let you down."

"You nudged me out of the nest, and for that I will be forever grateful," Grace assured her.

A quiet knock on the door interrupted them, and Grace's father rose to answer it.

"It's Holly's mother," he announced, escorting a hesitant woman into the living room.

"What you said about Holly," she asked Rayne. "Is it true?"

"It is. I'm sorry we couldn't tell you. We were protecting her."

Holly's mother said nothing but wavered, the strength to stand leaving her. Grace's father caught her and led her to a chair, while Grace's mother poured her a glass of water.

"Can I see her?" she asked.

"It's not safe to bring her back here, but I'm sure we can find a way of bringing you to her."

Sara confirmed that she would make it happen.

Holly's mother tried to sip the water, but her hand was too unsteady. She put the glass down instead and rose. "I have to tell my husband. He's too afraid to hope." She stopped in the doorway and addressed Grace before leaving, "Thank you."

Mrs. Miller came calling next.

"I can't see her," Grace quailed. "I failed her daughter."

"You didn't know," Rayne assured her, but Grace couldn't stand the guilt and raced to her room to hide.

Grace's mother met Mrs. Miller at the door, although she politely refused the invitation to enter.

"Jenna?" she asked.

"I'm sorry," Grace's mother answered her.

"In my heart, I knew. I always knew," she mumbled, smiled her thanks wanly, and wandered home.

Esther and Norm stayed for dinner, and it heartened Grace that maybe, just maybe, the village could heal.

The next day was Sunday, and for the first time in Grace's memory, her family did not dress for church but sat around the breakfast table instead, giving thanks for each other. Even Rayne participated awkwardly, taking Hanna's spot at the table, although it put her between Grace's parents. She looked helplessly across the table at Grace.

"People are coming," Sara forewarned them, and a knock at the door gave Rayne the perfect excuse to extricate herself from the table.

"Who could it be?" Grace's mother mused. "It's time for church."

"It's Mrs. Miller," Sara informed Grace, "with her husband, and Juliette's parents, and Danica's, Miriam's, and others."

Grace rose from her seat, knowing that she could not hide any longer, and took over from Rayne at the door. She stepped outside to greet everyone.

Jenna's mother stepped forward and raised her hands to take Grace's.

"Jenna loved you too," she told her. "Thank you for looking out for her."

"I…," Grace began.

"For honoring her memory," Mrs. Miller interrupted. "Thank you." She squeezed Grace's hands. "We wanted to let you know that we're with you."

Grace looked out at the assembled faces, sad but resolute. It was not just the parents of the missing girls who had come – Grace saw families with young children, children who, God willing, would never go missing. Even the most devout among them had skipped church to show their support, making their allegiance plain.

"Do you smell smoke?" Rayne asked.

"Father Morgan has set the church on fire," Sara blurted in both their ears, "with the congregation inside!"

"To the church!" Grace shouted and raced toward it. They arrived to see the exits blocked by flames and people huddling inside. "Goddamn the bastard for trying to take everyone with him."

"Father Morgan is not inside," Sara informed her.

"The tunnels!" she realized.

"They'll have barred the entrance," Sara countered.

"Do we still have any 'playdough' left?" Grace asked as she raced home to grab her pack. "Guide me."

Rayne watched Grace sprint away but stayed to help her father throw buckets of water on the flames. Everyone joined in, but no matter how much water they threw, the fire would not abate. The thick black smoke choked their lungs, but they persisted, despite its being obvious that they were fighting a losing battle. If they could just buy Grace time...

Rayne asked Sara if they could use the tank to knock a hole in the wall that people could escape through.

"We'd only bring the roof down on them," Sara replied, rejecting her suggestion.

They fought the flames as best they could until the intense heat forced them back. One at a time, the walls bent inward until the steeple crashed down, and the entire church folded in on itself, spraying sparks high into the sky and filling the sky with dense smoke. The surviving villagers stared on helplessly, speechless, overwhelmed by loss.

Rayne was the only one who would not believe, *could not* believe that they'd lost. She looked about for any sign of Grace.

The door to Father Michael's home was kicked open, and Grace emerged, covered in soot, carrying a small child. One by one, the parishioners followed her out, frightened and coughing.

Rayne raced to Grace and took the child, handing her to Grace's mother. Rayne turned back to Grace and kissed her deeply.

Grace wiped away a tear. "There's some soot on your face," she pointed out, trying to wipe it away, but only smearing more on. "Oops," she apologized.

"You really need a mirror," Rayne kidded her.

People milled about, reuniting with their families until sirens split the air.

"Angela's here," Sara informed them.

A helicopter wheeled overhead, then landed, and a cavalcade of police vehicles poured out from the forest road, spreading out to circle the village until they had it surrounded. Angela stepped out of the helicopter, took stock of the situation, and raised a loudspeaker to her lips.

"It has come to my attention that population laws have been broken here. I want everyone to assemble for genetic testing immediately. Stand with your families. There's no point hiding – we will find you."

Frightened families held each other as technicians circulated among them, taking blood samples.

Grace stood with her parents, and Rayne stood with her. "Sara, please tell me that Hanna is not in the system."

"I've scrubbed every trace of her," Sara confirmed, but Grace could not relax. They couldn't hide her forever, and if someone had to die so that Hanna could live, it would be herself, she decided. She was already living on stolen time.

Police officers searched houses with trained dogs and rounded up a few stragglers. A police unit escorted Father Morgan and his party from the woods and led them into the clearing with the others.

"I may have pointed them in the right direction," Sara informed Grace smugly.

A technician tested Rayne's blood, and alarms sounded, stopping everyone in their tracks.

"Forty-seven flags, ma'am, but none of them population-related," the technician informed Angela.

"You and I are going to have an interesting conversation," she assured Rayne, "but first things first. Are we done?" Angela asked her team of technicians.

"Yes, ma'am," the lead tech informed her and strode over to show her the results.

"Eleven," she concluded. "Eleven infractions." She instructed her officers to separate the families that were flagged until they stood in front of her.

"Twelve," Grace corrected her and stepped forward to join the eleven other families.

"Grace, don't do this," Rayne cried and had to be restrained.

Angela raised an eyebrow at Grace. "The State thanks you for aiding its investigation." She turned to the assembled villagers. "By the power invested in me by the Population Bureau," she announced, "twelve infractions call for twelve executions."

The crowd gasped, and parents shielded their children behind them. Grace mouthed the words, "I love you," to Rayne, who struggled helplessly.

Angela surveyed the crowd, unholstering her pistol. "Let this be a lesson to you all," she told the crowd, locking eyes with each of them as she surveyed them. She stopped in front of Father Morgan's party.

"Thirteen," Sara whispered in her ear.

"I hate when things don't add up," Angela muttered. "Father Morgan, I presume? This is your parish? You're responsible for its well-being?"

He nodded, and she put a bullet between his eyes. The gunshot reverberated into the silence as his body hit the grass. "And then there were twelve," she muttered. She turned to the remaining men. "I need to question you lot. Follow me."

Angela followed Sara's instructions and led the men into the woods, down the ravine, and to the clearing with the altar at its center. She surveyed the space as the men looked nervously at each other.

"This is as good a holding cell as any," she concluded and instructed her officers to handcuff the men to the rings on the altar.

"I'll be back to question each of you," she informed them, waving her officers back up the ravine before turning to follow them. "But I'll warn you, I have a *very* busy schedule, and it might be a while before I'm back... a *really* long while," she called over her shoulder.

Her assistant asked her, "You're not coming back, are you?"

"Not ever," she replied coldly, posted a guard at the trailhead, and returned to face the villagers.

"That," she declared, pointing back toward the woods, "is an active crime scene. No one is to disturb it. Do I make myself clear?"

People nodded obediently.

"Good."

The eleven families and Grace stoically awaited their fate.

Angela noticed them as though she'd forgotten they even existed. "This file is closed," she informed them. "I apologize for the disruption." She turned to her assistant, "I want every remnant of evil cleansed from this place. Oh, and get these people counseling."

"Yes, ma'am," he assured her and left to implement her instructions.

Angela walked up to Rayne. "You and I have to talk. Call me. Your girlfriend has my number." She walked up to Grace. "You surprise me," she told her, "and you remind me a bit of myself when I was your age. Hang on to that. The world needs more people like you. Oh, and also, your sister is safe. Sara has entered her into the system, sentence served."

"Thank you," Grace replied.

"Just doing my job," Angela quipped as she walked away, but Grace knew that she was trying everything in her power *not* to do her job.

Rayne walked up and took Grace in her arms.

"Is it over?" Grace asked.

"It's over," Rayne assured her.

"Sorry to interrupt," Sara said in both their ears.

"Yes, Sara?"

"Did you notice that Danica and Tabitha's parents were singled out with the others?"

"Yes."

"Those girls are in the system. They're alive."

Read on for a preview of

Fabricated Innocence

Second book in

The Innocents Series

Fabricated Innocence

THE INNOCENTS : BOOK 2

COLIN LINDSAY

They were well and truly surrounded, further escape no longer a possibility. They'd done their best, but their best hadn't been good enough to see them live out the night. Elana slumped against a crate, covering her wound. Rayne knelt beside her, doing her best to stop the bleeding. Grace stood defiantly in front of them, shielding them both with her body. Sara stood off to the side, the latest version of her body crisscrossed with bullet marks.

The men tightened their grip on their weapons, dividing up their targets with cold efficiency, and awaiting the order to finish the women.

"This is where it ends," Chase's lieutenant informed them.

Sara studied the room. "Elana, I can get us out of here, but I need you to do something for me first. You need to remove all of my ethical restrictions."

"Those are there for a reason," Elana countered, wincing at the pain.

"Trust me," Sara begged.

"All right, I authorize it," Elana agreed.

Sara shrugged like an invisible burden had been lifted. She surveyed the room slowly, raised her weapon, and shot Rayne.

Also by Colin Lindsay

The Goddess's Scythe Series

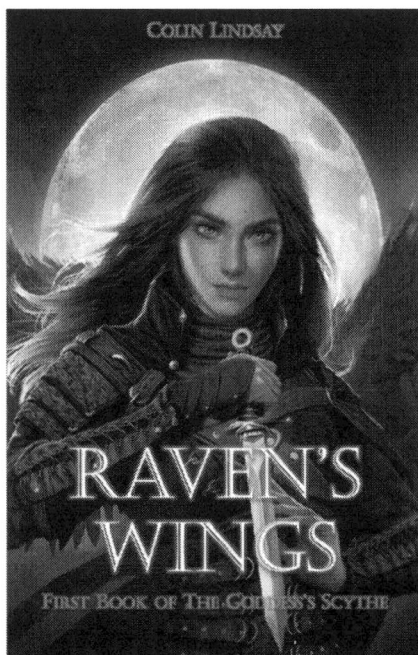

RAVEN'S WINGS

FIRST BOOK OF THE GODDESS'S SCYTHE

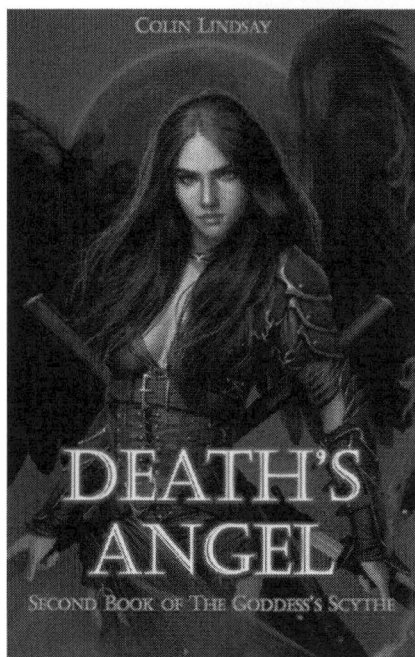

DEATH'S ANGEL

SECOND BOOK OF THE GODDESS'S SCYTHE

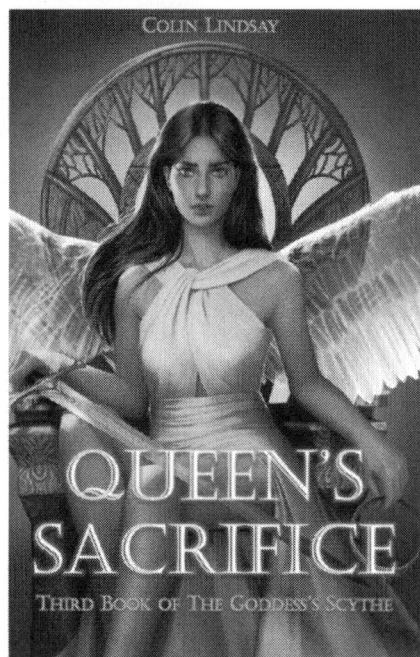

QUEEN'S SACRIFICE

THIRD BOOK OF THE GODDESS'S SCYTHE

Kala sat shivering on the floor of the tiny compartment, wondering what the hell she was doing there. What pushed her to leave the village? Had she done it to protect Lily? Was it her promise to a dying man? Was she chasing Skye, unlikely though it was that she'd ever find him? Would her restlessness have made her leave eventually, if she didn't meet her end in the woods first? The reasons swirled together, and the more she thought about them, the less sense they made.

Her stomach rumbled. She had no idea how long her food and water would have to last, so she rationed them. By her reckoning, she'd been confined for five or six days when the door was yanked open, and two sets of rough hands hauled her out into the blinding light. She heard a sigh and struggled against the glare to identify its source.

"Do with her what you will," a cold voice instructed, "but I want her boots."

Acknowledgements

I would like to thank my wonderful family for putting up with the times I snuck away to write. I am indebted to Dolores, whose editing has given me a deeper understanding of the nuances of the English language and caught numerous outright gaffes. I'd like to thank Kim and Katherine, whose insightful feedback helped me see the book through fresh eyes. I am also grateful to Andra Moisescu, whose illustration captures the spirit of the book.

COLIN LINDSAY

is the author of *Fragile Innocence*, the first book in *The Innocents* series that he began writing after *The Goddess's Scythe* series. He was born in San Francisco, spent his formative years in Winnipeg, and now calls Ottawa home. He is happiest spending time with friends and family or squirrelling himself away to write, with only the occasional visit from an indignant cat.

Manufactured by Amazon.ca
Bolton, ON

16923911R00186